ABOUT IT AND YOU'RE *MUERTE*. DEAD. DEAD!"

Carrasco kicked him hard, twice in the ribs, then walked away leaving Serafino in the path, his scratched and bloodied face smashed into the earth.

When he was sure Carrasco was gone, Serafino pushed his body slowly upward onto his hands and knees; his head bowed, his shoulders bent forward. The shock of Carrasco's warning and despair at losing his money gave way to bitterness and enmity. It was one thing to warn him, even beat him. It was another to steal his children's food and leave them to starve. That was an unpardonable sin. Carrasco would have to return his money. Serafino would make him return it.

Later, Serafino would try to see it all again in his mind. Try to reconstruct what was happening when he struck Carrasco with the hand holding the rock. He could remember no raised fist on Carrasco's part. And when Carrasco fell and he fell onto him, Serafino could not remember any struggle as his hands encircled Carrasco's neck . . .

Other Avon Books by
Patricia D. Benke

FALSE WITNESS
GUILTY BY CHOICE

ABOVE THE LAW

PATRICIA D. BENKE

AVON BOOKS ◆ NEW YORK

AVON BOOKS
A division of
The Hearst Corporation
1350 Avenue of the Americas
New York, New York 10019

Copyright © 1997 by Patricia D. Benke
Inside cover author photo by Kira Corsa
Published by arrangement with the author
Visit our website at http://AvonBooks.com
Library of Congress Catalog Card Number: 97-93004
ISBN: 0-380-79015-7

First Avon Books Printing: August 1997

AVON TRADEMARK REG. U.S. PAT. OFF. AND IN OTHER COUNTRIES, MARCA REGISTRADA, HECHO EN U.S.A.

Printed in the U.S.A.

WCD   10   9   8   7   6   5   4   3   2   1

For Marge and Bill Benke

Prologue

THE OLD WOMAN worked the broom over the dirt floor of her wood hovel. She moved stiffly, with determination. Everything she owned was in the cardboard boxes leaning in uneven columns against the sides of her house, awaiting the men from the city who would be coming to move her out, awaiting the bulldozers sent to level the encampment of Mexican laborers. She swept the same spot in the dirt over and over again in mindless repetition, as if her work could turn back the clock, could make any difference at all.

PART ONE

McGONIGLE CANYON

1

RIBBONS OF GOLD and orange split the clouds shortly before dawn as the encampment of migrant laborers nestled against the hills of McGonigle Canyon stirred from its sleep.

Somewhere in the shrubs a rooster crowed. Fires to warm hands frigid from the cold night crackled as security chains came unhooked from the cardboard and wood shacks, the cantons, where children still slept.

At the metal drums holding icy water, shivering women in sweatshirts and stretch knit pants washed their faces and slicked back their hair readying themselves for the day, then hurried to prepare lunches of tortillas and egg stew for the men who would soon be off to the fields.

In the distance a catering truck, its headlights still on, its horn blaring, rattled and creaked down the rutted dirt path toward the camp, coming to rest in a cloud of brown dust next to a grove of eucalyptus trees at the side of the road. A lone figure slipped from the driver's side and raised the quilted silver side section of the truck, banging it noisily against the roof of the vehicle.

Slowly at first, then more rapidly, men emerged from the shacks and rusted abandoned cars. They stumbled toward the catering truck and huddled together, their breath visible in the breaking light, hugging themselves and slapping their arms to ward off the cold.

As they waited for hot water and instant coffee, the driver silently, unceremoniously began throwing empty cardboard boxes, paper cups, and refuse from the back of his truck to the ground near the vehicle. One of the men fumbled for the cigarette lighter in his pants pocket and bent to light the pile, the small fire at once surrounded by men standing so close, their faces were obscured by the smoke. Still others walked quickly off into the high weeds surrounding the encampment, carrying rolls of toilet paper and newspaper with them.

With barely enough time for the men to drink a cup of coffee, a large flatbed truck rattled into position behind the catering truck. Slowly the men climbed onto it until it overflowed with laborers dressed in Levi's and T-shirts, baseball caps and straw hats. By the time it was ready to leave, twenty-two men were cramped against the cab and sitting along the edges of the truck bed, their feet dangling over the sides. Stragglers running alongside, hands outstretched, pleaded with the others that someone make a little room and pull them on board.

Another truck rattled to a stop, and soon it too drove away packed with men. Those laborers left behind began to walk toward the fields. Others climbed into old cars and pickup trucks while a few mounted bicycles and pedaled away.

With the men gone to the fields, the women re-treated into the cantons for a few more hours of sleep, reducing the camp to a sudden silence.

In the hills above the encampment, away from the rutted roads where the catering truck's horn did not reach to waken him, Serafino Morales pushed aside the roof of wood boards and tree branches that covered the hole in the ground where he slept. He closed his eyes tightly to shut out the bright sunlight. His ancestors had ruled the south of Mexico when the Spaniards invaded in the six-teenth century, dismantled its culture, and left it in ruins. What was left of his once golden, once noble heritage lay here, in a hole, in dispassionate accep-tance, on scattered blankets and a dirty mattress pulled from city waste bins.

Feeling far older than his fifty years, Serafino rubbed the wrinkled skin on his high, dark cheeks. He was a Mixtec Indian, an "inhabitant of the clouds." He did not feel so exalted.

Serafino stretched, his feet pressing against the edge of the hole. He was a small man; at five feet, average for a Mixtec Indian. In Oaxaca, in his small pueblo there, everything was tiny. The women scarcely reached five feet, and the horses were smaller than donkeys. His was a miniature world back home. Here he had easily become nothing.

Serafino crawled from the hole and dusted his gray T-shirt and blue Levi's. He would bathe to-night with one of the garden hoses in the Oaxacan encampment. For now he had barely enough time to relieve himself in the shrubbery and walk down to join the other men who were late for the fields. This was the second time in a week Serafino had been late waking up. He was growing slower, more tired every day. Soon the trips to the north would have to end for him.

It took only a few minutes to climb down the hill to the main encampment path, but walking, it would take forty minutes to reach the work station in the fields nearest the canyon. Along the dirt path that led to the fields, Serafino could hear the men's voices behind him, voices wondering if there would be more than three hours of work picking ripe tomatoes and cucumbers, voices worrying if there would be any work left for them at all by the time they arrived, voices wondering what price their lateness would cost, because there was always a price for being late.

Today the cost of a tardy arrival was placement on the crews assigned to kill malba, a nuisance weed, and so, dressed in a white suit and wearing a gas mask and gloves, Serafino spent the morning and afternoon walking slowly between the rows of cucumbers. In front of him a tractor pulling a tank of the herbicide paraquat inched forward as he held a metal applicator rod connected by hose to the container. He bent close to the ground, spraying the defoliant on his target, pausing now and then to stretch and relieve the aching in his back.

"Spread it more evenly," the field boss called out in Spanish, then in English. "Remember! It kills whatever it touches!"

At the end of the day, with the spraying completed, Serafino pulled the mask from his face and deposited the protective clothing in the cardboard box supplied by the field boss.

By then it was four o'clock, and a cool breeze persuaded him to forgo the crowded trucks and walk back to the encampment by way of the stream that cut through the fields and the base of the canyon. He lived alone, so he was in no hurry; no one was waiting for him.

Serafino had not walked far when something on the opposite side of the stream caught his eye. The tractor with the container of paraquat still attached to it was parked next to the water. Rogelio Carrasco, the driver of the tractor, was standing at the tank, an applicator hose in his hand.

Carrasco, a tall, heavy man with crooked teeth, lived in the labor encampment. He, like everyone else, knew the stream was the principal water supply. People bathed in the water. Children played in it and animals drank it. If he had to wear special clothing all over his body to keep the paraquat from his skin, it was certainly dangerous to put it in the stream.

On seeing Serafino approach, Carrasco hooked the hose to its metal lock on the tractor. He couldn't be sure how much the field hand—the man he knew as Serafino—had seen. Still, to respond directly to the intrusion on the crime would have confirmed the malignancy of his actions, so instead Carrasco turned his back and walked away, hoping the entire episode would end with his departure.

Dr. Ramón Partido was making the first of his house calls for the day at the place where there were no houses. Because the farm laborers of McGonigle Canyon could not come to him, he regularly went to them. Packing his medical supplies into his white 1993 Chrysler minivan, Partido scoured the canyon paths for those in need of assistance. His brown eyes moved from shack to shack, shrub to shrub, searching for the sick or injured. "It doesn't matter if you can pay me," he yelled to the field hands. "My services are free."

There was no set routine to his visits to the canyon dwellers, but they recognized his van, and it was not unusual for him to be waved down by someone with an urgent medical problem.

This morning as he drove through the mud ruts of McGonigle Canyon, Esperanza Ignacio flagged him down and in broken English pleaded with him to examine her five-year-old son Raúl.

Wringing her hands, the woman recounted the horrifying events of the previous evening. The boy had been out playing near the stream when his eyes began to burn. By the time he crossed the field and staggered into the canton, he was in great pain. She'd splashed his face with water, but it hadn't helped. His vision was blurred. Then he couldn't see anything. "All the time he was in pain, in pain," she wailed.

The doctor found the boy sitting on a mattress in the middle of the dirt floor, a white towel moist with water wrapped around his head, covering his eyes. Partido carefully unwrapped the bandage. The boy's eyes were blistered. He would need more than the care available at a clinic.

The boy's mother could offer no explanation. Nor could the boy relate what had caused the injury. He knew only that he was playing somewhere out at the edge of the stream when his eyes first began to sting.

Ramón Partido explained to the woman that her son's eyes might be seriously damaged. As she wept, he helped the boy to his feet and into the van with his mother for a trip to the hospital.

If he had to make a quick diagnosis, it would be that somehow a toxin had made its way into the boy's eyes. If that were correct, it would be the second case of toxic poisoning he'd seen in the canyon in three days.

The doctor remained silent, listening to the mother crying periodically as she comforted her child. He had a healthy practice of his own in San Diego. He didn't need such grief. But the first time he came to this canyon, it had pulled him into it, and now it would not let him go.

As he drove away from McGonigle Canyon, Raúl lying across the backseat and Esperanza Ignacio cradling her son's head in her arms, Partido scribbled on the white paper tablet he left on his dashboard "report Ignacio poisoning to county health."

2

FRANKLIN TALBOT'S 1956 Cadillac coasted
up the private tree-lined driveway from his estate
to the main road, where he stopped his car and
contemplated the thick fog obscuring all but several yards of his vision. The fog was far worse than
he'd expected. It would be a risk driving his favorite car into it. All it would take to ruin the vehicle was one punk going too fast. He considered
for a moment returning to the garage and changing
cars, but he glanced at his wristwatch. It was already eight o'clock, and he was late. He'd asked
Rex Cutter to meet him at his office for an update
before the other employees arrived at eight-thirty.
He didn't like crowds when he met with his closest
advisor and lobbyist. This morning's discussion
would be particularly important to Talbot Construction Company's latest housing development
project, so important that Franklin Talbot continued on, turning the car toward the freeway and
into the fog.

Talbot looked forward to his meetings with Cutter, an abrasive Englishman who had a penchant

for ridiculing the business that had made him a
rich man. He appreciated the man's wit and his
sarcasm. It was Cutter who first pointed out the
habit land developers had of naming newly built
communities after the very things destroyed in order to build them. Sort of memorials, he would say,
and point to Talbot's own Del Mar Hills development, reminding his friend that every last hill in
the area was leveled long before any construction
of homes began. He needled him as well about his
condominium project Los Arboles, Spanish for "the
trees," where every mature tree in the tract had
been cut down to build the houses. Talbot had re-
planted saplings, of course. But Cutter would never
call them trees. Why, they wouldn't be real trees
for ten years.

Franklin Talbot appreciated the truth in Rex Cutter's humor, truth that several decades earlier had
ended Cutter's promising political career. At the
time, land development in San Diego County had
been proceeding at an uncontrollable fever pitch,
and because of this, then city councilman Rex Cutter made developers uneasy with his pseudo anti-
development philosophy.

The uneasiness was compounded because while
the popular Cutter had not yet attained a power
base of sufficient stature or extent to slow the development industry, he was generally considered a
man on his way up. There was talk of his running
for mayor. His sarcastic commentary left his enemies and supporters alike wary of how he might
react to long-term development plans.

Of course he realized the developers he made so
nervous would begin to take their antipathy toward him seriously as his star ascended the political heavens and his growing clout became a thing

to be reckoned with. But in the end it was neither a bold position on land development nor his sense of misplaced humor that felled Cutter. All it took was one persistent private investigator out to find dirt. It was easy because Cutter and his mistress left a trail of motel receipts several blocks long. And there were photos, although no one ever *exactly* saw them.

Cutter managed to bail out of the public spotlight before the cards came tumbling down. He rationalized it was time anyway. There was too much money around him, moving, swirling, but ever out of the grasp of earnest public officials like him. He made forty-seven thousand a year and worked ten hours a day. The developers he watched move in and out of the mayor's office, watched dine at the finest restaurants with the highest city officials, made five, six, seven times his salary.

Cutter concluded this was one of those times when fate moves you unwillingly. That's how he saw the motel receipts—God's tickets outta there. Besides, if his enemies were onto him in one area of questionable, albeit human, behavior, would it not be long before they discovered his other weaknesses?

While his options were several, ironically he found himself heavily courted by the development industry he had vilified. He was eventually offered a lucrative position as lobbyist for Talbot Construction Company. It made sense. Three years on the city council. All that inside information.

His place in the city council chamber moved from the second seat on the dais, where he had addressed the public, to the back of the room, where he watched. Just watched. Which people came. Which went. Who sat with whom. Where the power could be brokered. Making the payments where and when he was ordered to.

He got very rich. Nice clothes, expensive cars. No wrinkled brown suit worn every day. He was a new kind of bagman. But a bagman nonetheless. Franklin Talbot's bagman. And this morning Franklin Talbot wanted an update on the assignment Cutter had undertaken for him.

For the last month Rex Cutter's assignment had been simple enough: deliver payments to Rogelio Carrasco, an itinerant Mexican laborer who lived in the McGonigle Canyon encampment. It was a delivery that brought Cutter to McGonigle Canyon this afternoon, sitting with Carrasco in the new black Mercedes with tinted windows and a cellular phone.

Carrasco ran his beefy hand over the leather-wrapped dashboard and the lobbyist winced. The car had just been detailed at a cost of one hundred dollars. The Armor All still glistened on the steering wheel. He looked closely to see whether the field hand's chubby fingers, caked with dirt, were leaving prints.

"I could get used to driving a car like this," Carrasco blurted in broken English. The lobbyist, ignoring the impossible, reached inside the vest pocket of his suit, retrieved a white envelope, and held it out toward Carrasco.

Before Carrasco could accept the envelope, Serafino Morales, on his way home from the fields and intrigued by the shiny vehicle, walked toward the car and looked inside the driver's window. He nodded to Carrasco, and making eye contact with Cutter as well, he walked on.

"¡Dios mío! My God!" Carrasco gasped. It could

not be. Serafino had seen him at the stream dumping the paraquat, and now he'd seen him being paid for dumping the toxin. Not twice in one week could the fates blow across his path and upset his work.

Shaken as well by Serafino's appearance, the lobbyist turned to Carrasco.

"Do you know that man?" he whispered, his hand shaking ever so subtly but unnoticed by Carrasco.

"Him? He's a dumb Indian. There is no worry about Serafino Morales, señor Cutter."

The lobbyist eyed Carrasco warily. "Have you ever seen him before?" Cutter asked, suddenly worried the intrusive Serafino might have more information than he should.

"Once. He see once."

Beads of perspiration forming on his brow, Cutter grew more insistent.

"*What* did he see once?"

Carrasco smiled and shrugged, sending the lobbyist into a fit of anger.

"Did he see you with the paraquat? Did he ever see you dumping the poison?"

"Maybe . . . I think. . . ."

Exasperated, Cutter pounded the steering wheel with his hand, then turned toward Carrasco, jabbing his index finger repeatedly at the man's chest.

"Don't 'maybe' me. Don't *ever*, *ever* let yourself be seen again! And I don't care how, but you'd better make damn sure this stupid Indian stays stupid and keeps what he saw to himself."

Carrasco's eyes followed the lobbyist's finger as it poked at him, and for a split second, Carrasco's eyes hardened and his body tensed. No one threatened Rogelio Carrasco this way. No one. If this weak excuse for a man hadn't been paying him so well for doing his dirt, he, Carrasco, would have reached out right then for his throat and choked the life from him with one hand. But he caught himself. There was far too much to lose if he allowed his temper to get the best of him. So he relaxed, allowing the facade of subservient ignorance to continue.

"He's my friend, señor Cutter. My *friend*. He won't say anything to anyone. I'll talk with him."

The lobbyist's temper subsided.

"He'd better not say anything, or you're in deep shit, Carrasco. I'll come looking for you, personally." He took a breath. "And next time we meet, I'd like to be a little further off the road, okay?"

"*Sí*. Okay. A little bit more off the road. I understand."

The lobbyist handed the envelope to Carrasco.

"There's fifty dollars in there and fifty more next week when the job's done at the tomato vines, okay? You meet me down the road more, near the end of the canyon. Next Thursday, same time."

"*Sí. Sí, señor*. I remain your humble servant."

Carrasco opened the door to leave. Cutter watched him run across the road and drive away in a decrepit truck, its exact identity having long since disappeared under dents and a patchwork of primer.

He found this part of the job distasteful. The man was filthy, and his shoes left ugly brown smears on the camel-colored carpet. The car had smelled fresh, new; now it was dirty. The lobbyist reached for his cellular phone and set off a medley of beeping sounds.

"Todd? Mr. Cutter here. Can I bring my car back in this morning for a quick clean? Just the interior." He glanced at his Rolex. "Swell. I'll be there in a half an hour."

3

SERAFINO'S MEMORY WAS *vivid. It was spring and the air was clean and warm. His father had motioned to come with him, and he'd left his mother behind in the adobe, weaving palm leaves into mats and sombreros, belts and lassos. A large mat took five days to make but could sell for six thousand pesos, about two dollars and sixty cents American money.*

They walked down the rock-strewn dirt road, Serafino struggling to keep up with his father, who was explaining what the child had, even at the age of five, already come to understand and accept. The rain had not been good. The land could not support a supply of food this winter.

As the church bells pealed, Serafino heard his father speaking of what was looming over them. Without rain, the arid land would yield only a meager crop of beans and corn. It would be a daily struggle to fend off starvation.

Serafino followed his father for a quarter mile to a field cracked by the sun and lack of water. The two stood next to each other for some time. Then the man bent down, lifted Serafino, and swung him onto his shoulders. His father remained silent, turning slowly toward the mountains. El norte. The child understood. His father was leaving, going north to the United States to find work to feed them.

In simple language he made the boy understand he would come back.

Serafino Morales pushed forward through the deepening darkness toward McGonigle Canyon, his black tennis shoes scraping against the dry cobbled earth of the footpath. With the spraying of the paraquat completed days earlier, he was working in the cucumber fields, picking the ripening vegetables. Tonight, he left the fields late, missing the flatbed truck crammed with hungry field workers anxious to return to the labor camp. There had been no choice for him but to walk the two miles back. Now, with the end of his journey a half mile away, the muscles in his legs were beginning to cramp.

Serafino was alone on the path, but one of hundreds who walked the same route to the fields. From Mexico into California they came, the nameless, faceless from Oaxaca and Veracruz, Sinaloa and Baja.

Northward thousands of miles from the eroded topsoil of their homeland, leaving behind the women and children to fend for themselves. Northward into the fields of Southern California. Into Carlsbad and Vista. Oceanside, Fallbrook, and Rainbow. All moving northward with one imperative: migrate or starve.

From the time of Serafino's birth in Oaxaca, deep in the south of Mexico, the die was cast. To escape the ever deepening poverty of his village, Serafino, like his father and grandfather, came north to

Southern California, working the fields, picking the tender vegetables, and sending money home to feed his family, keeping them from starvation. Each year he returned to his Mexican pueblo two thousand miles away when the planting and harvesting were done. Next year the oldest of his four sons, Alberto, would turn eighteen, and he too would come north to work, sending money home. Then Alberto's son would come. And so it would go on, generations coming and going, migrating ever northward for the reasons man has always migrated.

Serafino was never without work in San Diego. There was a certain touch, a gentle way of picking, that avoided bruising the soft fruits and vegetables. The men from Oaxaca had learned the touch, the right feel, for the softness. They taught their sons and their sons taught their sons, and because the farmers of the area knew it, he and his fellow Oaxacans were especially in demand during the strawberry and tomato seasons.

Serafino's work had begun at six-thirty that morning. He picked cucumbers most of the day, their thorny spines puncturing his cotton gloves, at day's end leaving his fingers numb.

He had no complaints. It had been a good day, so he did not mind the pain now. Moving along the four-foot vines, he loaded cucumbers into square wooden boxes, then loaded the boxes onto wheelbarrows for inspection by the wrinkled old woman, the "Leather One" he called her, who sat on the metal folding chair under the large sun umbrella.

Today the Leather One had been satisfied with all the boxes Serafino presented to her for inspection. Had she felt there were too many young ones, yellow ones, she could reject his labor, reject his boxes as poor work and refuse to punch the picking card he kept in his shirt pocket. No punch, no pay.

As Serafino continued along the path toward McGonigle Canyon, the fields, invisible in the darkness surrounding him, were alive with crickets, their uninterrupted chirping testimony to his acceptance on the path.

The first cool breeze of the evening brushed Serafino's face and the dampness of his body. He shuddered. The offensive odor he smelled was his own. If the hose was not running at the camp, he would be too late to wash himself, and he would have to wait until morning or try to make his way to the stream in the dark.

Serafino's hand dug into the right pocket of his jeans, feeling for his money. Five twenty-dollar bills were folded neatly into a square. Twenty dollars a day for five days' of work. Tomorrow he would take the taxi to Del Mar and send a money order home to Mexico. He would keep only enough to get him through the week. Here in the United States it was not much. In the north part of San Diego County, near Del Mar, a person could spend more than he earned in a whole week for one dinner at a restaurant. But back in Mexico it would feed his wife and children for several weeks. It was, for them, the difference between survival and death. So he did not care what it would *not* buy here.

Fifty yards more and the sound of the crickets abruptly stopped. Serafino froze, waiting. Perhaps a coyote was prowling the canyon for rabbits and squirrels.

The rustling in the fields around him neither

faded nor grew louder. Serafino walked on, his fear growing. Whoever, whatever had not changed its distance.

He knew the risks of walking alone in the canyon. Border robberies. American youths preying on Mexican laborers. Not all of the aggressors were Americans. Some were Mexican laborers who turned on their own kind for diversion or profit. These were bullies out to humiliate.

In the stillness Serafino realized he was no longer alone on the road. A man, bigger than he, moved in from the darkness of the fields and grabbed him around the neck from behind.

"Hey, stupid Indian," the man spat.

Serafino gagged and struggled for breath.

The man taunted him. "What?" he snarled, releasing Serafino.

Serafino turned to face his assailant, holding his hands up in supplication, still struggling for words. Serafino recognized him at once. It was Rogelio Carrasco.

Carrasco moved in front of him and snarled again, pointing to Serafino's pants pocket.

Did he know Serafino had been paid?

"*Dinero.*"

Serafino understood now. He wanted his money.

"*¿Tus pantalones?*" Carrasco pointed menacingly to the pocket Serafino had checked minutes before.

Serafino stood mute, able to discern the meaning of the gesture.

While moments before he had been calm, Serafino's heart pounded now, his brain screaming, *Flee. Run off the road into the canyon below.*

As Serafino's body lurched forward, Carrasco caught his arm and pushed him backward. Before Serafino could regain his balance, Carrasco punched him on the side of his head, and he staggered, his hands uselessly raised in self-defense. Serafino fell forward onto the ground, trying to protect the pocket containing his money, but from behind him a hand forced its way into his pants pocket. Carrasco stood above him.

"You saw nothing, Indian. No paraquat. No poison. Say a word about it and you're dead. Dead. *Muerto!*"

Serafino, despite great pain, turned his body slightly and looked up at Carrasco, the disjointed events and the threats now making ghastly sense to him as the English words "saw nothing" and "paraquat" fit together.

Carrasco kicked him hard, twice in the ribs, then walked away, leaving Serafino in the path, his scratched and bloodied face smashed into the earth.

When he was sure Carrasco was gone, Serafino pushed his body slowly upward onto his hands and knees, his head bowed, his shoulders bent forward. He remained so for several minutes until the urge to vomit had passed. Then he struggled to his feet and, still shaking, brushed the dirt from the front of his pants. His work gloves were strewn somewhere nearby in the dark.

Long before Serafino reached the encampment, the shock of Carrasco's warning and the despair at losing his money gave way to bitterness and enmity. It was one thing to warn him, even beat him. It was another to steal his children's food and leave them to starve. That was an unpardonable sin, and Carrasco knew it. Carrasco was just like him—he had come here and suffered so that women and children at home would not starve.

Carrasco would have to return his money. Serafino would make him return it.

How could he ignore me? Serafino thought. Twice this morning Serafino tried to speak to Carrasco. He had approached like a gentleman with his hands folded in front of him and each time Carrasco turned away, pretending he did not know what Serafino was talking about, pretending Serafino was not there. And when Serafino had become just a little more insistent, had raised his voice not in anger but imploring the man, there were others, Carrasco's family, who stood around Serafino with their fists in the air. Yet Serafino could not let this go unanswered. He had to keep trying until Carrasco gave him back his money.

All day Serafino watched Carrasco—where he went, what he did. Hoping there would be a time to appeal to the man again, alone, man to man with no one else there. Then maybe Carrasco's pride would not interfere.

Serafino saw his chance at last when the day ended and Carrasco walked alone toward the stream. Serafino followed quietly behind him taking deep breaths to keep the fear inside him under control.

"Señor Carrasco. Mister Carrasco." Serafino struggled with the words, calling politely when they reached a clearing next to the water. *"Por favor, mi dinero."* "Please, my money."

Carrasco only smirked again and turned away. Why would he act this way? He had no intention of listening to Serafino, and the betrayed man could feel the civility in him giving way to anger, to the realization he would have to confront Carrasco more directly.

Serafino looked quickly to his right and then his left. Where was the escape route if he needed to run? His heart was pounding as he splashed along the shallow stream, dragging his feet in the water, announcing his approach, aware now of a deeper growing anger, of his stooping down to pick up a rock from the stream. Serafino's mind told him to pick up the rock because he might need it to defend himself if Carrasco turned on him again, but another part of him wanted only to lash out with it.

As he neared, Carrasco's body began to turn. Serafino could have waited, but he struck him with the hand holding the rock.

Later Serafino would try to see it all again in his mind, try to reconstruct what was happening when he hit Carrasco. He could remember no raised fist on Carrasco's part. And as Carrasco fell and he fell onto him, Serafino could not remember any struggle as his hands encircled Carrasco's neck.

4

JUDITH THORNTON TIGHTENED the belt of her white terry cloth robe and brushed the loose strands of auburn hair back from her forehead. A thick wet fog lingered over Silverado Estates. If it was as bad all over the city, freeway traffic this morning was bound to be backed up all the way into downtown San Diego. It was seven o'clock. If she was out of the house in the next half hour, she might miss the worst of it. Judith didn't like arriving at her office later than 7:45. As chief deputy for the San Diego District Attorney's Office, she personally supervised the Major Violator Unit, where her duties included the assignment of trial deputies to cover thirty-seven criminal courtrooms, most of which were in full swing by 8:30.

There wasn't much to do other than get herself ready for work. Her eight-year-old daughter, Elizabeth, was spending the summer with Steven, her former husband. In Elizabeth's absence, the six-thousand-square-foot house was cavernous. The only activity surrounded the daily care of Judith's mother, a stroke patient who, unable to move or communicate, was confined primarily to bed. That wouldn't begin until the day nurse, Jean, arrived at 7:30.

Judith pushed down on the handle of the French door to the patio and stepped outside. She walked down the gray slate path to the large Spanish fountain, flipped the switch, and waited for the water to flow from the ornament at the top, fill each of the three layers, then fall to the fountain's circular concrete pool. She sat at the fountain's edge, her eyes sweeping the expanse around her. Alone wasn't so bad in an acre of grass and roses surrounded by sycamore and cypress trees. The yard had matured into a park, just as she and Steven had planned when they built the house. But he was gone now, and despite his monthly financial assistance, the burden of running the house was all hers. There were times it seemed more a business than a home, with gardeners costing as much each month as a small apartment. But as long as Steven was able to help, she could hold on okay.

And what had she to complain about anyway? Not her job. At thirty-nine she was the only woman ever to have held the highest administrative position in her office. And there was constant speculation she might be a candidate for a judgeship or even for the district attorney's position if Lawrence Farrell, the current D.A., accepted a judicial appointment. Nor could she complain about her mother. Her mother's care was a necessity and a moral responsibility. The emotional turmoil it brought was part of life. Her own life wasn't all that bad. She had a beautiful house, a healthy, happy daughter, and a former spouse she still respected. Despite the bills being an uncomfortable stretch, she was able to pay them each month.

Still, there were moments when however good the parts of her life were, the whole of it threatened to suffocate her.

Rogelio Carrasco. That was the name typed in bold print on the tab of the manila folder. Someone had delivered the file and deposited it on Judith's chair before her arrival in the office. The name didn't sound familiar, and in the Major Violator Unit, the names of repeat offenders became familiar very quickly.

Judith opened the file. Sixteen glossy black-and-white autopsy photos spilled onto her desk. She realized then that Carrasco was not the perpetrator of anything. He was the victim. But there must have been a mistake. Her unit handled crimes committed by career criminals. She got the toughest and the most violent—not the dead. To her knowledge, the Major Violator Unit had never taken a case based on who the victim was.

A short, cryptic note written in red ink was the only handwritten notation, and it was attached to the inside left page of the folder. She recognized the writing was from Lawrence Farrell, asking her to come chat when she'd had a chance to examine the file. The district attorney had been her mentor and friend during her tenure in the office, and for the past year she'd served as his chief deputy district attorney.

Given the thinness of the file and the brevity of the police report, her examination didn't take long. The facts were straightforward: Carrasco, a farm laborer, had been found dead at the edge of a small stream in the north part of the county. There was a laceration on the back of his head, but the cause of death was strangulation.

Other than some blood at the scene that matched Carrasco's, there were no clues. No suspects. And still no apparent reason for Rogelio Carrasco's murder file to be sent along to her unit.

"Okay, so I'm intrigued," Judith announced as she walked into Lawrence Farrell's office. "Who is Rogelio Carrasco, and what's he doing dead in the Major Violator Unit?"

Farrell looked up from the newspaper lying on his desk. He folded his arms behind his head and stretched, flexing his body.

"He's a Mexican national found dead two days ago up at McGonigle Canyon. A real bad actor too, from what little we've picked up on him."

"The canyon sounds familiar."

"It's in North County next to the big nursery up there—or what used to be a big nursery, near Black Mountain Road."

"That's a pretty rural area, isn't it?" she asked.

"Not anymore. It's where all the new building development's been going on, North City West. There's a big encampment of migrants stretching about seven-tenths of a mile up there on private property along the canyon. The camp's been there for twenty years or so, at least since the late seventies. At its height it had maybe two thousand residents. It's down to six hundred now, but the problem is, the migrants and the new condo owners surrounding the canyon are beginning to share each other's space. And the new homeowners don't like what they're seeing."

"Like what?"

"It's not a simple answer. Sit down and I'll give you a little history."

Judith grabbed a chair and pulled it to the front of Farrell's desk.

"Like I said, the camp's been there forever. It started as a small bachelor camp, and it's evolved into a community of sorts after the women and children came. Now there's trash pickup, a daily police patrol assigned by the city, Catholic church services every Sunday, portable toilets, credit systems, and food services. That's the okay part. But there's a down-side. Like crime—a real active trade in crystal meth. A stream polluted by human sewage. Not to mention the laborers standing on street corners in neighboring communities like Peñasquitos, waiting for someone to offer them work. The mayor and private developers are under a lot of pressure to clear the encampment out."

"With all the city and county code violations you just mentioned, that shouldn't be too hard to do."

"It *is* hard to get done. San Diego has a multi-million-dollar crop industry, and the farmers aren't going to find all the crop laborers they need in the classified ads. The laborers have almost always come from Mexico. The growers have to move their crops out. If you mess with the labor supply, the crops don't get to market."

"A standoff between laborers and residents, and now a murder in the canyon where the kids from the canyon rim households have been playing. Am I right?"

"You are. In fact, a kid out playing in the canyon found the body. So . . . you have Mr. Carrasco in your unit because we need to expedite the investigation and prosecution of whoever killed the man."

"Is there anything on this Carrasco besides what's in the file?"

"Just that he didn't have the best reputation. When we look more closely, we're probably going to run up against a number of folks who might have liked to eliminate the man."

"Is San Diego P.D. investigating?"

"It is. Pike Martin's been assigned. He's already been up to the canyon a couple of times. He's got some contact up there who knows the area pretty well."

Judith always had mixed feelings when Pike was on the case. He pushed the limits too far at times, and she had to watch him carefully, but he was tough. One of the best. And he spoke better Spanish than she did.

"Can you put some priority on this one, Judith?"

"I'll do my best. I'll give Pike a call as soon as I get back to my desk."

"Keep me posted. I just need to let the city council know we're on top of it."

5

JUDITH WAS NOT used to being told how to run her Major Violator Unit, not even if it was the district attorney himself who was doing the telling. There were times, however, when politics had to be considered. In such cases it was usual for Farrell to ask her to handle the matter. He could keep a close eye on the case, and she, one of his most trusted administrators, could give him the kind of direct feedback the sensitive cases often required. So although the Carrasco murder was not the kind of case her unit was best geared up for, she hadn't questioned Farrell's decision to send the case to her.

She'd spent the better part of the morning examining her political hot potato. At the end of the morning, however, she was disappointed. From what she could tell, the case was a dead end. The toxicology reports on Carrasco were negative. No alcohol in his system. No drugs either. She made several notations of her own in the file, closed it, and placed it on the corner of her desk. It would have to wait for Pike Martin's examination. Maybe he'd have some new approach. At worst, she'd send it over to Pike and get it off her desk. At this point she had nothing to add to the case and had nowhere to start.

To the right of the Carrasco file lay five other cases, all set for trial within the month: three murders and two strong-arm robberies, one of which appeared to be part of a violent string of robberies by the same defendant. She should have been spending her time this morning reviewing them, not who murdered Rogelio Carrasco.

Judith picked out the chain robbery file. She'd need to see that the witnesses were subpoenaed and that the eyewitness identification procedures had been set up. The police in El Cajon, just east of San Diego, had good reason to suspect the defendant who was under arrest was the same man who'd beaten and robbed a convenience store clerk nearly to death five months earlier. They wanted the clerk to get a good look at him. Judith examined her calendar. Perhaps tomorrow . . . No, it wouldn't be enough time to set it up. The day after looked better.

The phone rang. It was her daughter, Elizabeth, who had been spending the summer with Judith's former husband, Steven. That was part of the arrangement. Elizabeth spent the school year with her and two months of the summer with Steven. The postcards from her travels this year were pinned to the bulletin board on the wall behind her. So far they'd come from Seattle, Portland, and Victoria, Canada. They all said about the same thing: "Having a great time. Love you."

She'd missed Elizabeth terribly, even though her absence freed Judith to spend more time with her own mother, a mother crippled and silenced by strokes, a mother who'd lived with her for three years and was a daily reminder to Judith of how little control over life anyone had.

Elizabeth's voice was a welcome surprise.

"Hi, Mom?"

"Where are you, honey?"

"We're in Jackson Hole. That's in Wyoming, and tomorrow I'm going white-water rafting with Daddy. Daddy wanted to call and tell you I'm okay and I'm still having fun."

"Put Daddy on, Liz. Can you? And wear a life preserver! Promise?"

"I promise! Here's Daddy. . . ."

Steven's voice was strong and light. They were having a great time. They'd write again soon. Don't worry, he promised, she'll wear a life preserver and a safety helmet. Judith was glad Steven was so easy to get along with. From the outset of their divorce two years earlier, he'd been cooperative. It wasn't difficult because despite the pain and trauma of the separation, the truth was they hadn't ever been right for each other. They'd met in college and dated for three years, and somehow marriage just seemed the natural next step. Law school followed for them both. Judith thought those had been their best years together. Everything was small: their apartment, their bank account. They didn't need much. After law school and successful career starts—hers in the District Attorney's Office, his in a civil law firm—life moved faster. The small apartment eventually gave way to a six-thousand-square-foot house on an acre. The bank account measured out bills in thousands, not hundreds, of dollars. Maybe it was the pressure of debt or success or both, but by the time they'd reached their late thirties, they'd had enough of the pressure and of life together. By that time Elizabeth had been born, and they had the sense to part amicably, each remaining active in their daughter's life. Judith remained in the house with Elizabeth and her mother. Steven remarried. Everything, it seemed, had a certain friendly equilibrium.

Elizabeth's call lightened Judith's morning, and for a few moments after they'd hung up, she forgot about the Carrasco file and the series of robberies sitting on her desk. She stood and walked to the window. It was grimy, dusty, needed washing. She hadn't noticed how badly until just now. Below on the concourse the numbers of people leaving the courthouse exceeded the numbers going in. It was the ebb and flow of the day. Her mind drifted. River rafting. She'd like to try it sometime.

The light rapping at her door was Farrell.

"Come on in, Larry. I've looked at the Carrasco case. There's not much there yet, so I'm going to wait until Pike has a chance to look at it before I decide what kind of action, if any, we can take."

He came in and sat in one of the chairs facing Judith. "Well, I just got off the phone with Pike Martin." He put his elbows on her desk and rubbed the palms of his hands together in front of his face. She'd known him long enough to see the signs. There was something else on his mind besides Rogelio Carrasco.

"What's up?" she asked.

"Well, I have a new attorney coming on board, and I want to assign him to your unit here. I'd like you to train him.

Judith's voice dropped. "You want me to *what*?"

Farrell clasped his hands together and lowered them to the desk in front of him.

"I've hired a young man, Peter Delgado, and I'd

like you to work with him, train him, for the next year or so."

Judith stood and walked around the desk, sitting in the vacant chair next to Farrell.

"Just a minute, Larry. Do I have any say in this?"

"Of course you do."

"We've differed on how cases ought to be handled, right?"

"We have."

"You've never told me how to handle my office."

"I'd never do that."

"You've never asked me to do something I found personally or ethically repugnant, right?"

"Never have. Never will."

"And until today, anyway, I've been allowed to run this unit the way I think it ought to be run. I make the initial screening decisions in hiring."

"You have and you do."

"So why are *you* hiring a new attorney into my unit without as much as consulting me?"

"This is different."

"Mind telling me how? As I understand it, we had three hundred and five applications for six *starting* positions in the mid-forty salary range."

"And one of those positions went to Peter Delgado. He's twenty-six and passed the California Bar Exam in February. He's good-looking but too young for you."

"You're making light of this, Larry! I want to know how this brand-new attorney ends up here with me."

Judith's black-framed glasses slipped, and she pushed them upward to the bridge of her nose, an involuntary motion signaling this was talk of a serious nature. The Major Violator Unit handled only the most serious felonies, the worst and most violent of repeat offenders. The attorneys assigned to her were drafted from the top ranks of the 150 lawyers in the office and had a minimum ten years' experience. The best. The brightest. Nothing less. Until now.

Judith's voice rose, bordering on the shrill. She caught herself, lest she lose her temper.

"This is bad precedent, Larry. You know as well as I do that the attorneys in this unit are *asked* to join. They don't apply. This placement of a new attorney won't be good for morale. There are at least ten senior attorneys in the trial department who'd die for a shot at this unit. And they deserve it. Where am I supposed to put this kid? What am I supposed to assign to him? Has he ever even *been* in a courtroom?" She allowed several seconds of uneasy silence to pass. "Well?" she demanded, cocking her head slightly to the side, the curls of her auburn hair slipping just past her shoulder.

"What do I *do* with him?" she continued in a somewhat more exasperated tone.

"Train him," Farrell said quickly, confidently, without a hint of reluctance. "He has potential." Another pause before the staccato explanation continued. "You don't need to assign him a trial right off the bat. You have carte blanche to start him anywhere, doing anything you feel is appropriate."

Farrell was trying to cushion the impact. To some extent he was right. There were a number of places she could start a novice. The cases within the office were handled at different trial levels by different sets of attorneys.

At least Judith could tightly control her new addition until she could evaluate his skill level.

She pointed her index finger at Farrell, something only those closest to him dared.

"He's starting with baby steps, Larry. Even if I have to pull misdemeanor cases to give to him."

"That's okay too."

Judith sat on the edge of her chair, her arms folded across her chest. There was no winning this argument.

"This has been quite a day, Larry. First I end up with the murder of some field hand whose case would never meet the criteria for being in this unit; now I've got a new deputy who'd never meet the criteria for being hired into it. If it wasn't you who'd brought me these two men, I'd think there was a conspiracy going on to undermine my office." She looked toward the window, then at Farrell.

"What do I tell the senior attorneys who see this kid waltz in here without paying his dues?" she demanded.

Again Farrell's response was succinct.

"Tell them the truth."

"Which is . . . ?"

"This is his dues."

Now it made sense. The governmental trial agencies like the District Attorney's Office and City Attorney's Office were sometimes the places where the sons and daughters of senior partners in established law firms took short-term jobs right out of law school. In private law firms, new attorneys carried partners' briefcases into court and wrote trial briefs and memos for three years before they were ever allowed to make a solo appearance in court. And that was only if a partner was standing next to them supervising. Their experience in civil law firms for these first formative years was tightly controlled to minimize mistakes, maximize work ethic, and determine if the new young associate fit the law firm's profile. In the government offices, however, new attorneys could get immediate immersion into trial experience, making mistakes, meeting the judges and court personnel, and watching the best—and the worst—attorneys at work. They cut their teeth in the government arenas and honed their trial skills. *Then* they went to work for the larger law firms.

"He's not a career attorney," Judith said flatly.

"Peter's here maybe a year. Two at most. You don't have to tell anyone anything. But If you feel you have to, tell your leading contenders his spot'll be open again."

"Why here, though, Larry? Why this department?"

"I want him with you, Judith. I don't expect you to cut him any slack or make any other exceptions for him. I want him trained. And I can't think of anyone I'd rather have do that than you."

"Don't flatter me."

"You know I mean it, Judith. I want this kid to be successful."

Judith squinted at him. "Is this some kind of political payback?"

"Why do you ask?"

"Because this isn't like you, assigning an inexperienced attorney to a unit like this. Who is he? Or should I ask, who's the kid's family?"

"Peter's family and mine go a long way back. His grandfather came from Mexico to the United States in the early fifties. He brought along a wife and five children. They settled in San Diego; up in the North County working in the fields picking vegetables. After a year his grandfather started looking for work in the city and started a small gardening business. My grandfather was one of his clients. Anyway, one of the five kids, Peter's father, is Ramón Delgado."

"Federal District Court Judge Delgado?"

"The same."

Ramón Delgado was a local product. He'd attended the University of San Diego, gone on to UCLA Law School, and then returned to San Diego to practice civil litigation and help direct local political campaigns for the Democratic Party. Ten years earlier he'd been appointed to a federal judgeship, one of the most coveted judicial appointments available.

"So Peter's following his dad's footsteps into civil litigation?"

"It looks that way. Judge Delgado called me personally and asked if I could find a spot for him. He didn't mention this unit by name but he did ask if I could put him where he'd get the most direction and be the most challenged. That's here with you, Judith."

"Thanks."

"You'll have a chance to look at his résumé. I sent one up this morning. I'm sure it's somewhere in the mail there on your desk. Not Ivy League colleges, but excellent. Penn State undergrad. Second in his class at Virginia Law School. We know he can write. He was the law review managing editor. He might stay here in San Diego. But he needs experience."

Judith was nonresponsive.

"Look, Judith, I know it's a burden. I'm only asking that he be assigned here. What you choose to *do* with him is totally up to you. You can have him just sit and watch trials for a whole year if you want. But there's something else to think about."

Judith sighed. "What else?"

"How many minorities are in your unit, Judith?"

She thought for a moment. "Five women, one black." That was it.

"Women don't count for me anymore, Judith. The head of the unit's a woman, and almost half the deputies are women. No Hispanic attorneys. We're fifteen minutes from Mexico, and the criminal system's chock full of Hispanic witnesses and victims. There are no Hispanics at the top trial level and, as I see it, no immediate prospects for it."

"Okay. So you want this young man to get a glimpse of how it works."

"That. And I think we could benefit from a glimpse of him."

Judith shrugged. "Okay. You have a point. I don't like it. But I don't have a choice really, do I?"

Farrell was silent, and that was answer enough.

"When's he coming in?" Judith asked.

Farrell looked at the desk clock to Judith's right. "In about twenty minutes."

"Thanks for the warning."

"I thought you'd like to just kind of ease him into work. I took the liberty of having the support staff set him up in an office at the other end of the hallway, next to Ashby. You want me to stick around until he gets here?"

"No, I think I can handle one inexperienced twenty-six-year-old attorney just fine."

"I'll check back in a couple of days and see how he's doing."

Judith wrinkled her nose at him, one last act of futile defiance.

When Farrell left the office, Judith found Delgado's résumé in her morning mail and quickly made her way down a flight of stairs to the Municipal Court assignment desk, where she checked

out two case files, one a misdemeanor drunk driving trial and the other a sentencing hearing in a
prostitution case.

She'd size Peter Delgado up, and if it appeared
he was too inexperienced, she'd assign the sentencing matter to him. The defendant's sentence in
the case had already been agreed to in a plea bargain: six months in Las Colinas, the women's facility of the county jail. The judge would take the
defendant through her plea. All Delgado would
have to do is read the sentencing report to famil-
iarize himself with the facts, stand up in court, say
his name when the judge asked who represented
the People, listen to be sure the judge asked the
required questions, and state his agreement with
the plea bargain.

Judith was back at her desk less than five
minutes when the buzzer on her phone sounded.
It was the receptionist informing her Peter Delgado
was on his way to her office. Judith quickly
scanned his résumé, set it on her desk, and waited.

The announcement of his arrival was not dramatic, a slight tapping on her already open door.

"Peter?"

He poked his head into her office.

"Yes, ma'am. I think you were expecting me."

"Yes, I was—I am. Come in . . . please."

Judith hadn't been sure what to expect. The standard well-connected look, perhaps. Near arrogant.
Armani shirt. A smile some orthodontist spent
years perfecting.

Delgado was not of that mold. He wasn't much
taller than she was, maybe five eight or nine, 150
pounds. Soft waves of black hair flattened in a traditional part to the right, straining, she surmised,

against gel holding back a head full of natural curl. Full lips, high cheekbones, and olive complexion were distinctively Hispanic. Only the deep hazel green eyes suggested his Mexican ancestry might have crossed paths along the line with some other culture.

There was no Armani to be seen anywhere.

He was wearing a conservative navy blue sports coat and dress pants, a white shirt, and a gray-and-blue-striped tie. Not high fashion but very nice overall—strikingly handsome without being cardboard.

After his subtle entrance Delgado strode toward her confidently. His hand, which he did not extend until she held out her own, was soft and smooth; his fingernails impeccably and professionally manicured.

"Have a seat, Peter. I have some questions, and I'm sure you do too."

Judith retreated to the formality of her desk, motioning Delgado to take a seat at one of the two chairs facing her. He sat, relaxed under circumstances most new attorneys found uncomfortable.

"Mr. Farrell tells me your family and his have been friends a long time, back to your grandfather's emigration to California."

"Yes, that's what my father has told me."

"Did your grandfather come to the United States with your grandmother?"

"He did, yes. And with my oldest uncle. He was about six at the time."

"You must have shared some interesting stories with them."

"Actually, no." There was a hint of apology as his voice lowered. "I don't know very much about them. I'm afraid I haven't spent much time in Mexico. Some day, though, I'd like to make an extended visit."

"You've been to Tijuana, of course." Tijuana, less than twenty minutes south of San Diego, served as the party mecca for students in the area. Her assumption was incorrect.

"Not in the last fifteen years I haven't, no. I don't enjoy it down there. There's something about donkeys painted with stripes to look like zebras and little kids selling sticks of gum on street corners and begging for quarters . . ." He hesitated. "I . . . it makes me uncomfortable. I did study several summers in Mexico City, though, on student exchange programs."

"Your studies have been mostly . . ."

"In the East. I like the East Coast. Until this job opened up with your office, I'd thought I might want to set up practice there. I'd been offered a good job with a medium-size firm in Washington D.C., but I'm willing to look at other options. I'm not attached to anything or anyone right now."

"I saw on your résumé that you're interested in civil litigation."

"I am, yes ma'am. Actually, I think my father has plans for me to join his old law firm."

"You must be looking forward to that."

"I am, yes, somewhat. I'll give it a try."

"Have you ever handled anything in court before, Peter, as a law clerk perhaps while you were in school?"

"No, but I did take part in my law school's trial practice moot court program and I've observed cases. In my third year, you can see from my résumé, I was a research clerk for a federal trial judge in Virginia, Judge Martin Timlin. He's a reference and would be very happy to talk with you."

"I don't think that's going to be necessary."

He hadn't the slightest idea of how terribly out of place he was. Judith felt a compulsion to tell him. Before someone else did. Or before he made the mistake of concluding too quickly that he was prepared to be part of the unit.

"Before we go any further, Peter, I want to level with you. You're in my unit because you were personally placed here by the district attorney. I didn't hire you. I wouldn't have hired you. The attorneys here are selected by me personally after they've handled trials for a number of years. And they've all handled tough trials. You've handled nothing."

Delgado didn't flinch. "But you're here for training. So I'm going to train you. You do what I say, when I say it." He nodded in agreement as she continued.

"My preliminary plan is to take you through the system, starting in Municipal Court, with misdemeanor cases. How fast you go through the system depends on how good you are, how good you get, and what kinds of cases are available. You won't waste your time. You'll see the best and worst of the system—judges who'll move up to higher courts, judges who drink too much at lunch and nod off at two in the afternoon in front of juries. Same goes for attorneys. Watch the good ones. You'll spot them right away."

For the first time, it seemed, Delgado smiled. "When you handle your cases, you'll be critiqued, Peter. By me or one of the trial supervisors from our office. If you're really bad or really good, the judge might give you some pointers too. A word of advice—accept the critiques graciously. They're meant to make you a better attorney. You won't be protected here the same way you'd be in a civil firm as a new attorney. Our volume's too heavy. The People of the State of California can't afford to let their attorneys carry senior attorneys' briefcases around for a year. On the other hand, the baptism by fire is offset by freedom to develop quickly with your own style. You have any problems, you bring them to me. If you can handle all that, we'll get along fine."

Delgado sat upright in his chair and looked directly at Judith, who felt a twinge of guilt that her lecture may have sounded like a scolding. "I know how I got here, Mrs. Thornton. It's a favor to my father. I've had those before. But it just gets me in the door; that's all it does."

His sudden candor surprised her, interrupting her control of the discussion.

"Look, I'm sorry, Peter. I didn't mean to be so hard on you."

"It's all right. I understand. You don't know if I belong here." There was a brief pause, almost a sigh, before he added, "Neither do I."

There it was. She'd felt it from the moment he'd walked through the door. His calm demeanor, the subtle put-downs of the less fortunate, and his disdain for Tijuana. Mexico was a good place to study, perhaps, but not to be from. Some Hispanic representative Farrell had recruited.

Now they understood each other. Each had been foisted on the other, and in the very recognition of that, there was a mutual respect.

Almost against her will, Judith found herself liking Delgado.

"Can you start today?"

"I am prepared to, yes."

Judith pursed her lips and squinted at him. She had both the simple sentencing and more complicated trial files on her desk. Now, having listened to him and watched him, she'd made up her mind.

"Here's what I'd like you to do. Go down to the second floor, Municipal Court Department Ten. That's Judge Thomas Levine's courtroom. Spend at least two hours there after lunch today. They get started at one-thirty sharp. He does mostly misdemeanor trials, many of them DUIs—that's short for driving under the influence of drugs or alcohol. Watch him. Don't let him scare you. He has a very abrasive exterior, but he's a real softy. Watch and listen to the attorneys. Can you do that?"

"I can spend *more* than two hours down there," Delgado said enthusiastically.

"Don't be too eager to just sit and watch. I have something else for you to do." Judith picked up the two misdemeanor files she'd checked out at the assignment desk and offered the DUI file, the trial file, to Delgado. It was a calculated risk.

"Take this along with you. After you've observed in Department Ten, go into the office law library, or your office, and read the file. Every word of it. Especially the police reports and the toxicology reports. And take this along too."

Judith reached over to the credenza on the right of her computer and pulled a four-inch-thick black binder from between a row of notebooks.

"This is what we call our trial manual."

She passed it to Delgado. "Everything you need to try the DUI case I just gave you can be found in that trial manual. Every question is written out for you. You call to the witness stand the police officer who arrested the guy, and the questions you need to ask him are listed right there. Same goes for the lab technician who tested the defendant's blood. You'll need to call him to the stand and lay a foundation for his testimony. You'll see the stipulation is set out too for the blood alcohol level. Most of the time the defense attorney will stipulate, that is, agree to the blood alcohol level and launch his attack on how the lab got the results it did. If the defendant takes the stand, just listen carefully and ask about all the discrepancies between his version of events and the arresting officer's. The trial manual's your safety net for a while. It's got all the most common misdemeanor trial formats in it—prostitution, petty thefts—check out the index."

Judith stopped and looked at Delgado, who was at once curious, thumbing through the trial manual.

"Don't let it overwhelm you. Just observe for the afternoon. Then look at your case file. You'll see there are only two witnesses you have to call, and they've already been subpoenaed by the paralegals and served by the marshal's office. Both witnesses will be checking in up here in our office lobby an hour before trial so you can talk with them before trial starts. The defendant in this case has requested a jury trial, so you need to review how you pick a jury. It's there in the manual too. Then just call the witnesses to the stand and ask the questions. Tie it all together in a closing statement. You do know what a closing statement is?"

"I prepared several in my trial practice classes."

"Good. You're ready to jump into this, then."

She tried to sound positive, but he wasn't really ready. He was too new to be ready. The case Judith gave him was simple. Yet to a novice like him it must have looked like the beginning of Armageddon. She vaguely recalled the feeling. Anxiety driven by youthful ambition. Excitement tempered by sheer terror. For her first six trials Judith had copied every question from the trial manual. For every witness she read off page after page of pre-written inquiries. Only after the sixth trial did she dare venture outside the safety of that procedure, finally throwing off the form for substance.

"I'm sorry to toss so much at you, Peter, but there is no luxury of time here. It's the only way to do it. By next month you'll have done so many trials, you won't need the manual. Now go get some lunch and get ready for this afternoon."

As Delgado rose, Judith added, "By the way, Peter, your office is next to Len Ashby's. He's a great guy and a terrific attorney. Ask him lots of questions. That's the best way to learn."

At the door, Delgado suddenly stopped and turned toward her.

"Mrs. Thornton, I forgot to ask, when *is* this trial you assigned to me?"

"Tomorrow morning, Peter. Eight-thirty A.M. Department Ten." As he stepped out the door, she called after him. "And, Peter?" He thrust his head and shoulders back through the open door. "If we're going to work together, call me Judith."

"Judith," he repeated, nodding and closing the door behind him.

When he was gone, Judith poured herself a cup of coffee and took a minute to reflect. She'd thrown a lot at him.

Yet Delgado was an enigma. A Hispanic with a rich history but no knowledge of its impact on him. A young man apparently capable of deep sensitivity with no plan or desire to identify or use it.

Still, there was something she could not yet define. It was one of those judgments that came intuitively to her now, the result of years of hiring new attorneys, selecting juries, and interviewing witnesses, of looking into people's eyes while she listened to the inflection in their voice.

Peter Delgado was floating between two worlds, waiting to put his feet down somewhere, and she had this gnawing feeling that if he made the right choice, he could be a superstar.

Judith waited several days until she was certain Peter Delgado was deep into his trial before venturing into the courtroom to observe him.

The moment she entered Department 10 and took a seat at the back of the courtroom, Judge Thomas Levine glanced in her direction and nodded slightly, acknowledging her presence. It wasn't the usual practice for the chief deputy district attorney to sit in on a misdemeanor trial, and he undoubtedly realized Delgado was a new deputy.

Delgado was standing in the well of the courtroom, facing his own witness, Art Lutz. Lutz was probably the most experienced lab technician at the San Diego P.D., and as with all good experts, a simple, well-directed question put to him would elicit, unaided, a fountain of relevant information. However, the gruff and humorless gray-haired Lutz had a reputation for being particularly impatient with sloppy or ill-prepared counsel, and it was not beneath him to give even experienced deputy district attorneys a bad time. She would not have picked Lutz as Delgado's first venture into the broad world of forensics.

Judith realized at once that something was wrong. The defense attorney was leaning back, far back, in his chair. He was too relaxed. Both the judge and Lutz were leaning far too expectantly toward Delgado. And Delgado . . . where was his trial manual? Not in his hands or on his counsel table. He had nothing in his hands. No notes. No written questions.

Calm and collected, he strode casually before the witness and smiled in Lutz's direction.

"Now, Mr. Lutz," he began "did you, on the date in question or at any other time previously or subsequently, say, or even intimate, to anyone, connected to this case or not, that the testing of the defendant's blood was concluded and as a matter of importance or otherwise revealed he was intoxicated? Answer yes or no."

There was a moment of silence as Lutz's shrubby gray brows closed together.

"Yes or no *what*, Counsel?"

Judith grimaced and felt the judge's gaze shift to her direction.

"Okay . . ." Delgado paused, having no intention of answering a question he undoubtedly could not remember. "Okay . . . we've talked about, at length, how the blood-testing process works or does not work. Is there anything that we haven't covered that you can think of, anything in your mind that you're thinking about how that testing takes place that I haven't asked you and you're thinking, 'he hasn't asked me that' and 'I'm not telling him because he hasn't asked me.' Is there anything?"

Lutz was merciless. "My God, have you gone and lost your mind or something, Counsel?" he asked as the entire jury and spectator section erupted in a roar of laughter. When the noise subsided, Lutz turned and looked up at the judge. "I didn't understand the question, Your Honor." There was another, more subdued wave of laughter as the defense attorney shook his head.

Delgado blushed and stood helplessly as the judge took over the questioning of the witness.

"Mr. Lutz, can you please tell us what test you used to determine the defendant's blood alcohol level?"

As Lutz began to recite in monotone detail the test steps taken to determine the defendant's blood alcohol level, Judith looked toward the judge. He was staring at her again, surely wondering if Delgado really did have some connection to her unit and, if so, how that had come to be.

Judith rose to leave the courtroom. Delgado had not seen her come in, and for now, she wanted to keep it that way—chalk this performance up to inexperience and lack of preparation time. But the fool! To enter a first trial improvising questions to a witness like Lutz! He'd not yet learned how little he knew. Judith could feel Levine's eyes follow her as she left the courtroom.

6

"You've lost weight."

Judith's comment was directed toward Pike Martin. He had appeared, silently, in her office doorway, a white Styrofoam cup of coffee in his hand. She hadn't seen Pike for months, but it was one of the peculiarities of their relationship that they seldom greeted each other with extraneous salutations. Their conversations began as though they'd never ended.

"Thanks for the compliment. I've been trying. No beer. No pizza. No cigarettes." He walked to a chair across from her desk and sat down before he added, "No loose women."

He was dressed casually in a teal blue polo shirt and brown pants. She'd been expecting him to drop by. Normally she worked with the investigators from her own office rather than from the San Diego Police Department, and it had taken a full day to finally connect with him by phone. When she did, he was already up to speed on the Carrasco murder, although he didn't know much more than she already had in her file.

"You're not on duty," Judith said. His graying hair was cut shorter than usual, and his wiry eyebrows looked to have been lightly trimmed of their wild strands. Something else was new as well. It was the unmistakable emergence of a thin mustache. The overall effect of the new look was to soften his otherwise weather-worn face.

"Not this afternoon. And by the way, you're looking okay yourself." He craned his neck slightly over the desk and gave an obvious glance to the ring finger on her left hand. "You haven't hooked up with any eligible attorney yet?"

"You must be kidding, Pike. I haven't the time. Or the inclination. And even if I had the inclination, it wouldn't be with an attorney."

"Good. Then there's still hope for me," he said, and not waiting for a response, added, "I hear you've hired this good-looking eligible bachelor who's got all the ladies making detours to say hello."

"You must mean Peter Delgado. He's too young for me."

"Hey, says who?" he bellowed in her defense.

"Says the district attorney. Besides, I have my hands full just trying to keep him busy with cases he can handle."

"Yeah. I heard about what Lutz did to him in court the other day."

"News travels fast, doesn't it?"

"I got it straight from Lutz himself. It must have been quite a scene."

"You know I wish you pompous investigators would let up once in a while. What Lutz did was inexcusable."

"But, Judith! We get dead bodies. Blood. All day. The dregs of life. The courtroom's the only real entertainment we get sometimes. You wouldn't take it away from us, would you?"

Pike looked up at the wall clock. "I need to be back at my office in twenty minutes to interview a witness, but I'm planning to head up to McGonigle Canyon tomorrow morning on that Carrasco murder. You oughta come up with me. We can take a look around. Maybe I can take some photos of my own."

As Pike stood to leave, he ran the index finger of his right hand across his upper lip and, she thought, might have winked at her. She couldn't be sure. Pike had a nervous habit of blinking in times of stress, and the very mention of the Carrasco murder case might be sufficient to produce the effect. In any event, if it was a wink, it was a harmless wink. They'd met several years earlier when he was assigned to investigate the murder of a seven-year-old girl. At the time he was still recovering from the accidental death of his own daughter and the emotional roller coaster of an acrimonious divorce. He was one of the most thorough detectives she'd ever worked with. But he also exhibited traits she didn't admire in law enforcement: a cynical brutishness that jeopardized the case against a serial murderer by pushing a fragile prosecution witness to the brink of suicide. He'd mellowed, perhaps. On the exterior he was certainly more genteel. But to Judith's mind, people didn't change that completely that fast. The Pike Martin who had a disdain for the system and its formalities was still in there and was bound to emerge sometime again. Maybe not this day. Maybe not this case. She liked him, sure, but not enough to wink back. If it was a wink.

* * *

At ten o'clock the following morning Judith met Pike in the county parking lot next to the courthouse. She slipped into the passenger side of the county-issue unmarked green Dodge, shifted her brown leather briefcase off her lap to the floor, and buckled herself into an almost comfortable position on the flat bench seat. The county cars were all the same, bare-bones and smelling like cigarettes.

"I brought along the file on Carrasco. I still haven't been able to get hold of much more than what Farrell sent over to me. Farrell tells me you have a contact up near the canyon?"

"Yeah. Lee Ward. We're going to meet him now. His family's lived in the area for decades. They owned hundreds of acres on the east side of Interstate Five. He still owns about thirteen acres. The rest got sold off to the developers. I've known Lee a long time. We served together in Vietnam. He saw worse there than I did; he got shot up and was shipped home. After the war he went down to Mexico. Spent a long time there traveling, working for the government mapping or something. He even went down into Central America for a few years. I think he was married down south, but I don't ask too many questions. Anyway, he knows the Mexican people, their culture and languages. He's been living alone in North County for ten years or so. When I called him, he was pretty excited about helping."

Twenty minutes later Pike turned east off the freeway onto surface streets lined with palm trees.

"I remember when I was back in law school in the seventies," Judith said. "There was nothing up here, Pike, but tomato fields. Now look. Shopping centers. Malls. High-rise condominiums everywhere. You've got to wonder how there can be a

canyon full of migrant laborers anywhere near
here."

"They're here. How visible they are depends on
the season. In the spring when the crops are going
in and during the picking seasons they're almost
lining the streets. They sit on the corners in the
morning and wait until someone comes by looking
for cheap labor. Not just growers. The folks around
here keep their gardens and lawns manicured with
the locals. Look over there."

Pike pointed to the corner of a busy intersection
where a group of five or six Hispanic men in T-
shirts and Levi's stood leaning against a concrete
retaining wall, in no obvious hurry to cross the
street. As Judith watched, a gray pickup truck
pulled to the curb. When it was gone, so were two
of the men.

"The migrants are put up with as long as they're
not in the faces of the upscale folks around here.
When they get too visible, too close, the heat's on."

Pike turned his car east again for a mile to the
end of the development, and a few miles later he
made a sharp right turn onto a bumpy unpaved
dirt road and headed up a steep hill.

"Mind . . . telling me . . . where . . . we're going?"
Judith asked, fighting the rutted road for her
words.

"Lee's," Pike yelled over the noise of creaking
car joints and a suspension system not built for all-
terrain travel. He pointed to his right. "There it is,
up there."

At the top of the hill Pike brought the Dodge to
a stop in front of a square wooden box of a house,
its doors and windows screenless and wide open.
Pike got out. "I'll see if he's inside, Judith. Go
ahead and take a look around."

Judith stepped from the car into silence. She walked to the edge of the hill. In the distance, in every direction as far as she could see, were the pinks and browns of new condominiums.

From a pile of tires, a yellow striped cat appeared, meandering toward her legs, where it pushed against her ankles, purring. It was a domestic cat, yet it had a distinctively wild look, with strong back legs and a lean body.

Judith turned back toward the direction of the house and saw Pike walking toward her accompanied by a man dressed in blue jeans and a short-sleeved cotton plaid shirt; his sweat-stained straw hat was coming unraveled at the brim over his forehead.

Lee Ward was tall, maybe six feet two, his arms long and swinging languidly at his sides as he walked. His round eyes were bright azure blue, a stark contrast to his sun-browned skin and shoulder-length bleached blond hair pulled back into a ponytail secured with a rubber band. His mouth, a straight line with a slightly puckered upper lip, looked as if it had been slashed across the bottom of his face, giving him a reptilian quality. *He belongs to this place, to the arid land out here*, Judith thought.

"Pike's been telling me all about this case you have," Ward began. "He wants to get you out to McGonigle and let you take a look at where this Carrasco died. But if I might suggest we take my car instead of yours? Mine's been all beat to hell by the driving around here, and if we have to leave it in a gully somewhere, it's no big deal."

"Before we go, can you tell me what area this is?" Judith pointed to the condominiums in the distance. "I'm all turned around here."

Ward moved next to her, stretching his arm out near her shoulder.

"Out there about five miles is Del Mar. That's on the west side of the freeway. Where you were just pointing is Los Peñasquitos and Carmel Mountain Ranch. Beyond that, the big mountain out there, that's Black Mountain. Where we're standing here is about halfway between Del Mar and Peñasquitos. There's a proposal to build a new freeway through here, down near the high-power electrical poles you'll see in a minute. But it's stalled. The state's agreed not to begin it until the land is properly planned for development. So a good part of this area is in a holding pattern for another four years at least."

While Judith struggled to orient herself, Ward led them to his small Dodge Colt.

"Mind if I take some notes as we drive?" Judith asked as she climbed into the backseat and Pike squeezed into the bucket seat in the front.

"Okay by me," Ward laughed. His cause for humor soon became obvious. With each rut, each bump the car took, her pencil bobbed uncontrollably in her hand, leaving black lines scrawled on the yellow notepad. She was glad Pike was along. Between the two of them, they might remember what Ward was yelling as they drove.

"They call this camp Rancho de los Diablos, Ranch of the Devils."

"Why devils?" Judith yelled back.

"It's supposed to refer to the family that owned all the tomato fields around here where all the migrants used to work. I say 'used to work' because the tomato growers ran into some hard times, mostly because of the costs of water and lawsuits filed against them by the Immigration Naturalization Service. The INS gave 'em a real hard time. Some of 'em closed down."

The car continued its erratic, jagged route with Judith periodically pushing her head out the passenger window into the wind, her hair blowing wildly. Suddenly Ward's foot hit the brake hard, and his passengers were thrown forward.

"What was that?" Judith gasped as the furry gray animal causing the sudden slowdown raced past.

"Either a very ugly dog or the most beautiful coyote I've ever seen," Ward yelled, his foot pressed to the gas pedal again. "When you see the canyon where the migrants live, you'll think it's pretty bad. But it's known as the Hilton of migrant encampments. At least it has running water patched in by hose from the nursery a mile away, and a couple of chemical toilets that're serviced by the city about once a month."

The car took a sudden dive, forcing Ward into silence as he struggled momentarily to regain control.

Judith leaned forward over the front seat.

"Is it just migrants who live in the camp?"

Ward laughed. "Oh yeah. But about a year ago some white guy moved in and caused a real ruckus. You know, he was a homeless man who must have thought the place looked pretty good after living on the streets downtown. Now *that* really shook up the folks in the homes up along the canyon rim. It's one thing to have migrants down here. At least they work in the kitchens and fields. It's quite another for the place to become a homeless camp."

"It didn't last long," Pike shouted. "I remember when the city evicted the guy."

By now hundreds of acres of brown earth and scrub grass surrounded them, split only by the dirt road, metal towers, and utility wires. A mile ahead a thick ribbon of green stretched to the east and west. Without asking, Judith knew it was Mc-Gonigle Canyon.

Another five minutes passed before Ward pulled his car to the right and stopped the motor. "Let's get out for a minute. The camp's down below us. You can get a pretty good view from up here."

Pike and Judith climbed out of the car and followed Ward toward the rim of a canyon. "It's just down there."

"Down where?" Judith asked. "There's nothing down there but trees and shrubs."

Ward stepped next to Judith and lowered his head, looking in the same direction as she. He straightened his body and, placing his hands on her shoulders, moved her ten feet to the right.

The movement dramatically changed the landscape. The solid wall of green and brown vegetation below was suddenly dotted with red, white, and gray, colored mirrors reflecting the sun.

"What . . . ?" Judith was confused.

"Plastic. Plastic and wood houses—cantons. That, Mrs. Thornton, is McGonigle Canyon."

"'Incredible" was the only word she could say. Then, placing it all in the context she knew best, she asked, "Are all those people here legally?"

"Some are. But there are plenty who aren't."

"Where's the INS? Why don't they pick them up?"

"Ahh, *la migra*! Immigration. The INS. It doesn't do any good. They come in once in a while, but the few men they pick up don't even bother to stop and gather their belongings at the hovels. They're taken to the other side of the border, dropped off, and they're back over the border the same night and at work the next morning without skipping a beat. Everyone knows it. No one tries hard to change it. If the INS really rounded everyone up, they'd put the growers out of business. Everyone understands that."

"Haven't the trade unions been able to help?" Judith asked.

"Oh, a little after the Vietnam War, about 1975, César Chávez and his United Farm Workers came in. Chávez said the conditions were the worst he'd seen anywhere. The VFW recruited seventy-five of the farm hands, but the farmer fired 'em, just like that." He snapped his fingers to emphasize the speed of the firings. "A couple of Chávez's organizers were shot at, so they left; he picked a different battleground." He gestured with a wide sweep of his right arm. "This outlives everything."

Lee Ward lifted his sweat-stained straw hat with one hand, stroked his hair with the other, and pushed the hat back onto his head, tilting it down over his forehead.

"Most of the people down there come up for the growing and picking seasons and then go home to Mexico. They come up here because the earth around them down in Mexico dries up and blows away. The corn won't grow no more and the babies starve. This here is no different than what brought my granddaddy to California from Oklahoma back in the thirties. They get pushed here and there. Kinda like fleas. Someone scratches 'em and they move somewhere else. But they keep heading north. Some researcher up in Riverside says they're all the way up to Oregon and Washington."

Ward stopped, carefully choosing his words.

"McGonigle Canyon is a stinking stew of human debris and color. That's what it is. It's the best and worst, dreams and dirt all wrapped up together in plastic stuck together with pins." He looked, expressionless, at Judith. "Makes me want to puke and sing at the same time."

They were silent until Ward spoke again.

"You like canyons, Judith? Everyone has their own canyon. A place you go through or jump over. It can be fun or it can be hell. That's their canyon."

"It's scheduled for demolition in October. A couple of months from now," Pike added dryly. "That could cause us problems if our murder isn't solved. These folk'll be scattered everywhere."

Ward's response was reassuring. "Ah . . . well, I wouldn't worry. I'll believe it when I see it. It was scheduled for demolition before, in 1991. And it's still down there, like some shrub pruned every now and then, it grows back stronger. Just watch, when moving day gets closer, some church up here will get real noisy, the Good Samaritan groups will file a lawsuit, and some court, some judge somewhere, will grant a stay and the parties will reach an agreement. Those that have to move will scatter like so many weeds and just put their roots down in some other part of the canyon." Ward smiled at Pike, and Judith noticed for the first time that his teeth were bright, shiny white. He turned, heading for the car, and called to them, "The great thing about canyons is you don't know what's in 'em all the time. Wanna take a look?"

The car bumped and ground its way to the entrance of the encampment where the road smoothed out enough to lower the discussion several decibels. They were again in the middle of scrub brush, chaparral, brown-yellow dirt, and high-voltage power lines, the Dodge again bouncing from rut to rut. Judith grabbed the door handle to steady herself.

"Before we visit the murder scene down by the stream, I'll drive you through the camp and let you get a good idea what the place is like."

The car rolled onward, its occupants silent until Judith, suddenly cognizant of the fact there was no one visible in the camp, asked, "Where is everyone?"

"Out working," Ward yelled. "They'll be back tonight, and the place'll really liven up. What you're seeing is a series of small camps separated from each other by chaparral. Each of the camps is home to a different group of migrants. The Oaxacans live in one, the northern Mexicans live in another, and so on."

"They do that for what reason?" Judith asked.

"For the same reason my grandparents lived in Irish neighborhoods. They understand each other's language and customs. Some of the migrant camps get along with everyone else; some don't. Your dead man, Carrasco, was living in the camp of northern Mexicans."

Talk of possible clues, however, was set aside as Judith sat mesmerized by the primitive architecture passing outside the car window.

Houses patched together with wood, paper, plastic—every building material imaginable, anything that could provide shelter from the weather—were hidden back, away from the road, amid the tall weeds and shrubs. Other houses jutted out along the roadside itself—boxes of plywood and plastic, decorated with white lattice materials and graffiti-ridden cardboard.

Paper, bottles, and trash littered the side of the

road. Clotheslines, tied from the trunks of trees to the tops of houses, hung, laden with blue work pants and dresses in the sun.

Abandoned vans and truck shells dotted the area, some hidden in the shrubbery, clearly alternatives for those not fortunate enough to have acquired sufficient building material.

Ward slowed the car, twisted slightly at the driver's wheel, and turned his face to the backseat. "What do you think?" he yelled to Judith.

"Interesting," she shouted in reply.

In truth "interesting" would not have been the one word Judith chose to describe what she was seeing. "Disconnected" would be the word. It wasn't the poverty that elicited the emotion. Certainly there was poverty here. She was no stranger to poverty. She'd worked downtown and in San Diego's barrios, absorbed the violence and death that poverty brings to the gangs and the homeless. She'd moved in and out of those spheres as she pleased or necessity dictated. But still, despite the discomfort they brought, they were part of her world. This was different. She didn't belong here. She had no sense of connection to this place.

Between individual encampments, six-foot-tall weeds pushed out, scratching Ward's car and poking through the open car windows. Periodically there were signs of civilization, including a covered patio complete with picnic benches.

"*Carnitas*," Pike announced. "Can you smell that, Judith!" he exclaimed. Just like Tijuana." *Carnitas*, the spicy chunks of cooked pork, familiar to American tourists who frequented the restaurants and bars of Tijuana, were not one of Judith's favorite foods. To her the smell was heavy and dirty, and combined with the bouncing car, produced a slight nausea.

"That's a restaurant," Ward said. "It's empty now, but someone's cooking dinner, and it'll be full when the men come back from the fields this evening."

"A restaurant . . . Do people pay money for the food?" Judith asked, trying not to breathe too deeply.

Ward laughed. "They do. On Fridays, roasted goat night, dinner runs about five bucks. Everything else around here costs about ten dollars. Ten dollars for translation services. Ten dollars for a taxi ride to town. Ten dollars for five minutes with the prostitute who visits the camp on Saturday. It's a regular community." Ward's voice remained serious. "Actually, believe it or not, the life blood of the camp is the catering truck. It brings breakfast, coffee, and the newspapers. It's the only link these people have to the outside world."

The trio drove on, farther east, farther into the camp.

"Where was Carrasco's body found?" Judith asked.

This was Pike's second trip into the camp, and he was happy to share his knowledge of the area. "About a mile and a half east of here along the river."

Several minutes later, Ward brought the car to a stop amid a cloud of dust. "Here we are. The body was found about three hundred yards to the north there, through that underbrush. Is that about right, Pike?"

"That's about it."

Ward got out of the car and turned to his passengers. "Just a word of caution: we're going to be on a trail, and we may see other people. Keep your distance and let me do the talking."

Ward led Pike and Judith several yards from the car onto a trail marked by well-trodden grass. Every twenty feet or so, another trail led away into the canyon. Occasionally signs of human life appeared: food bags hanging from trees to protect them from the wild animals, garbage and feces, ash-filled open fire pits, and the remnants of plastic-covered lean-tos and wood sheds. With each step the greens and browns of the canyon more and more resembled some kind of subterranean world.

Then, not more than ten feet ahead, a tunnel of vegetation appeared. Ward led them forward into an artery wide enough for one person, a dark surrealistic conduit carved by the flow of human bodies, circulating them in the belly of the canyon.

Pike and Ward were walking fast ahead of Judith. She moved quickly, without slowing them by asking questions, pausing only briefly to push away the weeds and shrubbery grabbing at her sweater and snagging her hair as she walked past.

It's unreal, she thought. *It's out of some fairy tale or some bad dream.* It occurred to her that it would take a person with considerable anger and persistence to track a person through this to kill them.

"Do they have to live like this?" Judith shouted forward to Ward.

He turned back toward her but didn't stop. "They make about four bucks an hour in the fields. That's three times what they make in Mexico. Depending on how much work's available, a good laborer can make between seventy-five and a hundred and fifty dollars a week. It costs about seventy dollars a week to eat if you spend two bucks for breakfast, four for lunch and say three or four dollars a day for dinner. They save a little each week, then send it home. There's enough to live on but nowhere near what it takes to live like a human being in San Diego. So, they're stuck here in this." Ward stopped and motioned to the trail on his left. "This way."

They continued for another fifty yards; then Ward abruptly stopped. There were voices close by. Judith placed her hand on Pike's arm. He placed his own hand instinctively under his brown leather jacket, on the forty-five caliber pistol he wore during his field investigations. Ward, however, was relaxed. "Now," he joked, "*no one* yell *la migra.*"

As the three stepped into a circular clearing, they were confronted by four Mexican men. A small white dog was tethered by a thick rope to the hand of one of the men. They had heard Ward and his companions approach and were waiting for them, standing side by side in front of a plastic overhang propped up by large tree branches. To their right was a fire pit, and to the side of the overhang there was a gaping hole in the ground, half covered by a slat of wood.

As the men stood, confused, and suspicious of their visitors, Ward quickly summarized what they were seeing. "The hole there is a spider hole. Amazing! I didn't think any of these still existed. The men sleep there as long as the weather's warm enough." He turned his attention to the men, his Spanish impeccable. Judith and Pike knew enough of the language to say hello and maybe give some directions, but it was apparent Ward had lived among the Mexican people for a long time.

Within moments the looks of concern on the faces of the Mexicans gave way to smiles and amicable discussion. As they talked with Ward, Judith observed that three of them couldn't have been more than seventeen or eighteen years old. One, adorned with gold bracelets and a gold crucifix around his neck, grinned periodically at Judith and nodded. Ward must surely have been explaining who she was and why they were out walking the canyon. Their friendly talk, however, did not dispel her uneasiness, nor Pike's. His hand still rested inside his jacket, and his eyes never settled for long on any one thing or person.

"Judith, this is Paco here, the one who's smiling so broadly at you." Ward winked at Judith as Paco bowed low from the waist toward her. "This here is Antonio, and his dog Pollito—that means little chicken—and this is Marco, and this older gentleman is Gilberto." One by one the others bowed as they were introduced. "Gilberto has been here in the canyon for a year now. The others are new. They haven't been here more than a couple of months." He turned to Antonio. "*Dos meses, Antonio?* Two months?"

Antonio was suddenly animated. "*Sí, dos meses.* Two." He held two fingers up to Judith in the sign of a V . Then he emphatically slapped the pockets of his blue jeans.

"*Mucho dinero.* Much money go with me."

He needed no translator. He was leaving San Diego a rich man when he returned to Mexico.

More discussion and the name Carrasco was mentioned by Ward and again by Gilberto. And the word "*malo.*" Judith knew the word meant "bad."

"What did he say about Carrasco?" Judith whispered to Ward as they waved good-bye to the men and followed the trail farther into the canyon.

"Not much. Just what you already know—that he was a man who wasn't liked. But he has a lot of relatives up here, and none of them are happy he's dead. Beyond that, they claim to know nothing about the murder."

Several hundred yards from· the encampment, Pike stopped. "This is it, here." Judith recognized the area as having been marked off by the police. Yellow plastic tape still hung scalloped from the bushes, forming a loose circle. approximately ten feet in diameter around the spot where Carrasco's body must have lain. That was the only indication there had been anything out of the ordinary there.

They stood, not really expecting to find anything helpful. Finally they retraced their steps.

At the car Judith brushed the foxtails and bits of dry leaves from her wool skirt, and Pike relaxed sufficiently to remove his hand from under his jacket. Judith looked up toward the direction they had come. There was nothing but shrubs and trees. The trails, the men, and their camps were underneath it, hidden from view.

Ward shook his head and motioned toward the canyon. "How you dig into *that* for the murderer is going to be a real interesting thing to watch. I'd suggest you give it a couple of days and come back, talk to people around here, and see if there's any word of mouth circulating about the murder. I'll come up with you again if you'd like. I wouldn't come up here alone without an interpreter, either one of you." He looked at Judith's high-heeled shoes. "And if you come back up, Judith, you might want to wear tennis· shoes and pants."

As their car rattled through the bumps in the road, retracing the series of encampments, the sound of mariachi music drifted overhead. Men, home early from the fields, dragged themselves sweating and smiling up the trails.

Before they drove off onto the main road toward town, Judith looked back over her shoulder. It was all gone. The men. The clotheslines. The huts of plastic and wood. They were all invisible again, swallowed up by the canyon.

7

JUDITH WAS BACK from McGonigle Canyon and in her office at three-thirty feeling dirty and hot.

Pike called at four to ask if she wanted to return to the canyon the following morning. He pointed out that given the nature of the canyon inhabitants, it was advantageous to investigate Carrasco quickly before potential witnesses and leads disappeared. He and Lee Ward were planning to meet early.

Judith, however, declined the offer. There was nothing she could add by being out there. Besides, she didn't like the place. And unless she had to, she was never going back.

Judith finished reviewing the sentencing files for the following morning. They were all routine, nothing out of the norm or controversial. As she moved the files to her credenza for their morning transfer to Superior Court, Peter Delgado knocked at her office door.

"Come in, Peter. How's the trial going?"

He answered flatly. "It's over."

"Well, come in; tell me what happened." The end of a trial was always an exciting event, and she was anxious to hear how it had gone for him.

Delgado, holding an eight-by-eleven-inch brown envelope, took the chair facing her desk. Head bent, shoulders stooped, he looked at her, and she saw in his eyes all the signs of defeat. She knew, or thought she knew, the cause, and was prepared to give him her standard "it's okay, you'll do much better next time" pep talk reserved specially for new attorneys.

Her voice dropped. "You lost."

Delgado raised his head and stared at her. "No, actually, the jury came in guilty."

Attorneys, particularly new ones, did not react morosely to wins. A win was a cause to celebrate. The office gold star went up on your door the next morning proclaiming a success, a win. Some people in the office even kept track of the number of times the star appeared on each deputy's door! This sullen reaction was foreign to her, and she found herself grasping for words.

"I . . . I don't understand, Peter."

"The jury was out two hours."

Two hours was fast. Assuming a halfway decent case, a prosecutor whose jury came in that fast could reasonably guess the verdict was guilty.

"That's a fast verdict. Sometimes it takes the jury that long just to pick the foreman."

Delgado handed her the envelope he'd brought. "I guess I don't know *why* I won."

Judith lifted the flap of the envelope and immediately recognized the contents. Juror evaluation forms. Judge Levine handed the forms out to jurors after each trial ended in his courtroom; he was one of the few judges who did. Levine found the comments helpful to himself and to counsel, with whom he shared the information.

"Mind if I read these?"

"Oh no, please go ahead. But I'm warning you, they're enough to get me transferred out of this department. They're awful."

The first section of the form asked each juror what they thought about the judge, prosecutor, defense counsel, clerk, and bailiff. Even leafing through them, Judith could see the only person to merit much comment was Delgado. And, as he had warned her, it wasn't flattering.

"Can't form a coherent sentence." "Why is someone inexperienced handling this case?" Several of the forms were personally complimentary. "Nice young man." "Nice-looking young man."

"I've seen worse than this." Her comment went unanswered as she read on through all twelve juror forms plus the one from the alternate juror. "Okay. So they're not all that great, but you know, Peter, some cases you're going to win not because of how good you or the opposition may be but because of the kind of case it is."

He raised his head.

"You don't have to make me feel better."

"No, really. How can I explain this. . . . You see, Justice has a life of its own in the courtroom, Peter. Take your run-of-the-mill drunk driving case. Unless the evidence is totally screwed up, the jury will most often come in guilty. It's like the jury looks right through you and you're going to feel almost irrelevant. The DUI case you had? Think about it. It was a strong case. Fifteen, twenty years ago when drinking was more acceptable and there was more sympathy for the drinking driver, maybe the case would have taken a different turn; it would have taken two days to get a verdict. Juries don't tolerate drinking and driving like they used to. It's funny, maybe, but your competence in the courtroom isn't that critical sometimes. *Sometimes.*'' She paused to allow him to say something. When he didn't, she continued.

"On the other hand, there are going to be cases where you, the judge, and all the court personnel know the defendant's guilty, and no matter what you do, no matter how good you are, you're going to lose because the judge makes a ruling that the jury can't hear the most damaging evidence, or the victim was a scoundrel who some might think deserved to die, or your defendant is the kind of person the jury doesn't *want* to find guilty. My first murder case was like that. A wife shot her husband point-blank in the head while he was sleeping. It was a righteous first-degree murder. And that's how I prosecuted it. I expected to win it too. For the first time at trial we all learned her husband routinely beat her and their three kids. The jury was out an hour. An hour. And they came in not guilty. I was crushed. That was twenty years ago. Now, looking back, well, the jury might have been right. I guess, Peter, one of your jobs here is to learn the skills that'll help you. Those are the tough ones. Aside from those helpful things, the jurors are usually right about the attorneys. You've read the forms. You know what you need to work on. Your instincts are right and your presentation's fine. You just need . . . more experience.''

Judith reached toward the trash can next to her desk, slid the evaluation forms ceremoniously into it, and reached behind her, taking a file off the credenza.

"Forget the forms. Here's your next case. It's another misdemeanor set for trial two days from now. I had the assignment desk send it up for you. It's a solicitation of prostitution. If you look on the cover of the file where the case history is written, you'll see we offered the defendant a plea bargain and he's refused to take it. He's demanding a trial. There are two witnesses to the solicitation, the prostitute and the john who propositioned her— the defendant. It's the john who's on trial. It's a simple trial to put on—and it'll be a *miracle* if you get a guilty verdict."

"Weak evidence?"

"No. The case is a strong one. But the prostitute was an undercover policewoman, and the john is a good-looking white college student with a major in business administration. He'll be in court in a suit and tie. The jury's not going to *want* to find him guilty. They'll be waiting for you to make a mistake, watching you like a hawk.

Delgado reached for the file in her hand.

"You'll do fine. Just give yourself some time." There was one more thing she wanted to say that might make him feel better. "I don't mean to disillusion you. The point is the jury's the conscience of the community. Most of the time it's a pretty good conscience. It's not the cases where the jury does its own thing that worry me the most, it's the case that comes along where you emerge victorious doubting whether you should have won, wondering if your trial skills overpowered the truth."

Delgado stood leafing through the file. Maybe he hadn't heard the last part of what she'd said.

"Just do the best you can. After that, it's up to the jury. The people, they're going to do what they think is right."

Delgado spent a few silent minutes examining the file.

"You know, Peter, I was in the courtroom for a few minutes, and from what I saw, you *could* spend more time preparing your questions."

He looked up at her and blushed. "I know."

When Delgado left, Judith drank a cup of coffee and fidgeted at her desk, cleaning out the center drawer and several of her personal files. By the time she'd finished, it was six o'clock. The stickiness of McGonigle Canyon still clung to her. Between the canyon visit and reviewing the cases in the office, it had been a very long day. By the time she reached home, she'd be late enough to have missed dinner. But that was okay. The house seemed to run along fine without her. It was functioning efficiently. Not joyfully. Joy needed peace to thrive. Her life was not peaceful. There was too much pain for peace. But it was happy. For now that was the best she could manage.

Yet something had changed. An imperceptible something. There was a distance growing between herself and her mother. It was as physical as it was mental. Her mother was spending more and more time in bed. Judith was spending less and less time talking to her. There were quick good-byes in the morning, hellos followed by quick good nights as Judith rushed to get Elizabeth set for the next day. She couldn't remember when she'd last sat with her mother. Now, with Elizabeth away for the summer with her father, there were, theoretically, fewer obstacles to Judith's spending more time with her mother. So why was she delaying leaving her office?

Judith reached for the Rolodex next to her phone. She quickly located the name and phone number of her aunt Margaret, her mother's sister, in Canton, Ohio. Judith needed to call her. She should have called long ago. But why? What would she say? For starters she needed to tell Aunt Margaret that her sister was dying. But "dying" wasn't the right word. Dead. "Dead" would have been closer to the truth. But Judith didn't like the word, and the thought that she would even begin to categorize her mother as dead only heightened her own sadness and feeling of betrayal. Besides, Aunt Margaret could never understand the nuances of the word. She was the more literal of the two sisters. Judith had taken her to see King Tut's treasures when they were on tour in the United States. She'd viewed the entire exhibit in fifteen minutes, waiting impatiently as Judith spent several hours moving from one item then another. She'd be all in a panic and think her sister was really dying, as in "currently departing this world," and that was nowhere near the truth. Judith put the Rolodex back. She would call and tell Aunt Margaret what was happening when she knew what was happening.

Judith rose slowly and looked around. Her desktop was clear of all files. The next day's assignments had been made, all telephone messages answered. Even her conscience had been placated. There was nothing left to do. She pulled the file on the Carrasco murder, slipped it into her briefcase, and called her mother's aide to tell her she was on her way home.

Serafino sighed and stared into the darkness of the hole where he slept, the smell of earth filling him with remembrances of home, of his wife and children, and of the corn that sprung from the wet ground after a long rain. Sometimes if the rains were good, the corn lined the dirt roads as far as he could see. For now, it was no use to conjure such thoughts. He had killed a man.

He should have been feeling despair for his conduct or anger at himself. He should feel *something*. Carrasco was a man, like him. He ate, breathed, maybe loved. Yet Serafino felt nothing. This life had numbed his heart as surely as it had numbed his hands.

Serafino pushed away the wood roof of the hole just a crack and stared up at the stars. He breathed deeply the smell of the dirt around him, and for a brief moment he was back in Oaxaca, in his little village.

8

PIKE DUG THE toe of his heavy brown boot into the dry earth, waiting for the camp to come alive, waiting to talk to anyone who might know Rogelio Carrasco. He yawned. His eyes were stinging dry from the lack of sleep. It had been a rough night for his homicide detail. Shortly before 2 A.M. the first call came in. A man's body had been found by a bar owner just outside the back door of his downtown business establishment. No suspects were in custody, but a fight had broken out inside the bar between the thirty-five-year-old male victim and an acquaintance, over a debt.

As a member of the homicide detail, Pike had been awakened from a sound, unusually dreamless sleep. He'd put on his yellow police jacket and sped to the scene, where he helped interview witnesses and supervised the technicians and photography. He left notification of the victim's family to others. After decades of homicide work, he'd grown too dispassionate to feel adequate in such sensitive matters. An occasional case still moved him. Child murders. Kidnappings. Not much else.

The second homicide call came before he finished the investigation of the first. A homeless guy, fighting with another homeless guy. Words exchanged. A knife pulled. One man down. Permanently. No identification on the victim. When the evidence was processed, the body was dispatched to the coroner as a "doe," identity unknown. The wrap-up there lasted until four-thirty. Then there was enough time for coffee and a donut before the forty-minute trip north to McGonigle Canyon.

The early arrival time had not been his choice. Lee Ward suggested that if Pike wanted to do some serious interviewing, it would have to be before the men left for the fields.

Pike shivered. At fifty-two, his ability to work through the night had lost its allure. He'd been standing in the same place for twenty minutes too long, and the chill wetness of dew deposited a film on his jacket, melding him into his surroundings. There was an awareness of the smell of burning wood mixed with the still-frigid air.

At last Pike recognized Lee Ward's battered Dodge Colt. Pike and Ward issued perfunctory greetings and joined the men gathering at small fires. Ward immediately began a friendly discussion with the man next to him, and after a few minutes of chatter and laughter, Ward turned, grinning, to Pike. "He's a fisherman. He says someone told him if he goes to the ocean here, he'll see little children riding on wood planks on the waves."

The young fisherman smiled and shook his head. As Pike watched, the man took a bottle of hand lotion that was being passed around the fire, and rubbed his hands with the pink ointment.

Pike sipped his instant coffee as Ward made the rounds of the groups forming nearest the fire. Pike could catch bits of what was being said, and he recognized the name Carrasco. *Mal hombre.* A new name was repeated two, three, then four times. Serafino Morales. *A Serafino no le gustaba, y hace dos días que se desapareció.*

"What's he saying?" Pike interjected.

"He says this man, Serafino Morales, seems to have disappeared, been gone for two days now. And he didn't like Carrasco.

Pike took a small notebook from his jacket pocket and began to take notes. "Anyone here admit to knowing our victim, Carrasco?"

"Only a few men. No one liked him, but no one's willing to get more detailed than that. The man across from me there does say we'd better find this Serafino before Carrasco's family does."

"What do you mean?" Pike asked.

"Carrasco's two cousins are out to kill Serafino. Here in the camps, the men bring more than their language. They bring their cultures. Every one of the individual camps does things its own way. They have their own songs, foods, and their own law. Our law doesn't mean too much to them. In Mexico there are certain things one man does to another that call for certain things to be done. If this man Serafino has killed Carrasco, he's going to have to pay for it under the law of the canyon here."

Pike was direct. "Unless *our* law gets to him first."

A flatbed truck pulled into position behind the catering truck.

"That's a ranch foreman," Ward said, "coming for men to work the fields." The two listened as the foreman began to yell in Spanish. The men around him shook their heads and stared at their feet.

"What's wrong?" Pike asked.

"There's only three hours of work today and the men are unhappy."

Despite the expressions of unhappiness, the back of the truck began to fill with men until it overflowed.

Pike and Ward stood side by side watching the last of the men leave the camp. "So much for a labor strike," Pike mused.

Ward's eyes did not leave the road and the dust trail of the last flatbed, now a quarter mile away. "Today there's so little work, they'll be back here by noon, bored, frustrated, and hungry. Most will have scarcely earned twelve dollars. Enough for tortillas." Ward added, "These people are the poor ones. They do the work; they do the suffering. And always, in the end, they wind up with nothing. That's the way it is. That's the way it's always been."

Pike watched Ward's jawbone set firmly as the last truck disappeared from view. When it was gone, Ward turned to him. "One of the men gave me a name, someone we can talk to." He turned and began walking briskly down the road. Pike followed, content for the moment to allow Ward to lead the investigation.

At the end of the encampment, just before the weed and shrub dividing it from the next camp, Ward stopped and examined the canton nearest the road. Apparently satisfied they were headed in the right direction, he walked to a small footpath and followed it perhaps fifteen yards.

An old, gutted van with its two front tires flat nestled against overgrown iris, its rusting blue-

and-white exterior covered by a thick layer of dirt. Three-foot-tall weeds curled up the front of the vehicle between the bumper and hood. Behind it stood a long low wood shack with a white fiberglass roof. Old furniture and broken wood crates littered the yard.

Barely three feet high, the canton's door consisted of a dirty white sheet.

Ward knocked on the outside wall, and a high voice answered in English: "Come."

Ward pulled aside the sheet and allowed Pike to enter first. Inside, an old man sat on a tattered white wicker chair surrounded by long ropes hanging from the ceiling. Despite the cold, he wore only a pair of brown rayon pants. Pike stepped closer, his eyes adjusting to the dim light. The stringlike shapes hanging from the ceiling were dead snakes. To the left of the man, a plastic bag dangled. It contained what appeared to be five or six dead snakes. Pike grimaced.

The old man smiled broadly, revealing teeth in various stages of decay. "Snacks," he said, gesturing to the ropelike figures surrounding him.

"My God, they eat these things?" Pike whispered.

"No. He means snakes," Ward reassured him. "They use them as medicine."

"*Sí, sí*" the old man grinned. "*Para medicina. Para las vacas* . . . cows." He struggled for English words.

"I squash . . . send home to village in Mexico. *Vacas enfermas* . . . sick. Push snacks down the throats. Cows *se mejoran* . . . much better."

The man lapsed into Spanish as he and Ward spoke for what seemed to Pike to be an interminable length of time. Pike was unable to follow any of the conversation. Agitated by his lack of understanding and the musty odors of the canton, he was fidgeting, ready to leave.

At last Ward said good-bye and motioned for Pike to leave. Outside he pointed to the small notebook Pike was still carrying with him. "The snake man's the camp gossip. Take this down. Don Rufaldo, the owner of one of the restaurants, says someone told *him* Carrasco and this Serafino Morales supposedly argued. He doesn't know what they argued about, but Rufaldo says Serafino was beaten up by Carrasco. Word has it Serafino killed him in revenge, but that's all just rumor. There's another rumor too. When Carrasco's cousins get back from burying him down in Mexico, Serafino's a dead man."

"Where do we find Serafino?"

"The snake man says Serafino is a Mixtec, an Indian from Oaxaca. The Oaxacans are looked down on by the people from Guerrero and by everyone else, for that matter. They live at the very end of the camp system, and they cook and live separately from everyone else. None of the other twenty or so communities has any dealing with them mostly because the Mixtec language is so hard to understand. It'll be hard to track this Serafino down because he says he lives further up . . . in the hills."

"Can we find someone up here who can help us translate so we can interview Serafino's friends?" Pike asked.

"I'm not sure. He says Serafino speaks a little English, but we need to find someone who understands Mixtec."

"Are there any books we can get hold of to help translate?"

"Not really," Ward laughed. "There's no agreement on how the language should be written. It's a real liquid language—very musical and melodic. The meaning of the words depends on tonality, a lot like Chinese. If you change the pitch, you've changed the word's meaning. There's a lot of shading. Some people, me included, don't think it *can* be written down."

"So, who do we get to help us?"

"Damned if I know offhand. Let me think on it. In the meantime, if you want to come back up and canvass the hills for Serafino, give me a call. If you want to do that, we need to get some reinforcements. You and me won't be enough."

The two men walked back to the eucalyptus trees where the catering truck had been parked earlier. It was gone; the only evidence it had been there was the pile of ashes from the morning campfire. Ward got into his car and left, waving good-bye to Pike out the window.

Pike looked at his watch. It was seven-thirty. As far as he was concerned, they had their suspect. Serafino Morales. Now all they had to do was find him. And that wasn't going to be easy because by all indications he'd fled.

9

PIKE FILED HIS report on Serafino Morales, detailing the latest interviews and the investigation in the canyon. He'd called Judith at home and told her a copy of the report was on her desk if she wanted it over the weekend.

On Saturday morning she'd awakened early and, unable to sleep any longer, drove to her office to retrieve the report.

At 7 A.M. the hallways of the courthouse were cold and silent. Because it was Saturday, Judith signed in on the first floor with building security and took the elevator to the fourth floor. As she headed down the hallway toward her office, she noticed the light was on in Peter Delgado's office. She approached the open door and pushed it far enough to see Delgado's head was on his arms, folded on his desktop. He was asleep. She hadn't recalled seeing his name on the sign-in list with security. Certainly, she thought, he couldn't have been here all night, but she'd seen stranger things from young associates.

Rather than wake him, Judith continued on to

her office, leaving the sleeping deputy where he lay. In her office, Judith made a pot of coffee and separated out the Carrasco files, spreading the photos and reports on her desktop.

Thirty minutes later Delgado appeared at her office door.

"Good morning, Peter. You're in early." He was embarrassed, realizing she must have seen him asleep at his desk.

"Actually, I worked through the night. I'm afraid I fell asleep here."

"The case you're working on must be pretty important."

"It's the prostitute-against-college-student case you assigned. Remember the kid in college?"

"I remember. I think I told you it's going to be a tough one for you—"

He finished the sentence for her: "Even though it's an open-and-shut case."

"How's it going? If I recall, I predicted you were going to lose it."

"It's almost over, and I can't tell how it's going. We're in jury instructions on Monday. That's what I'm working on."

"Well, remember, don't feel too bad if you lose."

"I won't. I'm watching the jury. There's one lady crosses her arms over her chest every time I question witnesses. I think I've lost her already."

"Hey, how about a cup of coffee? It's ready. You look like you could use one. Have a seat and relax."

"Okay, thanks. Cream and sugar if you have it. I'm going to work a little longer, then go on home."

Judith handed Delgado a cup of coffee and waited for him to restart the conversation. He drank half the cup, then abruptly asked, "Do you like your job?"

Somehow the question was not entirely a surprise.

"I love it. I started here when I was about your age. It's all I've ever done. But then, I always fancied myself a public servant. Why do you ask?"

"I just wondered."

"How about you, Peter? Do you like your job?"

Delgado, who'd been avoiding eye contact with her, looked at her for the first time. "I don't know yet. So far so good."

"That's it? So far so good?"

"No, actually . . . I'm pretty miserable. I'm sorry. I don't mean to sound unappreciative. I know things got moved around to offer me this job."

"No offense taken."

"It's just that I'm not sure sometimes what I want."

Judith laughed. "It's okay. That's one of the luxuries of youth. After we get you good and trained, you'll probably find a firm specializing in insurance defense work, and in two years you'll be able to buy and sell every one of us here."

He shook his head. "No, no. I mean sometimes I don't know if I made the right choice going into law." He blushed. "I don't think I'm really very good at it. Maybe there's something else I should be doing."

"Well, your first attempt was a bit . . . rough." She smiled. "But you'll be fine. You just need the experience, that's all. Actually, if it means anything, I think you have a lot of potential."

He rose to leave.

"Thanks. It does mean a lot."

"You're welcome. Come back again, anytime."

Judith wished she could have offered some words of wisdom for him before he left. She would have liked to have told him to hang in there and learn all he could as fast as he could. That, she could honestly say, just comes with time. But she couldn't do it. It wasn't a matter of simply gaining more experience with him. He really didn't know what he wanted to do with himself, and there was nothing she could have said that would make him feel any better.

By the time she finished reviewing Pike's report, Delgado was gone.

Judith reached home shortly after eleven o'clock. Jean was in the bedroom, feeding Judith's mother, who was sitting propped up against pillows, her eyes wide open, her face showing the alertness that came so rarely, it brightened everyone in the house when it happened.

"You're looking good this morning, Mom. What's for breakfast?"

Jean answered for her. "Oatmeal and strained peaches."

"Maybe Mom would like to sit outside, Jean. It's overcast but comfortable if you put a shawl around her shoulders."

"Will you be home today, Mrs. Thornton?"

"Yes, but I've been thinking I might like to do a little shopping at Mission Valley."

Judith was looking at her mother when she made the statement about shopping, and ever so briefly, almost imperceptibly, her mother's eyes widened.

Judith wouldn't have been able to tell anyone why she did what she did next. Life was full of daily ups and downs with her mother, and sometimes life seemed almost normal. Those moments she seized unthinkingly.

"Jean?"

"Mrs. Thornton?"

"Get Mom dressed up, and can you call wheelchair transport? Sometimes they're busy, but they might be able to come over. Give them a call, can you?"

"Of course. I didn't know your mother had a doctor's appointment today."

"She doesn't." Judith looked at her mother and smiled. "Mom and I are going shopping."

Instantly she saw her mother's eyes brighten.

"But, Mrs. Thornton, she . . ."

Her mother's eyes moved to Jean, then back to Judith.

"I know, Jean. She can't walk around, but she can window shop with me, right Mom?"

"Well, okay—but—okay."

Judith slid open her mother's closet door and moved aside dress after dress no longer worn until she reached the bright pink flowered cotton one with short sleeves and ruffles at the shoulders.

"Here, put this one on Mom, Jean. I'll be outside. Let me know if the wheelchair transport's available."

Judith stood in the rose garden looking at the flowers, doing nothing more than that, until Jean came outside to tell her the wheelchair transport would be available in thirty minutes. Judith knew Jean could never approve of dragging her mother off to a shopping center. She had always insisted on gentle treatment, and she would never consider this excursion gentle. Moreover, like the doctors who treated her mother, Jean didn't believe there were any feelings or thought processes left in her mother. The doctors had said it expressly, and Judith hadn't believed them then. She could not believe them because they failed to see what she did.

A year earlier Judith's mother paid her last visit to her general practitioner's office. At the end of the examination the doctor asked to speak to Judith and did so in the presence of her mother, who by that time was unable to talk and was already quadriplegic and in a wheelchair. What the doctor wanted to discuss was helping to find a nursing home for her. He was standing behind her mother when he made the statement.

"If you need a nursing facility, you need to get on the lists now."

Judith quickly corrected him. "I don't have any desire to find a nursing home, Doctor. Mom's staying with me at the house, and I'll keep an aid with her."

At that moment she looked at her mother's face and saw her eyes were filled with tears, spilling down her cheeks. Contrary to what every medical expert had been telling her, her mother could hear. And, remarkably, she *understood*. She understood the medical advice Judith had been given. She understood the rejection the doctor sought to facilitate so cavalierly. From that moment on, Judith listened politely to medical advice, but she didn't believe it. Not for a second.

By the time the transport arrived, Judith's mother was dressed and sitting stiffly in her pink floral dress in her wheelchair.

The burly man who drove the wheelchair transporter had Judith's mother loaded before she could say good-bye to Jean. Ten minutes later Judith and her mother were outside the May Company in Mission Valley. Judith hadn't the heart to tell her that since her last visit in what seemed years earlier, the May Company restaurant she loved had closed and the store itself was about to join Robinson's Department Store.

Judith wheeled her mother to the center of the mall, and they strolled up one side of the mall and down the other. All the while her mother's sight was securely fastened on the windows, then on the people, and finally on the pretzel wagon.

"Sorry, Mom. Too hard to chew. Pretzels are out. Doctor's orders." Judith looked around. "But ice cream's not!"

Judith rolled her mother to the ice cream shop across the mall and bought a double scoop of pistachio in a cup. Then she parked her mother's wheelchair in one of the cement circles in the middle of the mall walkway.

Her mother ate the ice cream slowly, Judith feeding her a spoonful at a time, right in the middle of the busiest shopping hour of the day. No one laughed or pointed or thought it odd to see the old woman, her white hair whipped wild in the wind, being fed by a woman who was carrying on a conversation with herself. Periodically there would be a smile of approval on the face of some passing shopper, and it renewed Judith's faith in humanity and in herself.

They watched the shoppers until her mother nodded and closed her eyes. Judith pulled her cell phone from her purse, and in twenty minutes the wheelchair transport returned to the parking lot of the May Company and drove the two women home.

It took but a few minutes to roll the wheelchair from the transport van through the hall entry into her mother's bedroom and several minutes more to transfer her to the bed. Throughout the process she did not stir once.

When her mother was comfortable and covered with a light blanket, Judith sat on the edge of the bed watching her mother's chest move up and down, her thin white hair still disheveled from the afternoon's excursion.

Judith tried to remember what her mother used to look like. What she sounded like. It was so hard to do now. She worried that the woman growing thinner and more frighteningly pale each day would gradually become her permanent, lasting memory. Judith closed her eyes. Remembrances of her mother came to her like photographs. In the one she was seeing now, she was about six, sitting with her mother on the cement steps of the house where Judith spent her childhood. It was growing dark outside, and her mother, slightly overweight with auburn hair not unlike her own, had set a small plate of sliced apples and cut celery between them. They were eating like that, together, not saying anything to each other. Waiting in the quiet for the darkness to come.

Judith opened her eyes and took her mother's hand between her own two, feeling the smooth rice-paper-thin skin covering bulging veins. They were two people sitting, it now seemed, on opposite sides of a great void.

"You're in there, Mom; I know you're in there. You're in there."

A long time passed in silence before Judith took a shallow breath. "Are you in there?"

10

His ROUND RED face greasy with sweat, a balding, puffing don Cardona grinned widely at Serafino. It was eleven A.M., but the temperature had already soared to eighty-nine degrees.

"Come, have a beer with us! A cold beer. Cerveza!"

Serafino had been sleeping near the fields, away from the camps for several days following Carrasco's death. Unsure it was safe to return, he cautiously approached the man he knew in the fields as simply "Rojo," or "Red," a nickname derived from the fact his eyes were chronically reddened from the dust and insecticide of the fields. Although the men spoke different languages, in the course of working together, mutually understood forms of communication emerged.

But no communication was necessary other than the word "beer."

Don Cardona waved again for Serafino to approach as nearby, a man's baritone voice aided by electronic amplification swept across the canyon, the ending notes of each line held torturously longer than the writer could ever have intended.

Don Cardona was a rotund 250 pounds supported by a five-foot-four frame. A bricklayer by trade in Mexico, he was one of the first to come to the canyon in April of 1974. By month's end he was living in the loosely populated canyon, sleeping in a spider hole, and hanging his food in plastic bags from the trees to protect it from the possums and raccoons. Like the other men who settled in the canyon back then, he worked the tomato fields earning sixty-five cents an hour, harnessing himself to plows when the harvesting schedules of the field horses fell behind.

Soon the women began arriving, wives and girl-friends worried about men hundreds or thousands of miles away left to the devices of prostitutes. They came north, sneaking across the borders with the help of coyotes, smugglers. The canyon became home to families and children.

Serafino followed don Cardona off the path and into the encampment, and knew at once the reason for the music and the beer.

In the central area of the camp, between cantons of cardboard and blue-and-white plastic, a loose circle of metal folding chairs had been constructed. The chairs were occupied mostly by children and young adults, all attired in their Sunday best, sporting hair bows and new shoes, the women in the traditional bright-colored skirts, the men in dark pants showing no signs of field dust and dirt.

Clean faces. Clean hands.

At the farthest point in the circle sat don Cardona's fifteen-year-old daughter, Ana María, dressed in white, a wreath of delicate yellow and white daisies atop her straight black hair.

As the resonant singing grew louder still, a

young man approached Ana María, bowing
deeply. Smiling sweetly, she rose, holding the skirt
of her dress up to avoid scraping it along the thick
dirt and dust of the camp. It was a lost cause. The
camp's dirt had already left an ugly brown ring at
the base of her hem. On a gray card table behind
the dancing couple, a three-tier cake leaned to the
left, its white butter cream frosting melting in the
heat.

"*Quinceañera*," don Cardona announced, beam-
ing his approval.

The *quinceañera* was a coming-out party for girls
who reached the age of fifteen. It ranked second in
importance only to first Communion. Despite the
poverty of the family, costs were flaunted as no
extravagance was spared. The girl's dress cost $250.
The cake, from a bakery in nearby Del Mar, cost
$150.

To the right of the circle of chairs, the women
raced to keep up with the growing numbers of
people, throwing pieces of chicken and corn tortillas onto makeshift barbecues of five-gallon
metal drums, flipping the food with their bare
fingers.

Don Cardona thrust a cold can into Serafino's
hand and motioned to the barbecues. Serafino
shook his head. He did not feel comfortable. He
was dirty and sweaty. He would drink the beer
quickly and go.

A young boy, himself no more than seventeen or
eighteen years old, clad in blue denim pants and a
long-sleeved gray-and-blue-plaid flannel shirt,
clothing far too warm for the sweltering heat,
smiled meekly at Serafino from the barbecues.
Serafino recognized Antonio. Antonio lived, like
him, in a dirt spider hole, not far from his own,

waiting for the day he would take his millions of dollars home with him to Mexico.

The boy grinned again at Serafino and turned his attention to the party's guest of honor. He had waited patiently for a chance to dance with her, even though it obviously had taken a considerable period of time. He was a full foot taller than Ana María, and he held her snugly to him, his left hand comfortably against her lower back. The girl looked up at him, blushing. The others had kept their bodies distanced from hers.

As Serafino moved slowly toward the edge of the encampment, a man approached. Serafino knew him only as the snake man. He spoke some Oaxacan, enough that Serafino moved toward him as well, happy to find someone to talk to.

The snake man lost no time communicating the bad news.

"Serafino! You are a marked man, my friend."

Serafino's eyes narrowed to slits.

The snake man leaned toward Serafino's face. "People are talking about you and Carrasco, that wild man. They say you killed him. I told them no, no, you could not do such a thing. You are a good man, a calm man, not a killer."

"Who are these people?" Serafino asked.

"A policeman and a man. Then there are Carrasco's cousins. Both of *them* are looking to kill you if they see your face." He laughed sarcastically, slapping Serafino's shoulder. "You are a very popular man, my friend. But I will be honest"—he leaned closer to Serafino—"I would leave this place. If you do not, you are a dead man."

Serafino glanced furtively around the encampment. "Do others know these people are looking for me?"

"The police have not snooped too much. But Carrasco's brothers have told everyone. They are looking for you," he rasped. "They are in Mexico still, burying Carrasco. They took up a collection from everyone to help send his body back home and give him a Catholic funeral. The police, they took all his money because they thought he must have stolen it. There was too much, over a thousand dollars they say."

"You didn't . . ."

"No! In fact, I have not seen you today. You are not even here." With this, he patted Serafino gently on the right shoulder and strode away into the thick of the party.

Serafino drank down the last of his beer and left without thanking his host.

By the time Serafino reached his spider hole, his mind was set. He had no choice but to leave the area as quickly as he could. He would head north to his cousin's in Fillmore, where he would be safer and where there was work. He would make enough money to send home. He would finish the picking season and go home to his little village and to his wife. He wanted to go home and never come back. He would send his sons, and they could make a new life for themselves and perhaps send money home. But as for Serafino, he wanted his land and his small house. That was all.

11

SERAFINO STOOD LOOKING into the oncoming traffic. It seemed he'd been trying to cross the freeway for at least an hour. His body arched toward the pavement and abruptly stopped. The car was coming too fast. He would never make it across to the center median.

With no watch, he had no way to tell what time it was, but he was growing tired, and it had been dark for at least two hours. He guessed it was maybe nine or ten o'clock.

Soon the checkpoint would have to be dealt with. There, amid bright lights strung across the entire freeway, all traffic would slow to a crawl past uniformed border patrol officers who stared into the oncoming traffic, scrutinizing drivers and cars, looking at the furtive glances and Hispanic faces for any indication illegal aliens or drug runners might be in a vehicle.

He'd need to find some way past the checkpoint before the federal officers saw him. He wasn't sure just how he would do that. It would still be cat and mouse with the traffic.

Serafino walked on in the darkness. Then, just south of the border stop, the traffic unexpectedly halted.

Serafino blinked at the macabre scene unfolding before him.

In the dark, police flares directed traffic from four lanes to two, walking quickly on the freeway itself, heads down, flashlights in hand, beams of light fluttering back and forth, spotlights dancing in crazy patterns on the black concrete. There was no accident in sight, no cars with bent fenders or metal scrapes parked on the side of the roadway. The movements of the police were frantic and strangely different from what he had ever seen in the past.

A hundred feet more. Serafino first saw it out of the corner of his eye. A blanket wrapped around something bulky. He looked closer. The thick bundle was perhaps an animal that had wandered onto the freeway and been hit. But if that was true, what would the police be looking for so frantically?

The officer nearest Serafino reached down, his hand gloved, and picked something up from the asphalt.

What was it? It looked like a—no it couldn't have been.

He saw flannel. Blue-and-gray flannel. His mind locked helplessly on Antonio, the smiling boy who was on his way to make a fortune. Might the bundle have been him? Then he turned away. He did not want to look too closely. His worst thoughts would be verified, and he did not want to know. He hurried away again, north, along the shoulder of the freeway in the darkness and the protection of the pink-and-white oleander.

He wondered where Antonio's dog was.

In the midst of panic, the police had stopped all northbound traffic, and shrouded by the turmoil, Serafino glanced southward toward the body in the road. His fingers pinched together as he made the sign of the cross and slipped, undetected, across the freeway into the dark.

PART TWO

THE FIELDS

12

SERAFINO SAT MOTIONLESS across the street from the wood-and-stucco frame house. The people who lived there were farmers, making a go of it on their own, probably without many laborers to help. These were not the kinds of farms employing the likes of Serafino, so he would have to be content to steal some fruit, a ripe avocado perhaps, and go his way.

By his own guess he was somewhere in the northern part of the county, probably Fallbrook. Night had fallen, and he waited patiently for the lights inside the house to go out, signaling the occupants were going to sleep, leaving him to forage in the fruit trees near the back porch. He'd been canvassing the area most of evening, and as best he could tell, there were two orange trees, an apple tree, and an avocado tree, all bearing what looked to be ripe fruit. Beyond the house were more acres of avocado trees, but they were fenced in, and a large black dog within the compound of trees had warily eyed him as he waited in the road. The an-

imal still patrolled the acreage, although it was nowhere to be seen for the moment.

The road running in front of the house was only
one-way each way, and it wasn't particularly well
paved. The houses were scattered acres apart, their
mailboxes lined up at the crossroads down the
road.

When the last light in the house was turned off,
Serafino waited quietly, taking every precaution to
be sure the occupants were asleep before he
crossed the road. He could not have realized that
inside the house, as was her nightly custom, Pamela Healy was reading in bed. Beside her, her husband Art had plunged into a deep sleep and was
breathing heavily, oblivious to the crunching rustle
of the pages turning in her *Good Housekeeping* magazine or the reading light casting a glow over him
as well as the article on twenty-minute meals to
which she was giving her undivided attention.

For Healy, who had farmed in San Diego County
for thirty-five of his fifty years, from five-thirty in
the morning to eight or nine at night, six days a
week, the day had been especially grueling. The
account books for the previous winter had been reviewed and the news was not good. Summer bore
even darker projections of water costing upward of
ten thousand dollars a month, a far cry from 1972,
when water, the lifeblood of the insatiable avocado
tree, cost a mere sixty-five dollars per acre-foot and
the green thick-skinned tropical fruit fetched hefty
prices at the markets.

And his account books reflected water wasn't his
only skyrocketing cost. Insecticides had risen to
$165 per container. In the end, the scrappy farmer
with the gravelly voice thought they might try to
make a go of it one more year, and if at the end of

the year they were still in the hole, they could always sell the land to the developers who'd called every six months for the last two years, sharks smelling blood.

Art Healy was still in a deep slumber when the avocado tree closest to the bedroom window began to shake. The shaking stopped, then started again.

Pamela reached over and patted her husband's shoulder, startling him awake.

"There's someone out in the yard, Artie," she whispered.

There was a flurry of blankets; then he too listened and heard the rustle of leaves.

Pamela slid out of the bed toward the closet, and from there she took a rifle and walked toward the window, more intent on scaring whatever it was than on killing or maiming them. With her husband at her side, she heaved the window upward as noisily as she could, stuck the weapon out the window, and screamed at the top of her lungs, "Beat it or I'll shoot." Not exactly the most frightening of lines, but she aimed to startle, and Serafino, who had unfortunately chosen to climb the tree for the ripened fruit, was at that moment suspended between branches at the top, reaching for an avocado.

For her efforts Pamela was rewarded with the sound of cracking limbs as an object fell through the tree to the ground below and set to moaning from the pain emanating from his back and shoulders.

"You've got him!" her husband yelled, running down the stairs and out the back door, where to his surprise he was greeted not by a young thug but by the grimacing aging face of Serafino Morales.

Pamela was right behind her husband as he stood above Serafino, and it was she who first mentioned the fact that Serafino in his baggy Levi's and dirty blue jacket did not look the burglar her husband and she had feared.

"He's just an old man, Artie."

Art Healy bent down near Serafino and said in a clear loud voice, "*Yo hablo español.*" He waited for Serafino to respond.

"*Hambre.*" It was the only word of explanation Serafino could offer.

Healy, still staring at Serafino, addressed his wife. "He's hungry."

Art Healy could have given Serafino a swift kick in the pants and chased him from the yard. That was pretty standard operating procedure with some of his neighbors, one of whom, exasperated with migrating illegal immigrants shearing his trees of their fruit, defiantly cut the trees down.

But the sight of hunger was overpowering. Serafino, intruder and disturber of sleep that he was, offered a sad picture. And there was something in the desperation of his struggle that Art Healy understood.

"Make the man a sandwich, can you Pammy?"

His wife cocked her head to the side and struck the sides of her thighs with her hands.

"Do I make the regular or deluxe?" she whispered.

"Better make it the deluxe." He looked down at Serafino, who was not seriously injured, and asked, "Sandwich?" Serafino smiled and nodded as his benefactor pointed to the porch and several of the wood chairs there.

Serafino and Healy sat in the chairs as Pamela Healy busied herself in the kitchen carefully layering ham and cheese on wheat bread with tomatoes and lettuce. Healy allowed Serafino to eat without asking questions, but when he was done and bowed slightly to say thank you, the farmer looked into the window at the kitchen clock. It was eleven-thirty. Serafino clutched at the few words of English he knew, the important words, and said, "I eat, I work."

It took a moment for Healy to realize Serafino was offering to work in exchange for the food he'd been given. Serafino, in fact, was asking if he could continue to work in exchange for food. Thus misunderstanding each other, each said yes.

Healy ushered Serafino to the small packing shed a hundred yards from the house and showed him the cot and blankets routinely kept there for the laborers they used to hire. Had he been able to communicate in the Mixtec language, Healy would have apologized for the meager amenities. To Serafino, however, the packing shed was a palace, and he grasped both the farmer's hands in his own and shook them vigorously before Healy said, "*Mañana*, tomorrow," and went back to his house and to Pamela, who by that time had again retreated to the bedroom and her magazine.

As her husband climbed into bed, she sighed.

"Artie, we don't have any money to pay him."

"He's hungry, Pammy, and he might stay on and work for food and a place to sleep. It's a fair exchange, and besides, what other help do we have? I'll find plenty something for him to do."

"You stubborn old cuss, you just won't give up, will you? This old farm's going to kill you yet."

This was a desperate move, of that she was certain. But there could be no diverting him once his mind was made up, as it was then. Their farm was going down, like their neighbors', who were struggling along with them. She read for ten minutes more, then turned out the light next to her side of the bed. By that time Art Healy and Serafino Morales were already fast asleep.

Pamela Healy was the first to wake. There were kitchen chores to do and breakfast to make, and then she would open the produce stand several acres away where they directly marketed their avocados, apples, and sweet corn, slashing costs by avoiding a produce packer. At five-thirty her husband came downstairs and quickly ate the fried eggs, bread and butter, and coffee she'd set out for him.

"I wonder if our overnight guest's taken off," Pamela said as her husband pushed the bread into the coffee cup, lifted it out, and bit quickly into the soggy mass.

"My best guess is he's there. You got some extra bread and butter, Pammy, and a cup of coffee? He's going to be hungry."

She poured a thermosful of black coffee and wrapped three large chunks of bread in one of her thin red-and-white cotton kitchen towels, set them on the table to the right of her husband's plate, gave him a kiss on the top of his head, and left for the stand. Healy rose from the table and tucked the thermos and bread under his arm. The screen door slammed behind him as he headed in the direction of the packing shed.

He wasn't sure what to expect at the shed. If the man was gone, he was gone and a good deed had been done. But if he was still there, he might have the help he needed.

Healy found Serafino sitting in the dirt near the

door of the shed. On seeing him approach, Serafino quickly rose and again offered a slight bow.

Healy offered a short quick bow in return. Serafino eagerly took the bread and coffee and retreated to the place where he had been sitting next to the shed door. Healy waited until Serafino finished the improvised breakfast, then motioned for the laborer to come with him through the yard to the avocado trees beyond the house. Along the way he remembered to ask his name, and he in turn offered his to Serafino. Thereafter Serafino addressed him as "Meester Heelee," a title that made the farmer smile each time it was uttered.

Serafino's eyes narrowed as the two men walked through several flat acres, then a sloping hillside of avocado trees. The trees were sick, sagging with wilting, leathery leaves and limp branches. Fields of death, thought Serafino as overhead three black crows circled, croaking noisily.

Serafino walked to one of the larger trees and pinched a leaf with his fingernail. He bent to the ground and grabbed a handful of dry dirt, releasing it as dust into the wind, then turned to Healy again, taxing his English vocabulary.

"No water."

Healy, who tried not to walk among the trees if he could help it, turned his eyes from those planted by his own hand decades earlier. He rubbed his forehead, already glistening with perspiration. His response to Serafino was soft and sad. "No . . . no water."

Serafino stared intently into Healy's eyes. He did not know the words to tell him about the cold February morning he stood with his father before the long tunnels of clear plastic sheltering thousands of tiny cucumber plants. His father, always a proud man, was full of uncertainty that morning, speaking to Serafino about the possibility of disaster. With the boy peering curiously at the older man's hands, Serafino's father bent down and peeled back a side of the plastic so his ten-year-old son could see the plants inside. He placed his right hand gently under the green nodules protruding from the stalk and told Serafino the cucumbers were stubby because they were growing too close together. There would not be enough water for them. He explained the best use of water required the cucumbers be more spread out, and as he spoke, he used his thumbnail to sever two small fruits from the cluster of three in his hand. Then he stood up again, looked down at Serafino, and smiled. "You can live," he said, "with whatever God gave you."

Serafino nodded knowingly at Healy. Then he braced his back upward and, standing as erect as he could stretch, held up his right hand, his five fingers extended, and with his left hand motioned to the trees and then to his extended fingers. He bent to his palm the thumb, middle finger, and little finger, leaving two extended. The message was clear and not lost on the experienced grower. Cut down three and leave two standing. It would save water and give the remaining trees a chance to survive.

Healy pursed his lips and placed his hand firmly on the shoulder of the older man.

For the next week Serafino and Art Healy laced the avocado orchards, first ruthlessly marking with red paint those trees that were to be cut, and just as mercilessly cutting down first the youngest, most immature trees, then those that had been most damaged by the lack of water. This complete, they marked every other tree with yellow paint, thereafter cutting down each marked tree until approximately three of every five trees had been reduced to unsightly stumps.

13

———◆———

PIKE REACHED A detour, one demarked by
yellow plastic police tape. He'd seen the tape from
a distance, and although he'd intended to make a
right turn into the encampment to take photos of
the place Carrasco was killed, and could still have
made that turn, his curiosity and the sight of the
coroner's white van drew him from his original
course.

A gang killing or drunken fight was undoubtedly the cause. But there was a little too much excitement for a simple death by brawl. For one
thing, there were two television remote trucks. One
remote truck and maybe someone's doing a feature
story on life and death in the canyon. Two remote
trucks from two different stations and something's
going on beyond a story on habitat. Beyond the
numerical count, Marín Montoya, a lead reporter
for one of the local television stations, was engaged
in animated conversation with a cameraman. It was
a genuine news event.

The homicide detective in charge recognized
Pike even without the badge he flashed at him, and

waved Pike past. Once he reached the edge of the canyon, Pike saw the body of a man lying halfway to the bottom. The man was wearing a white suit. A white Panama hat lay nearby. This was no field laborer.

"What do we have?" Pike asked the officer standing next to him.

"Seems we have a city official, sort of," the officer said. "A guy named Rex Cutter, some big-time lobbyist for Talbot Construction. Used to be a city councilman way back when."

"What the hell's he doing out here?" Pike asked, leaning over the canyon edge.

"No clue. The coroner says he's been dead for maybe three hours. He left a big black Mercedes locked up a quarter mile down the road there. We haven't found any reason why he'd be here in the canyon. We took his car keys down and checked it out. It has gas and starts up."

"Possibly surveying the area for his employer. Maybe just taking a leak. Who knows," Pike offered. "Are there any signs the guy was murdered?"

"None. The coroner says he has all the signs of having died of a heart attack. There's a nasty-looking bite and swelling on the left leg. He thinks the guy was bitten by a rattlesnake and his heart shut down before he could get help."

Pike shook his head. "That still doesn't explain what he's doing so far from his car."

"No, it doesn't.

"Mind if I take a look around down there?"

"Just watch your step. It's slippery down there. We're treating it as an accidental death."

Pike maneuvered down the slope of the canyon, digging the heels of his leather loafers one at a time into the dry crusty soil to secure a foothold. The chaparral clung to his clothing, leaving brown foxtails and dry, curled leaves stuck to his pant legs.

He stopped next to the body and raised his head, his eyes sweeping the hot, silent canyon. Cutter got out of his car and walked a long distance. He'd left behind an expensive car. And he'd locked it. He wasn't intending to return to it for a while.

A brown hawk glided slowly above them; having framed its prey, it was forming circles of diminishing circumference. Cutter did not belong out here, of that Pike was certain. Although Pike had no cause to be involved in investigating the death of the lobbyist, instinct overcame protocol. What his instinct told him was that a piece or two was missing in the scene. There were explanations for why Cutter might be here, but none of them made clear sense.

Pike looked again at the body beside him and carefully considered the propriety of his next move. Rule one in homicide is that you don't move evidence or you risk tainting it. But this wasn't ruled a homicide, and who was Pike to question it? So he did what under other circumstances he would not have done.

Cutter's body lay in a fetal position on its left side, his hands clutching his chest. In the process of coming to rest, his suit coat had fallen open, exposing the white silk lining and an interior pocket into which a white envelope had been tucked, protruding an inch or so.

Pike knelt next to the body, and when the officers at the scene were occupied elsewhere, he reached over and pulled the envelope out by its corner, exposing half of it and the name "Rogelio Carrasco" hand printed in bold black letters just below the top right corner of the envelope. Pike stuck his thumb and index finger under the open flap, spreading the paper to look inside. His thumb pushed the money he saw there, revealing the corners of two crisp fifty-dollar bills.

Pike blinked, startled. What connection could a lobbyist like Cutter have with a murdered field laborer who was lucky to make thirty dollars a day?

And if the Rogelio Carrasco whose name was on the envelope was Rogelio Carrasco the murder victim, why was Cutter carrying money for him when the man had been dead for over a week?

Pike pushed the envelope back into the lobbyist's coat pocket and patted the pocket gently.

14

⊷

AS CASES WENT, the murder of Rogelio Carrasco was insignificant. So far no family or friends visited the police department or prosecutor's office demanding justice in his behalf. No one extolled his virtues because it didn't appear there were any.

Yet there was in his death a more generic importance. He had been killed in McGonigle Canyon, within earshot, within walking distance, of homes on the canyon rim—too close for comfort. Local homeowner associations and private security companies in the area called the mayor to stop the criminal contagion from escaping the canyon.

So the pressure to find Carrasco's killer had little to do with Rogelio Carrasco the man and everything to do with the politics of homicide.

Judith Thornton sat at the police department's property-room desk looking through Carrasco's personal belongings. Pike sat at the opposite end of the table, taking notes. It was Pike who had requested a closer examination of Carrasco's belongings. The money he'd seen in Cutter's pocket had created an additional wrinkle in the investigation of Carrasco's death. Fingers pointed toward Serafino Morales; then suddenly they pointed to something else as well, something far less defined.

For Judith it was always such a strange feeling, this sorting of the fragments of someone's life. Most of the time it yielded nothing of substance. Perhaps it served only to humanize the person whose body lay lifeless in the accompanying autopsy photos. But that was okay. It was too easy to forget the dead were human. Even in the worst, most notorious of murders, the case was known by the last name of the murderer, never the victim. So occasional reminders of the victim were welcome: Reminders the dead had died horrible deaths; had left behind children, wives, and husbands; had loved; had had feelings about things. Sometimes the items they possessed gave brief glimpses that helped the investigation, pushed her or the detectives one way or the other. Judith left herself open to all the possibilities when she sorted through victims' bagged belongings.

Carrasco's belongings were stored, as was the unclaimed property of all deceased crime victims, in brown bags marked with his name and the date of death. Judith tore the sealing tape from the top of the envelope and, discarding the thought of pouring the contents onto the table, reached inside the bag, pulling the items from it one by one.

Carrasco, it appeared, owned little: a pair of sunglasses, a small solid gold crucifix on a chain taken from around his neck, a portable Sony radio, a ring with a square turquoise inset engraved with a large C. There were papers, news clippings, all in Spanish, and two photos, one a color photo of three young men.

His sons?

Brothers, perhaps?

She looked for any familial resemblance in the photographs and thought she found some: the nose, the eyes. Maybe. She examined a three-by-five black-and-white photo of an old woman, wrinkled and unsmiling, with a look of great distance, almost mourning, in her eyes. It was his mother. Judith would bet money on it. Any relatives he may have had in the United States had not claimed his property.

Judith reached in yet again and retrieved a piece of paper, a small handwritten note from the property department clerk. Judith read it.

It had to be a misprint.

Sixteen hundred dollars in cash, all fifty-dollar bills, had been found rolled and secured with a rubber band in Carrasco's jacket pocket—a huge sum of money for a field laborer to have in his possession, far more than a month's salary. "Look at this!" She passed the property receipt to Pike and watched as he read of the money.

Judith reached into the bag again, this time for an explanation. There was none. But she retrieved a small black book, its pencil entries scribbled haphazardly in Spanish. She'd have it translated by someone who understood the language, but she knew enough Spanish to be immediately curious about the contents. Judith leafed through it. On the last page there was one short entry.

"*Serafino sabe.*" "*Saber*" was the verb "to know."

"Serafino knows." She repeated the words aloud for Pike and handed the book to him.

As he read, Judith fingered the property receipt for the sixteen hundred dollars.

"Serafino knows what?" Pike asked rhetorically.

"Maybe," Judith mused, looking first at the

property receipt, then the book, "he knows why a big-time lobbyist is handing out fifties to our field laborer, Mr. Carrasco."

Pike was fidgeting with the cup of coffee, turning it noisily on Judith's desk.

"If Serafino's in that canyon, I'm going to find him."

"How do we do that? You've seen the canyon, Pike. Serafino could be in any one of a million places there." She wrapped her hands around her own coffee cup on the table and squeezed.

Pike was silent, his head bent forward, his hands folded in front of him.

"There is a way, Judith."

"Which is?"

"A sweep."

"Sweep" was the term used for a concerted movement into or through an area for the purpose of rounding up a suspect or suspects. A sweep for illegal aliens could most likely be carried out by joint efforts of the Border Patrol, the county sheriff, and, sometimes, the city police.

"I don't think so, Pike. Lee Ward's already alluded to the fact that the Border Patrol agents have stayed out of the camps for months. We'd be disrupting an entire industry by looking for a murder suspect." Judith shook her head in opposition. "It's not a proper use of a sweep, Pike. You know someone's going to complain it's abusing people's rights."

"Do you want Serafino or not, Judith?"

"You heard Lee. Even if the Border Patrol picks up illegals, it'll take 'em a day and a half and they'll be back across the border," Judith complained as Pike's eyes blinked the way they did when he was excited. "They'll sign a form that the INS hands to them, get loaded on some bus, and get sent back to Tijuana. That's what, twenty minutes from San Diego? They'll have lunch and a beer down there, cross the border through the canyons or someone's backyard, and be back in McGonigle Canyon by the time they have to report to the fields the next day." She barely paused for a breath. "They don't even take their belongings with them, Pike. They leave them at McGonigle Canyon with friends because they know they're going to be back that fast." She emphasized the point with a snap of her fingers. "What're we going to accomplish with a sweep?"

But Pike's mind was made up, and there would be no changing it. "We need a sweep. I know Farrell's gotten letters from two city councilmen and one each from the Hillside Homeowners Association and the Friends of Immigrants Campaign. The pressure's on to solve the canyon murder. The neighbors are all fidgety, afraid to let their kids play anywhere near the canyon until this Carrasco's murder's solved. The pressure's on me now, and that, unfortunately, means the pressure's on *us*. We need to either find our suspect, this Serafino, or at least talk to someone who can give us some information on him. We need to do it now or we're going to lose him, Judith. We don't want anyone else; we want Serafino."

Judith still wasn't persuaded. She was staring at the table, shaking her head while Pike's attempts to persuade her continued.

"Like I said," she interrupted, " it's not a proper use of a sweep."

"Look, Judith, there are other reasons. We get a chance to show the property owners above the canyon that we're doing what we can to keep all the problems of the canyon contained, to keep Mc-Gonigle Canyon contained. Isn't that part of what this investigation is all about?"

Despite her concerns, much of what Pike was saying was true. They could never conduct an adequate search of the canyon area without a major law enforcement effort. And even if the sweep did net more than Serafino, who was to say the illegals weren't legitimately picked up as well?

"Okay, I'll defer to you on this one, Pike. We sweep. Hopefully we come up with something more than an expensive public relations stunt. I'll call the Border Patrol and see if we can get it moving."

"I'm calling Lee Ward in, just so I have someone who talks Spanish with me," Pike added.

As her investigator started to leave, Judith stopped him.

"But, Pike . . ."

"Yeah."

"I want it kept under control. No pushing people around. No physical *anything*. No intimidation. You keep the forces out there coordinated, okay?"

Pike was only superficially offended. "Would I do anything improper, boss?"

"Just please, keep it controlled."

A few minutes past 3 P.M., two days after Pike had persuaded Judith a sweep was necessary, the green-and-white Border Patrol vehicles began converging from all sides on the McGonigle Canyon campsite, kicking up moving clouds of dust and sending camp residents darting up hillsides, shouting *"la migra, la migra!"* Within minutes, khaki-clad agents dashed from their vehicles, sealing up the camp. They systematically walked the campsite, checking documents and rounding up those who could not produce adequate identification.

The men rounded up were not violent, and not one carried a handgun. They all relented to the questioning, complaining only that they didn't steal, they didn't stay drunk, and they were there only to make a living. They were not criminals and couldn't understand what to them was harassment.

Through it all, Pike and Lee Ward were present, waiting for the one person who might say a word pointing to the whereabouts of Serafino, or give them some shred of information about Carrasco's murder. Lee Ward was able to help, but on a limited basis. He was only slightly knowledgeable in the Mixtec language common to the Oaxacans and, knowing his own weaknesses, taped interviews with three men who claimed to know Serafino or Carrasco.

It took most of the afternoon before the Border Patrol units cleared out, and Pike placed the interview tapes in his canvas bag for review later, hopefully by someone who knew the language better than he and Lee Ward.

When the last law enforcement vehicle pulled away from the canyon and disappeared into the distance, an uneasy calm settled on the encampment. At first there was an eerie silence broken only by the sounds of chickens rustling the leaves in shrubbery. Then slowly, in small groups, camp inhabitants who had scattered into the hills at the first sign of *la migra* returned. Still frightened, some dazed, they retreated to their cantons. Women were weeping, men hugging relatives and friends they feared might have been taken away. Still others rubbed legs and arms scratched by the bush and ground as they had rushed desperately to the safety of the hills.

The sweep was complete but Pike was not yet ready to leave. A cool, strong breeze was moving through the encampment, and he wandered first down the main road, then to the stream.

He had just reached the edge of the water when the bullet struck the front of his left shoulder and he fell backward, hard, to the ground and passed out.

The first thing Pike saw when he regained consciousness was Lee Ward's face above him, eyes widened in horror.

Pike was lying on his back in pain, but he knew at once the wound was not life threatening.

"Get me outta here!" Pike growled up at Ward, who was already tugging Pike's 225-pound body from the edge of the river by pulling the man's jacket collar. Shaking, Ward shifted position and reached under Pike's arms, lifting him to his feet.

"My God, Pike, what happened? I heard the shots and when I couldn't find you—Don't say anything. There's a hospital close by."

Ward led Pike to his car and stuffed him into the backseat. The wounded man passed out again well before the car emerged from the canyon, not as much from the shock of being shot, Pike would later say, as from the viciously erratic drive up the hill.

Less than an hour after Pike reached the hospital, Judith walked, unannounced, into his room.

"Jesus, Judith, a little privacy, please!"

Breathless, she stopped short of the bed. Sitting

on its edge, clad in a white cotton gown, Pike was about to have a shot administered.

Judith, blushing, turned her back to Pike. "Tell me when you're decent."

"It's just a tetanus shot. The nurse is done, right, Nurse?"

The woman passed Judith and rolled her eyes. Pike would never be the ideal patient. Judith handed Pike a small stack of magazines.

"Lee Ward called and told me what happened. Did you see who it was?"

"No. I've already talked to a police investigator. The report's been written, but it doesn't say much. I was walking around and someone shot me. Lee tells me there's random shots fired up there all the time. Ballistics has the bullet they dug out of my shoulder. That'll tell us something."

"How long are they going to keep you here?"

"An hour or two more. They want to observe me. Hell, I told you, I'm fine. I'll call you as soon as I'm outta here."

"No, you're going to take it easy tonight, read the magazines I brought you, and call me in the morning."

Pike looked quickly through the magazines, a look of disgust spreading across his face as he called out their titles. "*Smithsonian*? *National Geographic*? *Good Housekeeping*?"

Judith called back to him as she exited the door.

"Sorry. I had to collect them in a hurry. And besides, I wouldn't have the nerve to buy the magazines you read."

Following Judith's departure, Pike slept. While his plan was to leave the hospital that same evening, he did not awaken until 11 P.M. when the nurse delivered his medicine and a small, white plastic bowl of strawberry Jell-O. He watched the news, looked at the pictures in the *National Geographic* magazine Judith brought him, and went back to sleep.

The next morning the doctors agreed Pike could be discharged. None too soon for the detective, who'd spent the early hours calculating the possibility someone may have ordered his execution at the river.

By the time he'd checked out, however, the conclusion drawn by the investigators was that Pike was probably wounded by someone who was out shooting too close to the camp. Despite reservations, Pike was prepared to live with that for the moment and admit to the possibility he'd been in the wrong place at the wrong time.

15

"INS SOMEHOW PICKED up a witness in the sweep who says he heard Serafino Morales say he was heading north to some cousin's home in Ventura County. And get this—he also heard Serafino say there was something bad in the water."

Judith, engrossed in reviewing the sentencing files for the following day, stopped reading and looked up at Pike. "What water?"

"I'm not sure and Lee isn't either. The words in the Mixtec language are hard to decipher. We have the guy's interview with Lee on tape, and we're hoping we can get someone else to listen to it."

"Where's the witness now?"

"They're holding him for us. He's got papers, so they can't send him back."

"What are they holding him on?" Judith asked.

"On being a material witness."

"A material witness to *what*?"

Pike was looking for help from the wrong person. "To an admission?"

"To *what* admission? *Whose* admission? Look, Pike, I'm not trying to be difficult, but we can't hold this man, whoever he is, on anything. If we have the information we need from him, we have to let him go."

"Judith, you know as well as I do that if we let this guy go, he's going to disappear. He saw or heard something from Serafino, and Serafino's our prime suspect here."

"Pike, this is exactly what I was afraid might happen out there. I even warned you it could happen. There's no legal cause to hold him. We don't keep people in jail because they're a witness to something. And based on what you've told me, I'd be hard pressed to even say this guy's witnessed anything. We don't need a false arrest case."

"Okay," an exasperated Pike whispered. "I won't lean on the INS. They'll spring 'em."

It was like that with Pike. She was always reining him in, watching and correcting. She was skeptical of Pike's announcement the witness had "somehow" been picked up by the INS. The guy had been interviewed by Lee Ward. More likely the INS had been *asked* to hold him by Pike. She was willing to cut him some allowances. He belonged to the good old days when the police had far more freedom in the field. But not at the expense of justice—or a false arrest complaint. Yet he had relented on the release of the interviewee, and that would be the end of her lecture.

"Can I listen to the man's interview with Lee?" she asked in a conciliatory tone.

"Sure, I've got it. I'll be back in a minute." Pike left for his office and in a few minutes returned and set a tape recorder on Judith's desk.

"As best Lee can understand, the man says Serafino was sure there's excrement in the water,"

Pike explained, snapping the interview tape into the machine.

Judith's voice elevated to light sarcasm. "There's excrement all over the place out there."

"No, no, hold on now, Judith. That's what the guy says Serafino told him."

"Maybe someone's *putting* excrement in the water?" she offered.

Pike snickered. "Serafino knows Carrasco's putting crap in the water?" He shook his head. "I'm sorry, I don't see how that's going to get a laborer who lives in the fields very excited."

The door behind Pike, which had been partially open, was pushed further, and Peter Delgado stepped inside.

"I'm sorry to interrupt, but I wanted to let you know I finished up my case."

"The college student and prostitute?"

A wide smile spread on Delgado's face, the white of his teeth a handsome contrast to his dark skin. It sent a clear, direct message.

"You won the case?" Judith asked.

He nodded.

"Congratulations. I really didn't think you'd pull it off. It's a big deal around here when you win a case no one thinks you will. I suppose I need to find you something else to work on now."

Delgado glanced quickly at the tape recorder.

"I heard you talking about the Mixtec language."

"Do *you* know anything about Mixtec?" Pike snapped.

"Some. When I was a student in Mexico, I minored in languages, and I spent a summer in something they called Mixtec Culture and Language One. It's basically the same today as it was three hundred fifty years ago. The meanings of words are determined by the pitch of the voice or the emphasis put on a part of the word. It's got long, short, nasalized, and aspirated vowels. It's real liquid sounding, and there's a glottal stop that makes it even more difficult."

"What's a glottal stop?" Pike interjected.

"It's where you choke the words." Delgado gestured toward his throat. "It's hard to explain. Let me show you how the language works." He pointed to the empty chair next to Judith. "May I?"

Judith pushed the chair away from the table.

Delgado sat and pulled a pencil and a yellow-lined writing pad to him. "Take the word 'bizi.'" He printed the word on the tablet. "If 'bizi' is pronounced with the first *i* as long and the second *i* high and choked, the word means 'bullfrog.' If *bizi* is pronounced with the first *i* choked and the second *i* low in pitch, it means 'seed.' If the word's pronounced with the second *i* high, it means the fruit of the pitahaya cactus. And if the second *i* is choked, then reticulated in a lower tone, it means 'returned.'" He paused and looked at Judith. "I could go on and tell you what happens if you add an *m* in front of 'bizi' if you want me to."

Judith and Pike were speechless at Delgado's rapid-fire explanation.

"No need. I think you've made the point. I didn't realize you had all this hidden linguistic talent," Judith said. "Could you listen to this interview tape we've got here? We have a suspect in the Carrasco murder who's told someone there's excrement in the water, but we're not sure that's what he said. We have the witness's statement on tape. Would you mind listening to it to see if he's saying there's 'excrement' in the water out at the canyon?"

"I'd be happy to, if I can take the tape recorder with me."

Judith picked the recorder up and handed it to Delgado. "It's yours."

It was Peter Delgado's choice to live in his parents' Point Loma home when he returned to San Diego.

After breakfast on the Saturday following Judith's handing the tape and recorder to him, Peter set to work listening to the interview with the Oaxacan field hand who claimed to have spoken with Serafino Morales. He had no dictionary because there was no Oaxacan dictionary. He relied on the notes from his summer class, notes he hadn't thrown away because he thought they might come in handy one day. He dug them out of the files in the garage, and with his own knowledge of the language and the library books he'd picked up on the Mixtec Indian culture, he felt he had enough to get started.

Delgado chose the wood-paneled library in which to begin his research, its large window opening to the backyard garden and fountain. From the window, he could see his father walking back and forth between the house and the gardens.

In the early afternoon Delgado rose and went outside. There he found his father digging in the vegetable garden in the corner of the yard. He could see the older man wearing a red plaid cotton shirt and blue jeans, leaning forward, weeding tomatoes with a long-handled hoe, the plants bending to the ground, heavy with the large red fruit.

"Papí," he said, for he called him by his childhood nickname, "you have a crop ready to be picked."

"You can help, then?" the older man asked, standing up straight, arching his back to stretch.

As Peter approached, he saw the sweat dripping from the man's face and the dirt caked to his fingernails. He wiped his brow with a white handkerchief dug from his shirt pocket and smiled broadly at his son.

"Papí, what are you going to do with all the tomatoes?"

"I take them to work in a big basket and give them away to whoever wants them. You should take some in on Monday!" He looked down at the half-weeded area and took a deep breath. "I used to be much faster at this."

"I'll help you finish if you'd like. Then maybe you'll let me pick."

The older man laughed. "I only have one hoe, but you can bend down and pull, like the *campesinos*. You can feel what it was like in the fields when I was a kid," he joked, "before I became the famous jurist I am today."

Peter watched his father grab the hoe with both hands and pound the metal end into the damp earth, overturning large clods of dirt. The thought occurred to Peter that he was the first generation of his family not to work in the fields, the first 100 percent American generation. He bent forward and grabbed a small weed, then another.

"¡*Apúrate*!! Pull faster, *campesino*!" his father laughed. "Or you get no pay today!"

The chiding, meant only in fun, stirred twinges of resentment in the younger man. He was *not* a *campesino*. He would never be a *campesino*. He wanted nothing to do with his family's past.

For an hour the two men dug and pulled, until

the tomato patch was stripped of weeds and every ripe tomato was picked.

"The word for excrement is '*gi*,'" announced Delgado to Judith the following afternoon. "It's possible that's what the man interviewed was saying. But I've checked a little closer, and what I found is that '*gi*' could also mean 'fire.' Your interviewee pronounced it closest to the 'fire' meaning."

Her position verified by Delgado, Judith was visibly excited, standing and walking toward the open window of her office.

"I've been arguing the 'excrement' meaning doesn't make sense, because supposedly Serafino got very upset about it. If the word means 'fire,' well that's a little more interesting. I think we can use you on the Carrasco case, Peter." She expected him to seize the opportunity, as would ninety-nine of one hundred new deputies. A chance to work on a case with senior attorneys? He'd snap at it, surely. His response surprised her.

"Actually, I'd really prefer not to. I speak the languages a little, but I don't think I'd like being out there. I just feel"—he searched here for the right word and found it—"uncomfortable."

"What if I *assigned* you to the Carrasco murder case?" Judith asked.

"I guess I'd have to then, wouldn't I?"

"You probably would. Would it be so bad?"

Peter shrugged.

Judith's voice was firm. "You're on the case, Peter."

16

JOEL HARRINGTON SWALLOWED the last
of his triple deluxe cheeseburger and trudged toward the bank of the stream cutting through
McGonigle Canyon. He glanced at his watch. It was
eight-thirty and the full moon was already casting
a soft light on the ground around him. Hurrying,
he crumpled and threw the burger's white paper
wrapper into the shrubbery. "One more piece of
trash in this hole of a canyon," he muttered.

He'd gained fifteen more pounds since Christmas, and he belched and grimaced with heartburn.
The walk up the encampment trail through the lilac
and wild roses was even more strenuous than he'd
remembered it being a year earlier, the last time
he'd made an investigative visit here, and he
cursed aloud its filth and squalor as he walked
through the odor of human excrement the canyon
winds blew into his face.

Harrington's whole day had been spent farther
up the coast at Batiquitos Lagoon monitoring the
comings and goings of the various water fowl some
neighborhood group claimed were being poisoned

by local youths. The sting operation proved uneventful, and he'd been on his way back to the field
office in downtown San Diego when the call came
through on his portable phone asking him to swing
by McGonigle Canyon and take some water samples from the stream and from irrigation systems
in the neighboring vegetable fields. Despite his discomfort at entering the canyon at night, he agreed
to stop by the encampment.

The overweight twenty-two-year veteran of the
county health department had parked his white
Ford van with the large blue SAN DIEGO COUNTY
HEALTH DEPARTMENT emblazoned on the doors into
the same eucalyptus tree grove used by the camp
catering truck. Testing kit in hand, he labored toward the stream, expecting it would yield strong
evidence of contamination of the human sort.

He'd been officially off duty as of seven o'clock.
Now, out of breath and sweating, he hurried toward the water anticipating the end of his workday.

Before he reached the stream, an excruciating
pain shot through his chest. Gasping for breath, he
stumbled to a flat patch of dirt under an oak tree,
finding both defeat and comfort resting his back
against its huge trunk.

Judith and Pike reached the mouth of the Mc
Gonigle Canyon encampment at ten o'clock the
next morning and were immediately besieged by
reporters. In truth they knew nothing more about
the death in the canyon than did the news media.

Only an hour earlier Judith had rushed into
Pike's office, her face flushed with the news that
someone had been found dead in McGonigle
Canyon.

The two sat in silence as the detective drove northward on Interstate 5 toward the canyon. Not until they reached the scene and were confronted by the group of reporters did Judith speak to her detective, cautioning him to refrain from giving out any gratuitous information about the prior deaths or what connection they might have to the death of the county health department employee.

Only when they contacted the police investigators at the scene did they learn Harrington appeared to have died of natural causes.

His body had been discovered the night before. When he failed to report back to his office, the dispatcher traced him to the location where he had died. Given the inaccessibility of the canyon for the heavy lighting equipment needed to conduct an investigation, the decision was made to secure the scene and wait for daylight. Had he been found during the day and the cause of death identified as an apparent heart attack, neither Pike nor Judith would have come to the scene. By fortuity they ended up at the camp eucalyptus grove, chatting with the lead detective.

"Was it clear what he was supposed to do here?" Pike asked him.

The detective checked his notepad, flipping the pages in search of history. "He was here to check out the toxicity of the water."

"Is there any information about why he was checking it out?"

The pages of the notepad flipped forward.

"Yeah. The county health department, his employer, sent him over to check it out because a doctor named Partido reported a case of poisoning up here. Partido treated a kid who got a toxin in his eyes, and someone at the county, for whatever reason, thought the stream should be checked."

"Anything else I ought to know?" Pike asked.

The pages of the notepad flipped forward, then back again as the detective reviewed the information he'd gathered over the last twelve hours.

"When the guy's supervisor came out here to identify the body, he mentioned there were several other cases of poisoning reported from out in this canyon. I don't have the names of the people who were poisoned listed. He didn't know who they were, just that they all got some kind of poison in the last two or three months. Oh, there was something else." He flipped the pages back again. "Here it is. The kid who was poisoned in the eyes has an attorney."

Pike looked at Judith, who after having cautioned Pike about saying too much, had herself maintained strict silence. His eyes began to blink as the detective continued.

"The attorney's name is Irene Talbot."

Talbot. The name had twice surfaced in the course of investigating Carrasco's murder. The dead lobbyist with the set of fifty-dollar bills tucked into an envelope marked for Carrasco worked for Talbot Construction Company. An attorney, Irene Talbot, was suing growers she claimed poisoned canyon children. There was a connection between the names, and it took little investigation to discover Irene Talbot was the daughter of Franklin Talbot, founder and current president of Talbot Construction.

While the coincidence was worth noting, that was all it was, a coincidence. There was no evidence that either Talbot knew Rogelio Carrasco or his suspected killer, Serafino Morales.

Still, for Judith coincidences had meaning, and she was not willing to dispense with the Talbots just yet. Like everything else, they were tethered to McGonigle Canyon, the sieve through which everything seemed to be strained.

17

PIKE HAD SEVERAL leads now that were the direct result of the visit to McGonigle Canyon following Harrington's death. One was the existence of a doctor who'd reported toxic poisoning in the encampment.

Pike caught up with Ramón Partido in the doctor's San Diego office. He waited patiently in the outer room until one by one the patients were called into the back rooms for examination. Finally Pike was the only one left, and he too was called in. The men shook hands, and Pike asked directly how many poisoning cases the practitioner had treated in McGonigle Canyon.

"I send the reports on to the county health department, but I also keep my own." He had in his hands a file thick with a rainbow of pink, white, and blue paper. "I've three cases here you might be interested in. One is a field laborer who became sick to his stomach after spending the day in the tomato fields. The illness occurred the afternoon following a major air spraying. There were no permanent injuries I could see, and I sent him home."

"How about the other two cases?"

"They were children. Would you like me to go over those?"

"I'd appreciate it."

The doctor shuffled the papers in his file and pulled several reports from the folder.

"Here they are. The first child I saw was Enrique Sandoval. He's eight years old. Lives in the Mc-Gonigle Canyon labor encampment. And ... let's see, he became sick to his stomach and vomited. I wasn't sure if it was the heat or the insecticide sprayed, but again, he wasn't bad enough to require hospitalization, so I recommended immediate removal of all clothing he'd been wearing in the field, a bath with soap, and rest at home."

"And there was another case, a child. . . ."

"Right. There was another child, a very young child, Raúl Ignacio. His case was a bit more puzzling because he came in from the fields just north of the encampment and his eyes were burning. By the time I picked him up, his eyes were blistered. I delivered him to the hospital myself because by the time I saw him, his eyes were in pretty bad condition."

"Did you do any follow-up on him?"

"No, I didn't. He needed help from more than one specialist, and as you can see from looking around, I'm just not equipped to deal with serious medical problems."

"Doctor, I'm curious about these poisoning cases. Are they random, or do you see a pattern?"

"I'm sure there are others who can speak to that issue far better than me. I've read studies about the toxic levels the field laborers have to deal with, and there are certainly horror stories of toxic dumping along the border that have caused identifiable birth defects. What I see out here is more subtle: people getting sick after a spraying, vomiting, dizziness, skin irritations. They seem like superficial problems, but they leave lasting medical injury. The only case that seemed really out of the norm for me was the Ignacio child. His was a gross injury, and while I don't know if anyone's isolated the origin of the toxin, he had to have contact with a major source. He just didn't know where."

"You at least saw enough of a pattern to report it?"

"I did. Actually, I did that right away. I filed a report with the county and gave the office there a follow-up call. They promised to send someone out."

"They did that."

"And what was the finding?"

"The man they sent to do the testing died of a heart attack out at the stream. As far as I know, they haven't sent anyone else out yet."

"It's a shame. They need to get someone out there. I might make another follow-up call."

The receptionist knocked gently and announced another patient had arrived.

Pike was anxious to hit one more topic before the doctor was called away. "Doctor, have you had any contact with an attorney named Irene Talbot?"

"That's the attorney representing the Ignacio boy. She's already called and asked me to send over my records on the boy. I did that. She said I'd be needed later, perhaps at trial, but I haven't heard back from her."

"Doctor, do you know who she's suing?"

"I do. She said she was suing the Tanekawas. They own all the land north of the encampment, where the boy says he was playing. From the little

I do know about it, the boy's suing for millions."

Pike nodded. "I'm sure he is."

"You know, it's a delicate balance out here, Detective. There's a kind of symbiotic relationship between the growers and the laborers. You put the grower out of business and you put the laborer out of work. One lawsuit like that could create a whole lot of unemployed people. There's pressure enough on the growers out here."

"Like what else?"

"Look around up there, Detective. All of San Diego looked like those fields once upon a time. Now taxes and water costs are up. Land values are far more than they were when the farms were purchased. Why should a family grow tomatoes when it can sell out to the highest offer from the developers?"

"You mean there are developers who want McGonigle Canyon for buildings?" It had never occurred to Pike that anyone would actually want to build a home inside the canyon itself.

"This is some of the most sought after land in the county. But it's on hold. Freeway Fifty-six is supposed to cut right through the area."

Pike was familiar with the unfinished freeway, its lanes abruptly stopping just to the west of McGonigle Canyon amid acres of leveled, carved-up land.

"Is that why the freeway's unfinished?"

"Uh-huh. The developers can't develop the land out here until the freeway's done. But that's not stopping them from making hard offers on it. In fact, with the freeway stalled indefinitely, the land's cheaper to bargain for right now."

"And the landowners won't sell?"

"They've been there for decades, since before

World War Two. They're farmers. If you have farming in your blood, it's difficult to let go of your land. If you don't have the land, you don't have anything. Money doesn't count for those kind of folk. On the other hand, the Tanekawa family's been through hell. Tax problems. INS problems. And they just had a horrible INS sweep." Pike blushed and turned away as the doctor continued. "It'll take its toll. You wait and see; it's just a matter of time. One more big hit at them . . ."

"Like a megalawsuit maybe."

"I'd think a million-dollar lawsuit could change a mind or two; yes, it could."

"Oh, Doctor, one more thing. The Ignacio boy's eyes, you said they were blistered."

"That's right. Blistering's a symptom of poisoning."

"How does the blistering occur?"

"The toxin, to make the story a short one, burns the eyes."

Pike had been heading toward the door and stopped, turning back toward Partido.

"It burns?"

"Well, it's a caustic."

"No, I understand, Doctor. It was your choice of words I found interesting."

Pike's mind was racing when he said good-bye to the doctor. He'd thrown out a large net and caught more than one fish. In particular, the multiple definition of *"gi"* had a whole new meaning. Something that *burned* was in the water.

18

PIKE WORKED ALONE. When Judith asked
him to take Peter Delgado along to interview Irene
Talbot, he balked. Only when the three conferred
and it was agreed Delgado would stay in the back-
ground and ask no questions did Pike relent. He
had no problems with Delgado tagging along pro-
vided he remain a trainee and observer only.

With Delgado at his side, Pike drove north on
Park Boulevard past the zoo entrance and the Reu-
ben H. Fleet Space Center.

Despite the overcast sky and chill, the parking
lot of the zoo was already half full, and school
buses bringing kids on summer field trips to the
space center lined the parking curbs.

At El Cajon Boulevard, Pike made a right turn
and watched the cross streets: Alabama, Florida,
Texas.

Irene Talbot's law office was located on the second floor of a white stucco building on the corner
of El Cajon and Vermont, once a lethargic district
of small businesses struggling to survive, held together by the auto traffic headed for the Sears Roe-

buck store. In the eighties the old Sears store was demolished to make way for a new upscale community of condominiums, bustling shops, a community center, and upscale restaurants.

For all his hesitation to bring young Delgado along, Pike enjoyed talking about the changes, pointing to the coffee shop that was new and the furniture store that was a landmark.

Amid the eclectic combination of business and residential buildings, Irene Talbot offered legal services to the poorest of the city. Her office sat above an antiques store. The second-floor window, facing El Cajon Boulevard, proclaimed in red block lettering IRENE TALBOT, ATTORNEY-AT-LAW.

Pike brought his car to a stop at the curb in front of the antiques shop. The entrance was tricky, a dimly lit interior stairwell to the right of the antiques store's door. They entered the second floor through a wood door on which a metal 2 was nailed. In the small gray linoleum-floored lobby were two doors. On the rippled-glass panel IRENE TALBOT, ATTORNEY-AT-LAW was printed in bold black lettering, as was SANDOVAL AND CHAVEZ, IM-MIGRATION COUNSELORS, which appeared on the second door. The same person had obviously painted them both.

Pike knocked gently on the glass. When no one answered, he opened the door and stepped inside. There was no anteroom. The entrance landed them in a small dimly lit office measuring no more than five hundred square feet, containing an oak desk flanked by two five-foot-tall gray metal filing cabinets. A young woman, no more than thirty, standing behind the desk, shuffling the files covering its top, greeted them. She was wearing blue jeans and a long-sleeved white cotton blouse with a Peter Pan collar. Her long brown hair was pulled back and secured at the nape of her neck by a bright red-and-blue-print scarf. The woman's dark brown eyes were partially obscured by the thick fringe of bangs hanging over her forehead.

"Irene Talbot?" Pike asked.

The woman stepped out from behind the desk and extended her hand. "I'm glad to meet you, Mr. . . ."

Pike reciprocated, extending his own hand. "Detective Pike Martin. This is Deputy District Attorney Peter Delgado."

It was the first time Delgado had been addressed in public as "Deputy District Attorney," and he enjoyed the respectful glance and the hand she extended to him as well. As she stepped away, both men realized there was someone else in the cramped office, sitting off to the side, next to the wall.

The man was of medium height, a very dark mestizo with an uneven haircut and heavy growth of beard. He wore baggy brown work pants and a white T-shirt emblazoned with the yellow thunderbolt insignia of the San Diego Chargers football team. His pants hugged his hips, and the T-shirt was two sizes too small, exposing his stomach. On his sockless feet he wore a laceless pair of black tennis shoes. Delgado gasped at the man's face and hands, which were grossly deformed, his skin rough and mottled brown, white, and pink. The skin on his neck was abnormally smooth and white. His eyes were slightly more than slits. Hearing Delgado gasp, the man raised his hands to his face, and for the first time the men could see his fingers were no more than stubs.

"I'm sorry. I didn't realize you had someone

with you," Pike mumbled, embarrassed by their awkward entrance and Delgado's audible shock.

Delgado, eyes riveted on the man, took a position next to the door and remained there with pencil and open notebook, only an observer and recorder of events as promised, but happy to be away from the center of conversation.

"It's okay, Detective. Señor Vásquez was just leaving." She turned to the man and spoke in fluent Spanish, telling him she would see him in two days. "*Si Dios quiere*," he answered. "If God wills it." He rose, nodded slightly toward Pike, and said good-bye in English, exiting through the door Pike and Delgado had just entered.

Delgado stepped further to the side of the door. As the man left, he bowed to Delgado, and noting he was Hispanic, spoke in Spanish to him. "*Adiós, compadre.*" "Good-bye, friend." His scarred face and hands were unavoidably three feet away from the deputy. When he exited, Delgado intended to write what he'd seen. He could not find the words to do so.

Ignoring the reaction to Vásquez, Irene Talbot motioned to the chair nearest her desk. "Come in and have a seat. What can I help you with?"

Delgado remained standing, an uneasy feeling in the pit of his stomach. "I'm not really sure, Miss Talbot, if you can help me at all," Pike said, choosing to sit in the chair Vásquez had vacated moments before.

"I'm happy to give it a try. Can I get you some coffee?" she asked, her eyes darting from Pike to Delgado. Delgado shook his head. "No, thank you."

"Thanks, I'd like some. Just black, please," Pike responded. As she turned to the coffeemaker on the credenza next to the wall behind her, Pike explained the reason for his visit. "I'm working on a homicide that happened up in McGonigle Canyon several weeks ago. A Mexican field worker named Rogelio Carrasco was murdered."

"You need some help documenting him or tracking down relatives, that sort of thing?" she asked, handing Pike an eight-ounce white foam cup of steaming coffee.

"No, actually . . . it seems one of your father's lobbyists died in the same canyon a few days ago. It would just be an unhappy coincidence, except the lobbyist had an envelope with money in it, and the envelope had the murder victim's—Carrasco's— name on it."

Her face was expressionless as she sat behind her desk. "So?"

Pike wasn't expecting the blunt reaction. "So, I need to cover all the bases here. I apologize. I don't want to seem too prying or accusatory."

"Accusatory? Of whom, Detective?"

"Of . . . well, I don't really know. I'm just covering the bases, that's all."

"I'm afraid I'm at a loss. I don't know how I can help you."

Pike took a noisy sip from the coffee cup. "Can you tell me a little bit about what you do?"

"Sure. I work for organizations that assist immigrants, especially those who work in the fields. We do a lot of fund-raising and offer pro bono, free, legal services to the immigrants, legal and illegal immigrants."

"Do you work with the field hands up in McGonigle Canyon?"

Her eyes widened.

"It's one of the worst areas in the county. You bet I do."

"What do you mean by one of the worst areas?"

"Have you ever been up there, Detective?"

"Yeah, as a matter of fact, several times."

"Well, then, you've seen the conditions the people live and work in."

"Yeah, it's pretty bad."

"Bad? It's a disgrace. No, I take that back; it's worse than a disgrace. That man who just left here is a great example. He fell asleep in his cardboard hut with a candle burning to keep him warm. He woke up in a hospital thirty days later, and his face looked the way it does now. The candle started a fire that burned seventy-five percent of his body. Four of his fingers had to be amputated."

"You're helping him?"

"I'm filing a lawsuit on his behalf against the grower whose land he was sleeping on."

"He worked for the grower?"

"No. But he was on the property with the owner's consent. He was actually working on the neighboring farm."

Pike shifted his weight on the chair. "Let me get this straight. You're filing a lawsuit against a farmer the man didn't work for? This guy was just sleeping on his land?" A broad smile spread across his face. "I hate to be simplistic, Miss Talbot, but we used to call those people squatters. How's a squatter got any right to sue?"

Pike's humor only increased the zealousness of her advocacy. "It's not quite that simple. The hut Mr. Vásquez was sleeping in was made of cardboard he pulled out of a pile on that grower's land. The farmers all put the cardboard out in piles. They know the laborers in the area are going to use them to make huts to sleep in. It's a cheap method of providing housing. We haven't proved it yet, but it's our position the farmer on whose land he slept knew he was there."

Pike looked at the floor and shook his head, forcing her to further defend herself.

"You know fire's not the only problem there, Detective. I've got a client—just a boy—who's been blinded by toxins. I've filed a million-dollar lawsuit on his behalf against the grower."

"That would be the Ignacio boy?"

"That's right, Detective. You know about him?"

"I've already talked to Dr. Partido."

"Then you know the toxins are a problem in the canyon."

"Just how much of a problem are toxins in the canyon?" Pike pressed her.

"Big-time problem."

"How big?"

"No one likes them. The field hands get covered. Neighbors on the rim of the canyon have had the stuff drift into their homes. My sources are telling me the tomato growers around McGonigle Canyon have applied to the county department of agriculture to ground-spray fifteen different chemical pesticides."

"Any problems with the stuff getting into the water supplies?"

She hesitated. "Only the case of the Ignacio boy, I think. I . . . I haven't been able to identify the poison's source yet. I have my own investigators working on it, but I might be able to put you in touch with people who can help you."

Pike looked up and waved his hands. "No need, no need." He stopped midsentence. She was biting the side of her mouth. Judith did that—when she was nervous. Irene Talbot was nervous, but just why, he wasn't sure. He let her speak next.

"You can get to the point, Detective."

"Your dad ever mention a man named Rogelio Carrasco?"

"I've never heard the name until you just said it."

"Do you know of any reason your father's lobbyist would be paying money to a field hand?"

"Maybe helping him out; that's all I can think of. Can I ask who the lobbyist is?"

"Rex Cutter."

Her eyes widened in disbelief. "Uncle Rex?" Uncle Rex is dead?"

"Uncle Rex?"

"He's not really a relative, but he might as well have been. Rex is one of my father's best friends. He's worked for him since I was a kid. How'd he die?"

"Rattler bit him out at McGonigle Canyon."

"Wait a minute. You don't think Daddy's involved in this Carrasco's death? Is that why you're asking about Uncle Rex? Is that why you're here?"

Even under the veil of accusation, she had the pleasantness and control of a seasoned attorney, and a smile crossed her face at the end of her question, as if she'd caught Pike before he could catch her.

Pike shook his head emphatically. "No, no. All we have is a good friend of your father with money in his pocket earmarked for Carrasco."

"So why do I suddenly get the feeling I don't want to talk with you anymore, Detective?"

"You got that feeling, huh?"

She nodded. "Loud and clear."

Pike's voice softened.

"That's too bad."

Again her eyes darted to Delgado, still standing but leaning now against the wall.

"Sorry, Detective. I'd be concerned the whole time you were after some dark secret."

"Is there one?" Pike pressed.

"Seriously, Detective, you're wrong if you think my father could ever be involved with anything as horrible as a killing. Especially the murder of a laborer." She motioned around the office. "He has *deep* feelings for the farm workers. "Without my father's help, this office of mine would have folded long ago. He pays the light bill, and he's the first to point out the cases that should be brought."

"Like the fire cases?"

"Yes. And the poison case. He's a good man, Detective."

"How's your father know about these great cases for you?"

"He has his ear to the canyon, Detective Martin."

Pike rose and tossed the empty coffee cup into the wastebasket next to him. "Well, it was a pleasure talking with you, Miss Talbot. Thanks for the coffee." He took a business card from his shirt pocket and laid it on the desk in front of her. "If you ever need to contact me, here's my card."

"Sorry I couldn't be of any help to you. If *you* need any information, Detective, on the conditions up there in the canyon, or if you need help tracking someone down, give me a call. I can help with that."

"No need, for now anyway. But I appreciate the offer."

Delgado followed Pike down the stairs and outside the office building. After an investigative interview or street contact, he liked to sit and think, sort out the important details and get them written down. As they sat in the car, Pike pulled his own pen and notepad from the glove compartment. There wasn't much to write: "Daughter nervous. Defensive. Brings civil actions for field hands. Fires. Toxins. Lots of money involved. Father gives financial support to daughter's office."

As an afterthought Pike wrote: "Father helps support the field hands."

Before starting the car, Pike glanced up at Irene Talbot's second-story window. The vertical blinds were parted a crack, just enough to recognize the form behind the curtain was unmistakably Irene Talbot, staring down at them.

It was eleven o'clock when Pike and Delgado left the curb outside Irene Talbot's office, and Pike invited Delgado to accompany him to his favorite Chinese restaurant.

Delgado pushed his lunch around on his plate. The China Camp lunch special came with egg flower soup, an entrée, and an egg roll. Delgado had been enthusiastic when Pike suggested the restaurant. It was close to downtown on Pacific Highway, and the prices were within the budget of cop and businessman, with the advantage that its high-backed wood booths offered the confidentiality he often needed.

"Not hungry?" Pike asked, taking a forkful of fried rice and muishi pork to his mouth. "Have some tea." Pike's large hands awkwardly poured the pale brown liquid into the small round white tea cup.

"Is everything okay?" the waiter asked, noticing Delgado had not touched his food.

"It's fine, really good. I had a late breakfast."

"You want to take it home with you?" the waiter asked, anxious to please him.

"Sure. I'll have it later."

"You didn't have a late breakfast, Peter. You had a late cup of coffee." He pointed his empty fork at Peter. "It's the guy in Irene Talbot's office, isn't it?"

"I suppose so."

"I've seen a lot worse. You will too if you hang around in this business long enough. You'll get used to it, though."

"You know, Pike, it's a horrible thing to have your body destroyed by fire."

Pike snorted. "Of course it's horrible!"

"No, I mean if he's Mixtec. In that culture it's horrible because you need your body after you die. Your body goes to the world below, to a large pueblo which has no name, where life goes on just as it does here. If you lose your body, you lose your soul."

Pike stopped eating and set his fork on the plate. "Who told you that?"

"My grandmother."

"So if I died young, my body would be young down there?"

"Yes."

"And if I die old, my body down there is old?"

"Right."

"And this man, Vásquez—he goes the way he looks?"

"Amputated fingers and scarred face, yes."

"My will says I'm supposed to be cremated."

Delgado smiled and shrugged his shoulders.

"Any other strange customs I should be aware of when you're out with me?" Pike chided, dipping his egg roll into the small plate of mustard sauce.

"Oh, there are a few. . . ."

The waiter interrupted again, bringing Peter a covered white foam food plate. He set two fortune cookies down on the table along with the bill.

"You pick first," Pike said.

Delgado picked the fortune cookie nearest him and cracked it open, pulling a thin white paper from it.

"What's it say?" Pike asked.

Delgado passed the paper to the detective. It was blank.

19

IT DIDN'T SEEM a turning point when it happened, the unmistakable sound of coughing, then choking coming from her mother's bedroom. Hearing it, Judith sprinted down the hallway and was joined at the bedroom door by Jean, who immediately ran to her mother. The old woman was bent forward, her false teeth half out of her mouth, her eyes wet from choking.

Jean pulled the lopsided upper teeth from her mouth and placed her hand on her mother's back, rubbing gently. Looking knowingly at Judith, she smiled slightly.

"Her teeth slipped, Mrs. Thornton. She choked on her teeth."

Judith relaxed. Jean set the offending denture on the dresser, pulled a pair of white plastic gloves from the box of two hundred on the nightstand, used her thumb to gently open her mother's mouth, and looked inside.

"The lowers are still in there!" she exclaimed, snapping the gloves off her hands.

Judith, her fear subsiding, considered putting the

uppers in the white ceramic cup with the lilacs on it that was used to soak her mother's teeth. All the while her mother's eyes were glued to the upper teeth, which were directly to her side.

"Her jaw's gone and shrunk, and the teeth don't fit anymore. Shall I put them back in, Mrs. Thornton?" The three women were now all looking at the teeth on the dresser. Jean's question went beyond the matter of what they were going to do right at that moment. They both realized her mother could choke on them if neither Judith nor Jean was around.

When Judith's mother had first become ill but could still talk, they'd joked about her false teeth. Judith would take them from her to soak them and as she sat puckered, would kiddingly tell her she wasn't bringing them back. It was funny and they always laughed. But Judith noticed that when her mother could no longer talk, it was more difficult to take her teeth away from her. On one occasion Jean's attempt to remove them resulted in her mother's clenching her teeth so tightly together, they couldn't be removed. An exasperated Jean pleaded, to no avail. Only when Judith promised to clean them herself, a job that always made her gag, and bring them right back, did her mother relent and slacken her jaw.

Her mother's eyes were still focused intently on the teeth.

"I can't take them from her, Jean. Not yet," Judith whispered to the aid. "Can we put them back in, at least for a while, if you can sit with her?"

The woman nodded. "Sure, I'll watch her."

It must, Judith realized, be one of the ultimate human degradations. Without her teeth, her mother was worse than immobilized. Even though she ate pureed foods already, having no teeth was a death sentence.

Judith approached the bedside and sat next to her mother while Jean donned another pair of plastic gloves and carefully slid the teeth back into her mother's mouth.

"For now, Mom, the teeth are back. But we need to watch you to be sure they don't slip. You can choke if they slip, okay?"

Her mother did not look into Judith's face but straight ahead, tuning her out.

Judith had tried to make her understand the danger. All her mother wanted was the teeth. Judith knew that at some point they would have to be removed for longer periods of time. Did her mother know? Judith hoped when that time came, and it was almost upon them, her mother would not know.

By the time Judith grabbed her purse and headed toward the garage door, her mother's eyes were closed, her teeth safely back in her mouth. The trauma of the event over, she had drifted peacefully off to sleep.

Such small things were starting to define the declining process of living.

"I am," Judith vowed half-sarcastically, "going to take good care of my teeth."

By the time Judith reached her office, Pike and Delgado had returned from their visit with Irene Talbot. She was ready for a cup of coffee after the disruption of her mother's dental emergency.

Pike summarized the visit and concluded by pointing out what he thought were inconsistencies in Irene Talbot's conduct, including her staring out the window at him.

"She said something that interested me, Judith. She said Rex Cutter was very close to her father. She called him Uncle Rex. If her father was so close to Cutter, how could he *not* know what the man was doing out in the canyon?"

"If Talbot is a savior of the field hands, maybe he was just giving Carrasco some financial help. That would end the mystery right there."

"I'd love to end it right there, but it still doesn't make sense to me. Why all in fifties? And what does Serafino know? I'm not buying it."

"Well, how do we find out if Talbot's involved?"

"We go visit him."

"Before we do that, I'd like to get a better picture of what I'm dealing with," Judith added. "Give me a day, and I'll go out with you to wherever he'll agree to meet."

"Shall we bring the kid with us?" Pike asked, referring to Delgado.

"I thought you considered him excess baggage."

"Well, he seemed to do okay out there in the field. He was a little shaken, I think, with seeing a burned guy in Irene Talbot's office. He was pretty quiet on the way back."

"Let's not overwhelm him, Pike. I don't think he's best used on this interview. Maybe we can start him to thinking about how we find Serafino Morales. The guy isn't in the canyon anymore. He's somewhere between here and Fillmore."

Pike and Judith walked down the hall to Delgado's office, where they found him writing a file report of what he'd observed in the field that day with Pike. They gave him a brief update on their plan to interview Talbot and asked what he thought about helping devise a way to find Serafino. This time he was quick to accept the challenge and offered to investigate the use of the media and distribution of a composite sketch.

For her part, Judith dispatched herself to the public library, where she could do some research on the elder Talbot.

20

A STERILE GRAY linoleum corridor on the second floor of the Central Library led Judith to a large room filled with tables. The walls stood lined with gray metal file cases containing files arranged alphabetically and again by subject. Several of the file cases stood devoted to the biographical clippings of San Diego's luminaries. The only other fixtures in the room were a receptionist assigned to give assistance and refile the research materials returned to her and, because nothing could be removed from the room, a copy machine charging five cents per page.

At Pike's suggestion, Judith spent part of the evening at one of the desks, reading two files thick with newspaper clippings on the life, times, and comrades of Franklin Talbot. The articles, ranging over at least three decades, were in no particular order and many were yellow with age, hopelessly frayed, or missing a second or third page separated somewhere in the pile of information.

As a whole the articles presented a visual and written portrait of the man. The more lengthy personal biographies offered a unique view into the man's past, and his personality.

One of the more interesting articles reported how in 1920 Franklin Talbot's father and mother walked the six-year-old out to the corral of their fifteen-thousand-acre ranch in New Mexico and proudly presented him with his first horse, an unbroken Appaloosa. Young Franklin balked at riding the animal and steadfastly refused to name it.

"If you name it," he protested, "it won't be wild anymore."

Two years later when the family was forced to sell its drought-ravaged ranch, pack up their cattle and possessions, and move to San Diego, it was Franklin who, with nary a hint of remorse, released the animal into the wild and, shunning the comfort of the sleeping compartment, climbed into a cattle car for the two-day trip west.

She read on. By the time World War II ended, young Talbot, his parents now dead, had parlayed the family holdings to include most of Mission Valley, extending over a radius of five miles. San Diego was as yet a vast sea of land, there for the taking, and Talbot and a close consortium of men of equal tenacity and vision, realizing the incipient power of raw land, acquired and expanded their holdings as quickly as their finances allowed.

In article after article the man's life was pieced together along with the history of the county. As the population of San Diego burgeoned in the sixties and seventies, and the demand for land along with it, the ranches were sold off to accommodate housing. Talbot's investments diversified to fit the needs of urban growth: quarrying, paving freeways, building the bridges over them and the homes alongside them. Yet even as he helped orchestrate the skyrocketing growth of the city, he remained a rancher at heart, establishing riding trails even as he poured the concrete slabs downtown.

As the obituaries revealed, of the early ranchers, only Franklin Talbot was left. He owned more acres than anyone cared to count and more men than anyone dared admit—in public, anyway. A spry widower retired from the day-to-day functioning of his business, Talbot still controlled every movement, every penny, of Talbot Industries. He didn't play golf or work out at the gyms, didn't visit the chic clubs and restaurants of the city's new Gaslamp Quarter. "Too busy to do that sort of thing," he had scowled to one reporter.

Judith viewed with growing reverence the succession of photos of the man. Youthful Talbot standing on a mound overlooking Mission Valley. Talbot in full regalia and silver saddle on horseback leading the New Year's Parade. Dedicating a freeway. Leading Boy Scouts on a backpacking trip he financed. Dedicating a parcel of land for city park land. Mr. Downtown San Diego. Mr. Chamber of Commerce. A seemingly endless list of citations and awards.

Even Pike, a seasoned investigator, would later admit to some trepidation over confronting a man like Franklin Talbot about his lobbyist's holding money for a murder victim. Yet it was Talbot for whom Cutter worked, and it was Talbot who might clarify what Cutter was doing out at McGonigle Canyon. Armed with a seemingly accurate idea of what Talbot was like, Judith and Pike drove north to meet with the man, who had requested they come to his home.

The directions from Talbot's secretary were for

the most part based on landmarks. Drive north on Interstate 5, exit Lomas Santa Fe Drive, and head east four miles to the oak grove just past the polo field. Turn right at the black iron gate. Drive a quarter mile down the road. "It's lined with Monterey pine and cypress," she said. "You'll see the red tile roof in the distance, and the road will lead directly to the house."

The house was a two-story Spanish-style with a nine-foot hand-crafted oak door costing more, as Pike quipped, than he made in two months. There was no doorbell. Visitors were required to use the huge polished brass door knocker at eye level. Pike and Judith knocked and were ushered into the gray-and-pink marble-floored entry by a smiling Mexican housekeeper. She led them out sliding glass doors to the patio.

Judith, who had seen a dozen photographs of Talbot, instantly recognized him. He was seated at a round white wood table, shielded from the sun by a blue canvas umbrella. Beyond the patio lay rolling green lawn interspersed with mounds of orange daylilies and pockets of sycamore and Monterey pine. A three-tiered Spanish fountain surrounded by clay pots filled with red and pink geraniums dripped noisily to the right of the patio.

Talbot's thick gray hair was combed straight back. His long face and straight jaw were covered by wrinkled skin more pale than Judith expected.

Talbot looked up as they approached, and he addressed Pike.

"Good afternoon, Mr. . . ."

"Martin. Detective Pike Martin." Pike drew his wallet and flashed the badge inside it.

Talbot's deep voice was a low, lazy drawl, giving his pronunciation a languid, elastic quality.

"And this pretty little lady is . . ."

Judith's eyes widened. "Pretty little lady" was not a designation she could ever remember having applied to her, at least not out loud. It rendered her speechless long enough to prompt Pike to make the introduction.

"Chief Deputy District Attorney Judith Thornton."

Judith extended her hand, and Talbot clasped her hand in both of his, winking at her in the process.

"Mr. Martin, Ms. Thornton, pleased to meet you. Have a chair. Would you like some lunch?"

Pike, only slightly offended by Talbot's purposeful lack of reference to his title, slipped onto one of the thickly padded chairs across from Talbot. Without waiting for Pike or Judith to respond, Talbot waved the housekeeper back toward him.

"Bring our guests some lunch, Flora. You like *carne asada*?" he asked the pair.

Pike spoke directly to the housekeeper. "*No, por favor. No tengo hambre.* I just ate." Judith shook her head. The woman looked at Talbot and, as she'd received no further commands from him, stepped away from the table and waited.

Talbot nodded approvingly toward Pike. "You speak Spanish, Mr. Martin. It's a useful thing in San Diego. You must find it helpful in your line of work, all the Mexican gangs and such. Uh, Flora, take my plate and bring us some ice cream . . . *helado.* I'm assuming Ms. Thornton would risk her girlish figure for some of your homemade ice cream?"

Judith squirmed. All the reverence she'd brought along was rapidly disappearing in the face of this awkward chauvinism. She had no clever comeback.

Meanwhile, Flora sprinted toward the house before either Pike or Judith could decline the offer of ice cream.

"I don't suppose this is a purely social visit." Although Talbot directed the comment to Pike, Judith seized the opportunity before Pike could respond, and her brisk reply startled both men.

"As a matter of fact it's not, Mr. Talbot. We're investigating the murder of a field worker, a man named Carrasco. Rogelio Carrasco. Have you ever heard of him?"

Talbot's smile disappeared, replaced by a look of such serious intensity as to be purposely disingenuous. He leaned forward but not toward Judith, who had asked the question and naturally expected Talbot to respond to her. Instead, he directed his response to Pike, as if to tell him a secret. In staccato, every word emphasized, Talbot whispered, "No, can't say as I ever have. You see, I haven't much cause to use farm help. My people at the house and on my jobs are all legal. I pay them often enough to keep them loyal, and I pay them enough that they don't need to work a second job. Take my little girl, Flora, now. She's thirty-three years old and has two kids, a fifteen-year-old boy and a twelve-year-old girl. She ran away from a drunkard husband down in Tijuana and lived in a hovel up in the canyon till I hired her. I pay her three hundred fifty dollars a week, and now she's in a little apartment."

As if on cue, Flora emerged from the house and approached. On a tray she carried three bowls of Neapolitan ice cream. One she set perfunctorily before Pike; another, before Judith. The third, containing four times the amount in either of the other bowls, an inedible portion, she set ceremoniously before Talbot. The disparity, embarrassingly noticeable, was ignored by the host.

"Now, where were we.... Ah, yes, you were talking about a field hand who's met ... an untimely death. A Mister Carras."

"Carrasco," Judith corrected.

"Carrasco, yes. Like I said, I've never heard the name before. Do you have a suspect in the man's murder?"

Judith pressed him further. "We're looking at a possible suspect. Serafino Morales. We think he's heading for Fillmore. How about that name? Does it sound familiar at all?"

"Nope, sorry," Talbot shot back at her.

"Actually there *is* a tie between you and Carrasco," Pike added. He watched Talbot's eyes narrow, waiting for more information, and Pike obliged. "It seems your lobbyist, Rex Cutter, might have known him."

Talbot looked down and shook his head. "Ah yes, poor Rex. Bit by a rattler. " He pushed a spoonful of the ice cream into his mouth and pulled the spoon out half-full. "Felled by one of his own kind. That's a truly fucked up end to a brilliant career." He was silent for a moment, then turned to Judith. "Oh, I do apologize, Ms. Thornton."

The expletive was a purposeful insult directed at her to embarrass her. Judith felt her face burning.

Pike, now fully cognizant of the tension between Talbot and Judith, watched Talbot's face carefully as he made the next statement. "Cutter died with money in his vest pocket and an envelope with Carrasco's name on it. You wouldn't know of any reason why one of your lobbyists might be paying money to a field hand?"

Talbot's face was expressionless as he lifted another spoon of ice cream into his mouth and pulled it out, still half-full. He smacked his lips and pointed the spoon at Pike. "Not one. Actually, Cutter always was one to go and freelance on me now and again." He shrugged his shoulders. "Perhaps he'd taken on another, somewhat smaller job." Another spoon of ice cream slipped into his mouth and was drawn out half-full. Neither Judith nor Pike had touched their dessert. Talbot addressed his comment to them both. "You'd better eat your ice cream there; it's melting."

Pike looked down at the softening mound and shook his head. The information Pike hoped would shake him seemed only to stimulate his appetite.

"Too bad. It's good stuff. Now, if this Carrasco left a wife or kids and you're looking for help for his family, I can—"

"No. That's not why we're here. Pike turned to candor. "Let's just say, Mr. Talbot, that we find the connection between Talbot Industries and a murdered field laborer curious. It was too, shall we say, 'interesting' to pass up."

Talbot swallowed several spoonfuls of ice cream and pushed the still half-full bowl away. "I'll tell you what, folks. I don't know anything about this Carrasco, or why Cutter was carrying money for him in an envelope, but if I find out anything, perhaps I can give you a call?"

"I'd appreciate that," Pike replied, reaching into his shirt pocket and placing his business card on the table. He stood to leave, Judith following suit.

Talbot remained seated, without extending his hand to Pike or Judith, without rising. "I trust you can find your way out okay?"

"I'm sure we can," Pike replied.

As he reached the patio door, Talbot yelled after them, "Sorry I couldn't have been of more help, Mr. Martin."

Pike, eyelids blinking, bit his lip, not from the rudeness of his host as much as from the realization Talbot had slipped. Judith, however, was far too angry to have caught any of Talbot's faux pas. At the car she whirled around to face Pike, her eyes narrow slits. For the first time it occurred to Pike that she was angry. Seated in the car, she spoke at last.

"That awful man! I might as well not have been there. That—"

"That liar," Pike said, finishing her sentence.

"What do you mean?" she asked, caught off guard by Pike's proclamation.

Pike turned his face to her.

"I never told him the money was *in* the envelope."

PART THREE

THE RIVER

21

SERAFINO EXPECTED HE might leave the Healy farm the way he arrived—unannounced. But the Healys had been kind to him, and the courtesy of a thank-you and a good-bye were necessary.

At the end of the eighth day of Serafino's stay on the Healy farm, the last of the marked avocado trees were cut down and chopped into a pile for firewood. Like Healy, Serafino felt great pride in having come up with a plan to save the trees and maybe give the farm new life for another year. But he also saw the dreams of the farmer turning to dust. It was like that sometimes. Any farmer knew it. Anyone whose life was in the soil. When the soil stopped growing plants or the rain didn't fall, part of your insides died too. But farmers were made to suffer. It was always work and much grief unless you were rich, and not many people had wealth enough to immunize them from the grief of growing food and relying on what grows.

Serafino rapped gently on the wood frame of the kitchen screen door. Pam Healy called Serafino into the kitchen, and he removed his sweat-stained straw hat from his head as he entered the house and looked around. He'd only been in the kitchen twice before; on both occasions the Healys had persuaded him, much against his wishes, to eat dinner with them at their table. But it was uncomfortable for the field hand. He was used to eating small amounts in short periods of time, and the prolonged small talk at the table was difficult for him. He was far more comfortable having his food brought out to the packing shed, where he could sit outside and watch the brown falcons circle overhead.

On this cool evening Pam Healy offered Serafino a glass of cold water with ice in it—it was a luxury to have ice—and returned to standing at the stove stirring something in a large pot.

"Stew for dinner," she announced. "Do you like stew?"

Serafino had never heard the English word "stew" before and looked perplexed when she said the word. But when he walked to the stove and peeked inside the pot, he recognized the contents. "Stew" was putting what you have left over into the water with a little meat and heating it until it was all mixed together. If he could have found the words, he would have told her the contents of the pot smelled much better than any stew he had ever made. At a loss for the words, Serafino smiled and nodded his approval.

"Have dinner with us here tonight, Serafino, please?"

She was asking. And under the circumstances Serafino said, "Yes, tonight yes."

Pam Healy took an extra plate from the white wood cabinet above the sink and pulled a set of silverware from the drawer. Art Healy came in as she was setting the place at the table. He was smiling. Pam looked at his face. There was a feeling of hope in her again. If the farm went under, they would cope. They had talked about it many times before the night Serafino fell from the tree. Once the cutting of the trees started, though, they had not talked of quitting. And now Art was smiling.

Art and Pam talked while Serafino ate. He watched them, his hands before him at the table waiting to be served. Periodically they addressed him or asked a question of him, repeating themselves, using simple words until he understood.

"Good," Serafino said at the end of the meal as Pam picked the dishes up from the table. "I . . ." He didn't know the words for "must go," so he raised his right hand and pointed his arm northward.

"Okay, good night, Serafino. I'm glad you liked the dinner," Pam said, unaware of the import of Serafino's announcement.

Art Healy, however, understood immediately.

"No, Pammy, he's saying he's leaving."

Pam Healy put the plates in the sink and came to the table, where the two men were still seated.

"Can't you persuade him to stay?" she asked her husband.

"I'd love to, but I think Serafino's made up his mind. Serafino, must go?" He asked the field hand.

"*Sí*, must . . ."

"I . . . I don't know what to say, Serafino. Thank you." Art extended his hand to him, and Serafino grabbed it with both hands, vigorously shaking it.

"Where . . . *¿Adónde . . . ?*"

Serafino struggled with the words in Oaxacan, but he could tell neither Healy understood any of the sounds he was making. He could say the name of the location though, "Fillmore . . . Ventura County . . . cousin's trees."

As Pam Healy rose and finished clearing the table, her husband raised his hands and pushed his palms toward Serafino, motioning for Serafino to stay seated. He went to the phone, dialed two numbers, and wrote something on a piece of paper as he talked. Several minutes later he returned to the table and took his wallet from his front pants pocket. He removed two twenty-dollar bills and placed them in front of Serafino.

"No," Serafino said, pushing the money back toward Healy.

"Please, yes. I'll make it up when I sell the firewood. I called the bus. *Autobús*. It costs thirty-two dollars to go to Fillmore. It leaves at seven in the morning, and you can be in Fillmore at one o'clock that afternoon. *Cinco horas*—five hours—San Diego to Fillmore." Healy mixed English with the Spanish he knew and repeated himself until Serafino understood.

At last Serafino seemed to stop protesting but made what at first seemed a strange request. He took a small pencil and piece of scrap paper from his pants pocket, then printed an address. Neither Pam nor Art Healy understood what he was saying about the address, but when Serafino placed one of the twenty-dollar bills on top of it, they realized he wanted them to send the money to that address.

"Money—*dinero*—send there?" Healy said, holding the bill and pointing to the paper with the address on it.

Serafino smiled and nodded vigorously. He would give up the bus ride to send half the money home and keep twenty for his trip north. If they sent the twenty dollars, it would give his family enough to buy food until he could join his cousin in Fillmore and earn more money to send home.

Even with this help, time was Serafino's enemy now. The sooner he could make his way to Fillmore and the work his cousin could offer him there, the sooner he could make up the money stolen from him by Carrasco.

Serafino took the twenty-dollar bill, folded it into a square, and shoved it far down into his front pants pocket. He rose from the table and bowed slightly to Pam Healy. Until that moment they had no idea when he was leaving. Drying her hands on the front of her white linen apron, she approached Serafino and extended her hands, which he took and held for a moment before releasing them.

Pam Healy placed a half loaf of white bread, a package of sliced American cheese, and two fresh peaches on the table. She wrapped them lightly in a thin red-and-white-checkered cotton towel and put the wrapped package into a sturdy blue canvas bag on which SAN DIEGO, AMERICA'S FINEST CITY was printed in large white letters. As an afterthought she grabbed an avocado from a bowl and held it up for Serafino to see. He grinned widely and, nodding, watched her place the fruit into the canvas bag, a souvenir of his visit.

Art Healy had left the kitchen briefly and returned with a map of California in his hand. He opened it fully on the now cleared table.

Serafino had never before seen a map of the entire state, and he stood over it, silent until Art Healy put his hand on the map and said, "California." Then he pointed to a large black dot. "San Diego," he said, and Serafino recognized the printed words designating the city. Healy moved his finger and pointed to another dot, this one much smaller. "Fillmore" it said. It did not appear there was much distance between them, only inches, but Art Healy tried to make him understand there were about a hundred miles between the dots. It would take him days to walk it.

Next Healy tried to explain the highways. There were several ways Serafino could travel to Fillmore. He could see on the map that the lines would take him different ways. Mostly he had to decide if he wanted to go through Los Angeles or not. He could cut across to Interstate 5 and go through the big city, or he could go up Freeway 15 all the way to Norco and then cut across north of Los Angeles and go up the coast highway all the way to Fillmore. The advantage to going through Los Angeles would be that he might find temporary work there. Many laborers had spoken of the barrios in Los Angeles and the need for workers in the restaurants and stores. He might give that city a try.

Healy folded the map and gave it to Serafino. Then he extended his hand to Serafino, who took it and squeezed it gently with both his own.

The sun was setting in a blaze of red and pink as the Healys walked with him to the road and watched as Serafino disappeared down the dirt street.

As he reached the bottom of the hill, the leaves in the shrubbery next to Serafino rustled and a large black Labrador retriever emerged, padding along behind him, wagging its thick tail. It was the dog belonging to the Healys' neighbor, one of the dogs that he suspected must have barked at him eight days earlier as he sat waiting for the Healys to go to sleep. Now it was escorting him to the intersection at the bottom of the hill, and then it would go home.

Serafino patted the top of the dog's head and scratched behind its ears. He reached into the canvas bag and pushed his hand into the towel-wrapped package. When he pulled his hand out, it contained a large jagged piece of bread, which he placed in front of the dog's nose and which it eagerly ate.

Believing the dog satisfied, Serafino walked on. But the dog followed him, wagging its tail wildly, leaping toward the hand carrying the bag of food.

Serafino knew better than to ignore the animal. As a young boy he had watched a skinny black mongrel steal bread from Delfino, a baker far too poor to give away his merchandise. Confused by the pleasure Delfino derived from allowing the dog as much bread as it wanted, Serafino challenged the man. Why, he demanded, had Delfino given the thief of a dog such a generous gift whereas if he, a boy, stole the bread, he would surely have been beaten?

Delfino only frowned, a look of great concern coming over his face. "When you die, you cannot cross the river into the next world unless you are carried across. At the river you will find a black dog and a white one. The white one will not take you because you are Indian and you will soil its fur. But the black dog will carry you across, unless during your lifetime you have mistreated a black dog or deprived it of food when it was hungry." He'd looked even more sternly then at Serafino and shook his finger at him, adding, "Never mistreat the black dog. And if it is hungry, you must feed it. If it wants to steal food from you, you must let it. It is testing your soul."

Serafino looked down at the black dog sitting expectantly at his feet. He reached into the canvas bag again and pulled another, larger piece of bread for the animal. Satisfied, the dog lumbered off in the direction of home as Serafino set his course for the highway.

22

JUDITH WAS IN her office late, reviewing exactly where they were in the investigation of Rogelio Carrasco's murder. A murder was a murder. You find the suspect. You arrest him and prosecute. If all goes well, you get a conviction. Despite the canyon sweep and the interviews, they were no closer to an arrest than they had been the day after the murder. They knew a lot more about McGonigle Canyon, but they were nowhere near arresting Serafino Morales.

Judith reached for the phone and called Pike, then Peter Delgado. It was about time they all compared notes and shook something up.

Both men were in her office within thirty minutes, coffee mugs in hand, tablets and files spread out over her small conference table. Even before they'd arrived, Judith had made several decisions, and she wasted no time telling them of her new plan.

"We know Serafino's not in that canyon. I'd like to issue a press release tomorrow announcing we've identified a suspect in the Carrasco murder.

We give his name and set up a hot-line number so anyone who knows the man or has seen him can call in. Pike, the hot-line number's yours."

"Do you really think the field laborers are going to be watching television?" Pike drawled.

Pike was right. It was highly unlikely the television stations were going to be a big help.

"Maybe not, but we'll pick up radio too, and who knows. We need all the help we can get. It's too bad we don't have any other way of identifying the guy. No photo, no driver's license. I say we go for what we can."

"Why don't I call 'Crime Stoppers?'" Delgado added.

"You mean do a reconstruction of the scene?" Judith asked.

"It can't hurt anything. We go out to the canyon, to the spot where Carrasco was murdered. Put some drama in it."

Pike nodded approvingly.

"Good idea, Peter. I think you should be in charge of that."

"Okay, then, Peter, you and I will work up a press release for immediate distribution. You can go ahead and see about a 'Crime Stoppers' episode. Just a couple of minutes' worth. San Diego P.D. will put that together for you. Pike, you can help there. If the press release gets some coverage tomorrow, let's meet again and see what we've got, if anything."

Pamela Healy was making dinner when she heard the news break on the small television set on the kitchen counter. It was only a fifteen-second report, and she wasn't sure she caught the full story. It was the name Serafino Morales that first

jarred her. An older Hispanic. Lived in McGonigle
Canyon. Wanted for murder. Murder? Could there
be more than one Serafino Morales?

Nervously she turned to another channel and listened to several news stories before the anchor-
woman paused and reported the San Diego police
now had a suspect in the strangulation murder of
Rogelio Carrasco, a field hand, in McGonigle
Canyon's encampment. He was described further
as an older man, a Oaxacan Indian. Pamela reached
for a pencil and jotted down the information number broadcast to the public.

As the reporter segued into the next report, Art
Healy came through the kitchen screen door. He
listened to Pamela's excited summary of the news
story and shook his head in disbelief. Still, it was
a murder. How were they to know what the man
did before he fell from their tree? Though Art
doubted it, maybe Serafino *was* capable of killing
someone. They hesitated, yet felt obligated to report. They had some knowledge of the man.

Art Healy reached for the phone and called the
number his wife had jotted down. The voice on the
other end took his telephone number and told him
a detective would be calling back.

The morning after Art Healy called the hot-line
number, Pike pulled his county car into the driveway of the Healys' house. Delgado was with him.
It was Pike who had returned Art Healy's telephone call and on hearing the description of the
Healys' employee, asked if he could come talk to
them as soon as possible. The door to the Healys'
was open, and through the screen door, Pike could
see Pam Healy at the sink. He knocked and Delgado and he sat at the kitchen table while Pam ran

outside to tell her husband the detective had arrived.

The three men sat at the kitchen table. Pam finished washing dishes, glancing over her shoulder now and then as the preliminary talk turned to more serious discussion.

"From the outset I just want to tell you my wife and I feel very uncomfortable talking to you about Serafino."

"If you're concerned he might come back and harm you in any way—" Pike began.

Healy waved his right hand back and forth rapidly. "No, no."

"We can be sure you have plenty of protection."

Pam Healy turned to face the detective and Delgado, a wooden spoon in hand, as her husband rubbed his eyes. "No, really, we're not concerned about our safety, Detective Martin. My goodness— Art and I wouldn't ever be afraid of Serafino."

"That's right, Detective. I can't imagine our Serafino harming anyone, let alone killing someone. If he ever did something like that, he had to have been pushed to do it. Why, the man could hardly walk straight most days."

"You said *our* Serafino. Have you known him long?" Delgado asked.

"Not really." Healy shot a quick glance at Pam, a look she knew. It meant "Don't say anything." When he spoke again, he wasn't completely candid. "He was looking for work for a few days, and I gave him some." Pam smiled. He hadn't told them Serafino fell from their tree trying to steal avocados. She wasn't about to tell them either.

Delgado continued. "Did he give you any indication he'd killed anyone? Ever mention a man named Carrasco?"

"No to both questions." Healy's voice grew more soft when he spoke again. "Serafino helped me save my avocado grove. He stayed in the packing shed out back and never bothered us. He ate what we gave him and never asked for money."

"We didn't have any money to give him anyway," Pam added.

"Did he say where he was going when he left?" Pike asked.

"To Fillmore, I think." Art Healy looked at his wife. "He's walking there, Detective."

Pam added, "That's what he said. Fillmore, because his cousin lives there and can give him some work."

Pike looked at Delgado and nodded. "He's our man."

It was not what the Healys wanted to hear. Both were hoping against hope he was not the man they were looking for.

"Would you mind if we dusted the packing shed for prints, Mrs. Healy?" Pike asked.

"I don't see why not, Detective. Art can show you where it is, can't you, Artie?"

"Of course, Detective. I'll take the two of you over there right now."

At the door Pike turned and addressed both husband and wife. "If we needed a composite drawing, can we get the two of you to come in and do some describing? If we're going to track him down in Fillmore, we'll need some kind of picture of the guy to pass around. He's got a name. We'd just like to give him a face. I'm warning you, though, it might take a little time, so we can arrange for you to come in even on a weekend."

Pam Healy would have said it but her husband

spoke first. "We don't have weekends, Detective. Just let us know when you want us."

"Detective," Pam asked as they were about to leave, "just who is it you think Serafino killed?"

"Another field hand—" Pike started to explain.

"Well, if he did, the man must have been a terrible person," Pam interrupted as the men pushed aside the screen door and headed for the packing shed.

The following Saturday the Healys met with Pike and Delgado at the San Diego Police Department. It took four hours, including breaks, but at the end of that time the police sketch artist had produced what the Healys believed was a very close likeness of Serafino Morales. Pike had the sketch reproduced, and after showing it to Judith and discussing their tactics, it was agreed he would take three days to travel into the Ventura County area to distribute fliers with Serafino's portrait at the farms and ranches near Fillmore in an attempt to locate his cousin and hence, the precise location to which he was headed.

23

◄―►

JUDITH HAD BEEN at the auto mechanic's in
Mission Valley since seven o'clock having him
check out the intermittent electrical problem that
made her car stall unexpectedly. After checking the
systems, the mechanic announced it was fixed. By
the time Judith paid for his services, it was eight-
thirty. If she was lucky, she'd be in her office by
nine. Before heading out onto the freeway, she
stopped at the gas station and filled the tank, then
pulled out into the busy left-turn lane of traffic. The
car abruptly stalled.

Judith sat in the vehicle. Just sat. She had no intention of getting out nor was she interested in
somehow maneuvering to the right curb. She had
no feelings about the vehicle or the mechanic, and
several minutes passed before Judith tried to start
the car again, to no avail. Finally, at the driver's
window a sweaty face appeared, and a young man,
perhaps in his twenties, who had been bicycling
asked if he could help. Judith got out of the car and
allowed him to push it back into the gas station,
where she had just been and from where she was

quick to note no one had emerged to help her. She thanked the man, locked the car, and telephoned the mechanic to report the location of the vehicle. Her next call was to her secretary, who promised to pick her up in ten minutes. When she arrived, Judith gave the car key to the gas station attendant and left, telling him to give the key to the mechanic.

There had been a time when such an event would have given Judith a mild migraine or a fit of pique with the mechanic or car. Judith found it interesting that she hadn't felt any such emotions. Then it occurred to her that she hadn't had a headache in some time. Given the degree of stress in her life, it was a revelation of sorts; perhaps, she thought, a sign of increased strength.

At work and safely behind her desk, Judith forgot about the car. This morning her desk was cluttered with unrelated debris: several short piles of paper needing responses, errant paper clips, and, for unknown reasons, a small folding map of San Francisco and an old grocery list. A second list, this one of things she was supposed to remember to do, was under the grocery list. She was becoming a person whose life was being directed by lists, lists that she wrote and scratched out.

Judith organized her desktop, throwing away what could be discarded. At ten o'clock she left for her monthly administrative meeting with the trial deputies in her unit.

By the time the meeting was over, several telephone messages lay unanswered on her now clean desk. The one from her mechanic she read and discarded. He had the car and would call her when it was fixed. The second message she read was from Irene Talbot, and the third was from Jean, her mother's health aid. It was marked "Not urgent."

Judith called Delgado and asked him to come to her office; then she called her house. Jean answered. It seemed the weekend aid would not be able to come. Judith would ordinarily cover the weekend herself in such a circumstance. That meant complete surrender of herself to being on call: feeding her mother, getting her up, readying her for bed, responding to the coughs and sneezes and hunger and changes of clothes and wet diaper pads. It meant a weekend of retreat to infancy. It was wrong, she knew, to feel this way. Yet there was growing resentment to her role of caregiver, and she could no longer deal with it by ignoring it. Even though she had no pressing demands for the weekend, she asked Jean if she might be able to work during the weekend. Saturday yes. Sunday no. It was an acceptable compromise.

When she hung up, she realized Delgado was standing outside the door waiting for her to finish her telephone conversation. Hearing her say goodbye, he knocked and came in.

"Take a look at this," Judith said, handing Irene Talbot's message to Delgado.

"The message is for Pike, but while he's chasing Serafino up in Fillmore, I'm screening his calls. Anything coming in on the Carrasco murder I'm going to pass along to you. I think you might want to follow up on this and call her back. If it's anything dramatic, let me know."

Back in his office, Delgado dialed the return number Irene Talbot left with the message. A secretary answered and asked him to hold briefly. Then there was a familiar voice at the other end.

"Irene Talbot."

Delgado spoke with a less than assured voice.

"I . . . this is Peter Delgado with the District Attorney's Office? I'm calling for Detective Martin . . . I mean in his behalf . . . since he's away from the city. I think you called him?"

He thought he detected a giggle on the other end of the phone.

"Uh, yes I did."

He could tell she was probably smiling. She was not making it easy for him. Delgado tried to relax and leaned back in his chair, allowing himself to smile as well.

"Can I help you?" he asked.

"I'm not sure you can, actually. I have some information for Detective Martin, and I don't know if it can wait. Do you know how long he's going to be gone?"

"At least two days, maybe longer."

There was another pause, but it was a thinking pause. She was trying to decide if she should divulge her information to him.

"Miss Talbot—it is Miss, isn't it?"

"It's Miss."

"I'm working on the Carrasco murder with Detective Martin. If there's something important about the case, you can tell me."

Her voice was surprisingly hushed.

"I don't think this is something I should talk about over the phone. Maybe I can meet you somewhere?"

Delgado hesitated.

"How about your office?" he suggested.

Her voice was direct. "No. Not here."

"Well how about my office, then?"

"I'd really prefer not."

There was an awkward pause before she spoke again.

"I'm going to be out at McGonigle Canyon tomorrow. It's Sunday and I have several clients there I need to talk to. Can you meet me at the end of the encampment road, at the mouth of the encampment?"

"I haven't been there before. I think I can find it okay. What time?"

"Is ten-thirty too early?"

"Not at all. I'll be there."

"And Mr. Delgado?"

"Uh-huh . . ."

"I'd rather you didn't bring anyone with you."

Delgado reached the encampment at ten-fifteen. Irene Talbot was already there, standing next to a white Ford Explorer. She was dressed in tight blue jeans and an oversize purple T-shirt. Her hair was drawn up into a ponytail secured with a white scarf. She waved when she saw his car approach.

As he stopped his vehicle, a van drove up and parked behind him. A group of six men jumped out, followed by a priest, overtaking Delgado and passing Irene Talbot.

"The priest's here to say mass," she announced. "The others are the choir. Despite what you see around here sometimes, the men are deeply religious. Want to go to church?"

"I don't think so, if you don't mind."

"That's okay. I've met with my clients. Let's walk down toward the fields where we can talk."

Several yards down the road, they passed a large covered patio with wooden benches. A hymn began as the men of the camp filled the rough pews in the impromptu outdoor auditorium. Since she seemed to know the camp well, he let her lead the way toward an open field, where she abruptly stopped and turned to him.

"I hope you don't mind my dragging you out here."

He tried not to sound too serious.

"That depends on what you dragged me out here for."

"You're going to think I'm pretty stupid, but I'm not sure what I dragged you out here for.

"Now this just might get interesting." His voice was lyrical.

"You're flirting, Mr. Delgado. And I'm dead serious."

"Tell me something, Miss Talbot, can we just use first names? It's easier."

"Okay. First names."

"What're you doing out here? I mean working with the field laborers. Your father's wealthy. You went to an Ivy League law school, I'll bet."

She turned her back to him. On the T-shirt was printed HARVARD.

"See, I was right—Harvard," Delgado said, laughing gently. "I guess that explains it."

"Harvard had nothing to do with my job here. I didn't decide to represent indigent field hands while I was in law school. Actually, I was home for Christmas vacation one year, and we had a particularly bad rain. It was so bad, the San Diego River down in Mission Valley overflowed and the water spilled over into the Fashion Valley parking lot. Made things pretty hard for the Christmas shoppers. Anyway, my father had some land down near Otay Mesa. They were just starting to build, and he needed to go down and see if the lake there had overflowed. I went along. I'll never forget sitting in his big truck with a cup of hot coffee and looking up into the hills, and all of a sudden these *things* began to move from one bush to another; then they'd move again. It took me awhile to realize those things were people. They were men, living up in the hills. They were holding plastic trash bags over their heads to keep the rain off, moving from one bush to another for protection. It was tragic and almost funny. They were drenched and they were still trying to keep dry. When my father was through and got back into the truck, I remember asking him about the men. He said they were laborers. Not his own. He didn't know whose. And I thought, how sad that no one cared."

"So you became the resident representative for your father's laborers?"

"No. I moved back to San Diego after I took the California Bar Exam and went to work for the public defender for a year and a half. I didn't care for criminal law. This seemed the natural thing to do. I set up my little office with my dad's help, and I take referrals from the various legal aid agencies. It just so happens I do a lot of immigration work. How about you? A Hispanic working for the district attorney. It must make your family pretty proud of you."

"Why do you say that?"

"I'm sorry. I didn't mean to offend you. I assumed . . . and I'm sorry. I assumed—"

"That my family came from a place like this?"

Her face had turned bright red.

"Don't feel bad. Your assumption's correct. My family came from Mexico, and my grandparents worked in the fields. So'd my father when he was young. But my personal story's not as interesting as yours. My father grew up to be a federal judge."

"Judge Delgado?"

"Yes."

"He has a wonderful reputation. I've never been in his courtroom, though."

"He's great all right. It's hard to do anything but try to follow in his footsteps."

"I see...."

"Anyway, what's this information you're now thoroughly embarrassed to tell me about?"

"Before I say anything, Peter, you have to promise me you won't repeat anything I tell you."

"Not even if it's about the murder case I'm working on? I can't make that promise."

"It's not about the Carrasco murder. I don't think so, anyway. It's about this canyon. You know I have a case involving a little boy who got some kind of toxin in his eyes out here?"

"The boy you told us about in your office?"

"That's the one. Well, I'm filing it against the farmer who owns the land around here, where the Ignacio boy was playing. You can appreciate the problems putting the case together. The first one being, where did he contact the toxin? I sent my investigator out to the fields and hired a soils person and a toxicologist, and I've spent close to twenty-five thousand dollars."

"And you found?"

Irene was hesitant to speak. After all, it was her case she was talking about here, perhaps giving it away too soon.

"I ... didn't expect what I got back from them."

She stopped there, and Delgado was not sure she wanted to continue. She was choosing her words carefully.

"Not only is the stream periodically polluted with a toxin called paraquat, so are the irrigation tanks. And not just here at the farm but this entire area surrounding the canyon."

"How can you be certain of that?" he asked.

"I trust my experts."

"Do you think the farmers are poisoning the crops or water?"

"That was my first reaction, but now I don't think so. It wouldn't make any sense. Why would they do it? To kill their own crops? Farmers don't poison their land. Besides, there's not enough of the stuff in any soil sample we've taken to kill a tree or a whole crop. It's a low-grade poisoning, and it's not a systemic poison. It won't flow to the plant through the roots. If a farmer out here wanted to get rid of his land, all he'd have to do is to poison it, and he wouldn't use paraquat in the soil. And if they got caught doing something like that, they'd be facing incredible state and federal penalties. It would put them out of business."

"So what are you going to do with this information? You've got to report it to someone."

"County health's going to know soon enough. I'm filing the case this week, and I've subpoenaed all of their health complaints on the area soils and water quality testing if they've done any."

"Did you want to report it to my office to file some kind of criminal complaint or investigate?"

"Oh no! That's not why I wanted to tell you about this. I don't want you to tell anyone!"

"All right, all right, I'm sworn to secrecy. You say the farmers wouldn't have any reason to poison the fields. How about an accident of some kind?"

"All over the area, a hundred acres? I don't think so."

"Maybe someone's trying to undermine the farmers somehow."

"Huh! The thought has crossed my mind. But it puts me in a terrible position, doesn't it? My lawsuit's against the owners—"

Delgado finished the sentence. "—for *their* poisoning the water."

"Right. If they're not poisoning the water, then who is? And I have to prove who's poisoning it to win my case."

"I hate to raise the issue, but if you don't think the owners are doing it, you have an ethical obligation not to sue them. It'll cost them thousands of dollars to defend the case. And if what you say is correct, you might be filing a bogus suit."

She ran her hand through her hair and closed her eyes tightly.

"I think I know that." She opened her eyes and looked right at him. "If I ever found out it wasn't the farmers, don't you think I'd drop the case against them?"

"You do have an interesting case. I'm not sure, though, what it has to do with our investigation into Carrasco's murder."

"I . . . I really don't know if it has anything to do with it. It's just . . . well . . ."

She knew what she wanted to say, but she didn't really want to say it. It was too horrible to be repeated out loud. But it was there, as plain as anything she'd ever worked on.

"I need to think about it a little more. Maybe I could call you sometime. I mean if I find something else you should know."

"I have a better idea. Why don't *I* call *you*? I promise I won't make you talk about any more of your trial secrets."

"I don't know, Mr. Delgado; this is a dangerous liaison here." Suddenly she brightened. "I know this is short notice, but this next Friday I'm going to a charity event at the Hotel Del over in Coronado. Have you been there before?"

"Once, maybe twice. It was a long time ago."

"It's a crime victim's fund-raiser. You'd be able to meet some of the movers and shakers in San Diego politics there. Daddy's a cochair for the event." He looked hesitant. "I could use an escort," she added.

He smiled at her. "You Harvard grads—always an ulterior motive."

"Then it's settled."

She reached into her purse, pulled out a business card, and handed it to him.

"My home telephone number's the second one listed there. Give me a call around Wednesday, and we can work out the details."

Delgado walked her back to her car, and the two watched the van, now filled with the still-singing choir and priest, drive past them out of the canyon. As she was getting into her car, she turned to him.

"This is a very interesting canyon, Peter."

"I'm beginning to get that feeling."

"If you haven't been out here before, take a look around."

"I might just do that." The engine revved as Irene began to pull away. He called after her, "Hey, if you find out anything else about the source of those toxins, you'll give me a call, won't you?"

There was no response to his question. Delgado stood alone in the settling dust of her car. He felt happy—he liked her and he wanted to see her again. But he also felt confused. He looked out over the encampment road, at the three dirty children playing in the weeds to the left of an abandoned car. The whole encampment was poisoned to one degree or another. She'd wanted to tell him that, but it wasn't just him she wanted to tell. She'd called Pike first. She'd wanted to tell the detective investigating Carrasco's death, and despite their conversation, he was no closer to connecting her information to the Carrasco murder than he was when he first drove into the encampment.

24

FOR AN HOUR, Irene Talbot's conversation with her father dealt with the mundane. In the wood-paneled library of the family home they sat, he behind his mahogany desk with the *San Diego Union* newspaper before him, she on the white wing chair next to a small table upon which her case files lay. Although she no longer lived at home but in one of the gated condominiums her father's company built, Irene Talbot was a frequent visitor. This afternoon she was a visitor with an ulterior motive.

She casually slipped the question in as they drank iced tea and discussed which congressman was where on what issue of importance to the construction industry.

"Why would Uncle Rex give money to farm workers?"

From the moment Pike Martin passed the information about Rex Cutter's money along to her, she'd been determined to ask that question. It provoked her while she worked and as she lay awake in bed. On several occasions she'd thought about calling Pike to ask if there was any other information about Uncle Rex, but she'd stopped herself for fear too mány questions would only fan the detective's curiosity.

More than the question itself, Irene Talbot was bothered by the discomfort it caused her. She finally had the opportunity to ask her father the question and gauge his reaction. His response was surprising.

"You've been talking to that detective. What's his name—Martin?" He continued reading the paper.

"He came to my office, Daddy, and asked me some questions about what Uncle Rex was doing out at McGonigle Canyon. Detective Martin said he had some money for a field hand."

"And you told the man what?" he said, turning the page and noisily folding it back.

She too continued examining the case file before her, flipping papers over, ostensibly reading them.

"Nothing. There was nothing to tell him. I couldn't imagine Uncle Rex paying a field hand anything unless he was doing a kindness."

"Well, I can't imagine it either. All I can think is that it's a horrible coincidence the guy he's giving some money ends up murdered by someone."

"That's what I told the detective."

"Mmm," Talbot mused, his eye catching a photograph at the bottom of the page, "Congressman Deering's going to be in town for the victims charity at the Hotel Del. Remind me, Sugar, he ought to be assigned close to our table. Did he seem satisfied with that?"

"Was who satisfied with what?"

"The detective. Was he satisfied with your explanation?"

"I guess so."

Talbot stared at his daughter.

"And you. Are you satisfied?"

"I'm not sure what I am. Uncle Rex was a nice man, but I never envisioned him the kind of person who'd be handing out fifty-dollar bills to field laborers. Is it possible he was doing some other job for someone else?"

Talbot stared at his newspaper and shook his head.

"I just don't know, Sugar; I just don't know. Rex was a man of many mysteries. This will just have to be one of them."

Irene Talbot closed the file on the desk before her.

"You know, Daddy, there's talk that some other field hand's involved in this."

"Oh? Like who?"

"A man named Serafino Morales. He supposedly knew what was going on between Uncle Rex and this Carrasco."

She'd purposely implied something might be going on between the two men, and she was curious to see if there was any response from her father. At first he continued reading. But she knew her father. If there was anything going on and her father was even remotely aware of it, he would be careful how he responded.

"I think I've heard that name before. Help me here." He wanted information from her and she obliged.

"Serafino Morales is a field hand who the police think killed Carrasco. They're trying to find him."

"That's where I heard it . . . when that detective came here with the deputy district attorney. They mentioned the man Morales."

"Peter Delgado came here with Detective Martin?"

"No. It wasn't a man. It was some woman."

Talbot set the paper down and looked at his daughter.

"Who's Peter Delgado?" he asked.

"The deputy district attorney who came to my office with Detective Martin. In fact, I asked him to come to the charity dinner with me."

"He's a—"

"He's a Chicano, yes." He caught the edge in her voice.

"Don't get me wrong now, Sugar. I didn't mean anything . . . politically incorrect. I was just going to ask if he's a *young* man."

Irene Talbot could not let his insensitivity slide. She made allowances for him, but not when it came to her personal life. "He's a *young* Chicano. And a very nice young man too."

"Well I hope the two of you will join the center table."

"I'd like that."

"Well, now, this young man, you say he's working on the Carrasco murder?"

"I know he is."

"Well, I'll enjoy meeting him, yes I will." He returned to his newspaper and spoke again. "I hope they find the man, that Morales. Is there any possibility they'll arrest him soon?"

"I think they said he left the area and went up to Fillmore to his cousin's. They're trying to track him down."

"There are a lot of farms up there."

"There aren't that many in Fillmore. That's where he's heading. It's a farming area southeast of the city of Ventura. He'll be easy to find."

"By the way, how's that horrible poisoning case coming along? The one where that poor little boy's eyes got all scratched up or burned up."

"I'm taking my time with it. He's terribly hurt. The doctor says he's lost seventy-five percent of his vision in one eye, twenty-five percent in the other. I'm about to file the case against the farmer whose land he was on."

"Tanekawa?"

"That's the one."

"Well, I hope you sue the hell out of him! You'll let me know if you need any help, now. The costs of a case like that can get pretty high."

"I will. You know I will if I need to."

Talbot looked at his wristwatch.

"I'm sorry, Sugar. I have to call the office at three P.M., and it's a quarter past right now."

Talbot rose. "Can you stay for dinner?"

"No. I don't think so. I have a pile full of work to do in the office. I'll call you tomorrow. If the police call me again, I'll let you know."

"Thanks, Sugar, especially if they get the whereabouts of that killer, I'd like to know. It would make me feel good to think they'd figured out where he was hiding out from the law. I'll see you at the dinner."

A ring of water had formed at the base of Irene Talbot's glass of iced tea, and she rubbed her fingers up and down the glass, over the beads of water condensing on the outside. From where Irene was sitting, she could see her father through the library door, pacing back and forth in the entry, the cellular telephone at his ear.

25

JUDITH WAS WEIGHTED down with packages. During lunch hour, she'd walked from the Criminal Courts Building on Broadway to Horton Plaza on Fourth Street and wandered in and out of the department stores and specialty shops looking for a birthday gift for her mother. Since she had drawers full of clothing she no longer needed and jewelry she could no longer wear, her birthdays taxed the imagination. Judith finally decided on a Bruce Willis movie—*Die Hard with a Vengeance*. It was a strange movie to bring home to an invalid mother. But one evening as Judith changed the channels of the television in search of a program, she'd noticed the woman's eyes widen with apparent interest as the image of Bruce Willis climbing through an elevator shaft flashed across the screen. It was *Die Hard*. Her mother's attention was riveted to the screen for the entire hour the movie remained on. Thereafter, Judith looked for action movies and found her mother's reaction the same— intense interest. They were not the kind of movies her mother used to watch. They were violent, even

gory at times. Her mother had always leaned far
to the side of Rodgers and Hammerstein. The mu-
sicals only put her to sleep now. Judith worried
briefly that the violence wasn't actually entertain-
ing to her mother but rather was frightening her.
Yet, she reasoned her mother could close her eyes
and not watch if it truly bothered her. She'd never,
ever done that when Bruce Willis was on the
screen. So the sequel to *Die Hard* seemed the natural choice.

She also bought an experiment, a food processor,
and regretted the impulse purchase. The large box
was heavy and bulky. She shifted it frequently,
slightly irritated it was ruining what was intended
to be a relaxing outing.

At the corner of Fourth and Broadway, Peter
Delgado caught up with her when she stopped for
a red light. He took the food processor from her
without commenting on its weight.

"Out for a walk?" she asked.

"Yeah. It's been so long since I've been in the
city, I forgot how beautiful it is."

"Where'd you go?"

"Just down to the B Street Pier. Then I went to
the post office in Horton Plaza. I feel a little like a
tourist."

They walked a block before Delgado asked when
Pike was coming back.

"He called this morning but I missed him. By the
time I called back to the motel he's staying at, he'd
left. I hope he can wrap up the investigation there
soon. I've gotten two telephone calls from Ricardo
Corona, who says he's Rogelio Carrasco's cousin."

"He speaks English?"

"Well enough to make some demands. He wants
to know when we're going to arrest the man who

killed Carrasco. He's pretty adamant. It's a geographical thing too."

"How do you mean?"

"Serafino Morales is Oaxacan. Carrasco and his family are from northern Mexico. The Oaxacans are Indians. I know an expletive when I hear one in any language. Several times in the conversation Ricardo made derogatory references to the Oaxacans. He's pretty angry."

"Do you think Carrasco's family would try to hurt anyone?"

"I don't think so, but the last thing we need is some kind of tribal family fight starting up out there in the canyon."

"Maybe someone should talk to them and keep it calm up there."

"That's not a bad idea. It's actually one of the things our victim assistance program's designed for. I don't think it's assistance they want though; it's more like revenge. What do you think about going up and talking to the family, Peter? It wouldn't be bad public relations either."

"What do I do when I go out?"

"Just talk to them. Listen. Let them vent. Then assure them we have the investigation well in hand. They don't need to feel they have to take any kind of action on their own. It wouldn't hurt to warn them to keep a lid on it. Have you been up there yet?"

"I was there once, after Irene Talbot called. She wanted to talk to me, and I met her up at the encampment. She really didn't have anything directly on the Carrasco murder. It was more like she wanted to express her concern over the toxins out there in the canyon."

He'd promised Irene he would keep her discovery of toxic poison to himself. But he felt comfortable telling Judith of her concern about the use of toxins in the fields. Judith's curiosity, however, was aroused.

"That's odd. Why would Irene Talbot call you up there to talk about toxins?" she asked.

Peter shrugged, ending the inquiry. He felt no sense of betrayal to either woman. He had kept his promise to Irene, and unless some stronger tie developed between the toxins and the Carrasco murder case, there was really nothing more to report to Judith.

For her part, Judith allowed the subject to be dropped, accepting Peter's explanation for the moment. She was far more interested in Irene's father.

"She's got a pretty interesting father."

"I'm going to meet him this weekend. She invited me to the crime victims fund-raiser."

"At the Hotel Del?"

"Yeah."

"Do I detect some personal interest on your part?"

"So far, we're just acquaintances. Not even friends."

Judith was silent a moment, and Delgado asked, "Is there a problem with that? I mean, because of the case?"

"No, not really." She grinned at him. "Not yet anyway. Seriously, though, in an investigation or trial, Peter, you want to keep some distance between you and the people involved."

"Is she involved?"

"No. But her father's out there, you know, on the fringes of this Carrasco murder. Hey, look, I don't want to spoil your fun. Just be cautious is all. I'll be giving one of the community service awards at the dinner, so I'll probably see you there. I understand Talbot Construction's helping underwrite the event this year."

"That's what Irene says."

"Irene?"

He smiled. "I mean Miss Talbot."

"Well, I'd be interested in your impressions of Franklin Talbot when the night's over. He's an icon in San Diego, but . . ." She stopped. "Let's just say he's an interesting character."

Outside the courthouse Judith took the food processor from Delgado and headed toward the county parking lot. She'd picked up her car the previous evening, and so far, at least, the persistent electrical problem seemed to be resolved.

26

◆

It was six A.M. Delgado guided his car through the rutted road and parked at the base of the encampment. At Judith's suggestion, he'd telephoned Lee Ward for advice and Lee told him he should get to the fields early, before the men left for whatever work they'd found for the day. Although Ward could not accompany him, he told Delgado where he would find the encampment of northern Mexican laborers.

A stubborn chill hung in the air as Delgado watched the camp spring to life, chickens running from bushes and the smoke of fires crackling in metal drums. He watched the steady procession of men walking toward the catering truck for coffee, and he too casually strolled over to it. The men standing near the vehicle with white Styrofoam cups in their hands gawked at him as he ordered a cup of coffee in Spanish and said good morning in their language. Several smiled hesitantly at him.

It occurred to Delgado that in his fine office clothing he must seem quite odd to the men. They stared at his polished leather shoes and colorful print tie, his pale blue shirt and linen pants and jacket. He walked to the nearest fire and stood with the laborers. Some were old and they, unlike the young men looking at his clothing, stared at his hands. Against the white of the cups they held, theirs were rough and stained. Their fingernails were lined with the brown of soil, while his hands were clean, his fingernails manicured.

In Spanish, Delgado asked if anyone knew where he might find Ricardo Corona. Two of the men nodded and pointed to a group of men standing at a second fire not more than twenty yards away. He thanked them, again in Spanish.

Delgado was not sure which of the four men standing at the fire was Ricardo Corona, but when he asked, the heaviest of the men identified himself as Ricardo. Delgado was surprised his communication with the men had been so easy. He stumbled here and there over a sentence or word, but his recall of the language was complete. Pretty good, he thought, for a man whose parents no longer spoke Spanish in the house and who'd left the language behind when he entered law school.

Even after a few minutes of discussion it was clear Ricardo Corona was an angry man who spoke for his entire family. He told Delgado of Carrasco's funeral and the grieving wife he'd left to suffer, to wonder why her husband, the father of her four small children, had been killed. Life would be even harder for her now. Although he tried to comfort Ricardo Corona by telling him they were hot on the track of Serafino Morales, the suspected murderer, Corona would not be comforted. Not until he could see the vultures circling the dead body of the killer would he be satisfied.

Delgado warned the man directly to avoid trouble in the camp. And he told him any violence, even from those grieving, could not be tolerated. He was direct but, he imagined, ineffectual. Particularly when he mentioned the name Serafino Morales and Carrasco's cousin leaned toward the ground and spit.

As the flatbed truck pulled into camp to transport the men to the fields, Ricardo Corona promised he would not seek revenge. But, he scowled, if Serafino Morales should ever return to McGonigle Canyon, he was a dead man.

Delgado watched the truck pull away laden with its cargo of field hands. He stood in the now silent camp until the sides of the catering truck slammed shut and it too drove away.

Delgado glanced at his wristwatch. It was six-thirty. He was not ready to return to downtown San Diego, to his windowless office filled with files and paper. Curious, wondering what lay beyond, he walked down the encampment road, past the point where Irene and he had stopped to talk, past the waist-high weeds tugging at his jacket. He saw the clotheslines hanging from trees and the rusty cars. He smelled the food in the crude restaurant where the Mixtec women cooked tortillas over an open fire. For the first time in a long time, it seemed, he smelled something other than air-conditioned air and dusty books. He walked, and a calm settled on him. He did not care where he stepped; he was not uncomfortable looking into the fields at the signs of an unfamiliar lifestyle.

When he reached the end of the second encampment, Delgado turned back. To his left, a small canton of cardboard and black plastic leaned precariously away from the road. Outside the shack, an old man, too stooped and stiff to work the fields, glanced up from the small garden he tended. His red cotton shirt and blue Levi's already showed the sweat and dirt of his task. Delgado spoke in Spanish, asking what the man was growing.

"Tomatoes," the man called back.

Delgado walked through the tall grass to the man and watched as he pulled a large ripe fruit from one of the plants and held it out to him.

"Thank you," Delgado said, taking the tomato into his hand.

The man offered another, and Delgado took it as well. It was smaller, and he ate it slowly as he walked back to his car.

27

WHEN PETER DELGADO walked into the Crown Room of the Hotel Del Coronado with Irene Talbot, his eyes instinctively looked to the ceiling. The last time he'd been in the room was for his high school prom almost a decade earlier.

"Mag-nif-i-cent, isn't it?"

The man who asked the question moved to Delgado's side and looked upward with him at the architectural masterpiece of sugar-pine paneling.

"One hundred fifty-six feet long, sixty-six feet wide, and thirty-three feet high. It's hand-fitted without a single nail in it. Support-free. One of the last in the country." He looked downward again and greeted the couple. "I'm Franklin Talbot." He extended his hand to the young attorney. "And you're Peter Delgado. I've heard a lot about you. And I already know this beautiful young lady." He reached out for Irene, and she gave him a hug.

"I'd like to introduce you to Frances Shipley. Irene, you know Liz." The two women embraced as he turned to Delgado. "Fran's husband Mark is president of Technic Industries."

The introductions out of the way, the men continued their discussion of the hotel.

"I haven't been here in years," Delgado said, again casting his eyes to the ceiling. "When was it built?"

"Eighteen eighty-eight," Talbot replied. "A Chinese crew of two thousand men brought down from San Francisco worked round the clock to finish it on schedule. They were paid about three dollars a day to work a six-hour shift."

"You can't find laborers like that anymore!" Fran said, her eyes wide. "Why I have to pay my housekeeper, Martina, fifty dollars a day."

"What does Martina do for you for fifty dollars?" Delgado asked, half-curious, half-critical of her complaint.

She threw her hands into the air. "Whatever people do who clean houses. What a silly question."

Talbot, sensing a turn in the conversation was appropriate, placed his hand gently under his daughter's elbow. "Peter, Irene, if you're both inclined, I've got two places for you at my table there in front of the speaker's podium. Fran, you lead the way."

The older woman stepped forward. As the four walked to the table, she leaned toward Irene and in a clearly audible whisper offered, "You couldn't have found *that* handsome thing out in your fields, Irene."

Irene, realizing Delgado must have heard the comment, shot a quick glance over her shoulder to him and saw the embarrassment on his now red face.

Next to the arrangement of flowers in the middle of the table was a note card marked RESERVED in black calligraphy. Not even the award presenters ventured to the table's empty seats, and it occurred to Delgado that those who were eventually standing around the table ready to be seated were white-haired men dressed in black tie accompanied by women in black- or white-sequined dresses, and they all seemed to be talking about the companies they owned. All, that is, except him.

No one purposely said or did anything to make him feel uncomfortable, but with his black hair and dark blue suit, he was simply conscious he was a combination of different colors. His discomfort grew as the news photographers grouped the white hairs and sequins together.

Delgado was relieved when Judith Thornton, accompanied by Lawrence Farrell and his wife—all in business attire—stopped at the table to say hello. Judith took special care to glance approvingly at him as she was being introduced to Irene. She grew more reserved when Delgado introduced her to Franklin Talbot.

"We've met," she responded tersely, extending her hand.

"Indeed we have," Talbot said. "I believe it was over a bowl of ice cream."

She couldn't resist. "A very large one, I recall."

"Very good, Mrs. Thornton! It was indeed. I understand you haven't made an arrest, though, in the death of the field hand we discussed over that very large bowl of ice cream."

"We're getting closer, Mr. Talbot. Any day now."

"Well, I hope so." His voice trailed off.

That was the extent of the conversation concerning Carrasco's murder in Judith's presence. But when the group sat, Talbot positioned himself next to Delgado.

"So tell me, Peter, has there been any luck in tracking down this Serafino Morales into the Fillmore area?"

Instinctively, Delgado repeated Judith's response. "We're getting closer," he assured Talbot. He tried to steer the conversation back to the history and architecture of the hotel, both subjects that seemed particularly interesting to Talbot's table guests.

Irene Talbot was silent much of the drive home. She finally asked whether he'd had a good time. He assured her he had. More specifically, she wanted to know if he'd been offended by Frances Shipley's offhand comments about laborers.

"Fran just is that way. Offensive as it is, she tends to speak without thinking."

"No problem," he'd responded. "Actually, I could have been a little kinder to her."

As the car stopped in front of her condominium, Irene laughed. "Kinder? She never knew what you were talking about."

There was a much deeper truth in Irene's comment, and as he walked her to the door, he observed, "I guess Fran and I are even, then."

28

SATURDAY MORNING. HER mother's birthday.

Judith awakened early and drove to the grocery store. She pushed the cart down one aisle and up another, in her regular pattern. Her shopping list was minimal today. The usual for her mother: Cream of Wheat. Oatmeal. Malt-o-Meal for variety. Nothing chewy. Nothing crunchy. Past the baby food section and the pureed fruits. Peaches, pears, more peaches. Breakfasts for the week. Snacks. Jean was pretty good about being creative, but there was no chewing mechanism left, so the choices were few, and they all had to be smooth.

Dairy foods were easier. Yogurt, cottage cheese. Eggs—she liked them scrambled, even though her beloved Tabasco sauce was gone from the menu.

And meats—they were the worst. She'd tried the strained beef once. Only once. Her mother had grimaced at the spoonful of thick pink and then spit it out of her mouth. That alone looked bad enough that Judith never bought it again. So her mother had become a sort of lactovegetarian.

Enter the food processor. Judith was determined to get some meat into her weakening mother, and today, on her mother's birthday, a new system of meat consumption would hopefully begin.

She gathered chicken and pot roast. Carrots and celery. Potatoes and onions.

On the way out of the store Judith grabbed another bouquet of flowers—white lilies and something lavender, she didn't know what it was—to add to the one she'd purchased earlier in the week.

Armed with food and flowers, she drove home.

It took the pot roast three hours to cook in her Dutch oven. While it cooked, she assembled the food processor, and the weekend aid got her mother washed and dressed. The newest flowers combined with the older bouquet to form a huge display of summer color in her mother's bedroom.

Satisfied the food processor wouldn't fall apart when she turned it on, Judith scooped the pot roast and vegetables into it, closed her eyes, and pushed the button. It whirled and ground, and much to her satisfaction, produced a thick—and smooth—blend. She added more broth to it, and turned the machine on again. It was thinner in consistency, one she thought her mother might tolerate.

Judith spooned a small portion of the pot roast puree into a bowl and carried it ceremoniously outside to the rose garden, where she found her mother sitting. The food actually smelled quite good. On seeing Judith, the aid excused herself to change the bedsheets, and she was left to try out the experimental meal on her own.

Judith took a small portion into a spoon and held it to her mother's lips. She opened her mouth and swallowed.

"Mmmmmmmmmm."

Judith's eyes widened. It was the first sound she'd heard from her mother in months. And it was the first sound of pleasure she'd heard from her for as long as she could remember. A second spoonful was followed by the same hum of approval. Spoonful by spoonful, the bowl of pot roast disappeared.

A small victory.

Back in the kitchen, Judith realized she'd underestimated—greatly underestimated—the quantity of food a two-pound pureed pot roast and vegetables made. She filled her pudding bowls, then her salad bowls, then her small plastic bowls with it. Into the freezer it all went, to be thawed one serving at a time.

While her mother napped that afternoon, Judith read the paper. For the first time in weeks she felt life was a little more under control than it had been the day before.

At three o'clock the telephone rang. Pike apologized for calling her on a Saturday, but he had good news that couldn't wait. He'd been carrying copies of the police composite, and after almost a week in the Fillmore area talking to growers, he'd located one of Serafino's cousins who worked as a foreman on an orange farm in Fillmore. Yes, Serafino did know where this cousin worked, and yes, he did have work for Serafino if and when Serafino ever came to Fillmore. Serafino, however, had not called the cousin or otherwise notified him he was on the way north. His cousin could not imagine Serafino killing another person.

"Shall I stay here?" Pike asked.

Judith had no trouble answering that question.

"No. I don't want you spinning your wheels up there. We have no idea when and if Serafino's going to arrive. Notify the local police. If he shows up or calls his cousin, we need to be sure we get a call immediately."

"I've already taken care of that, Judith."

"I'm sure you have. What kind of insurance do we have that he'll call?"

"His cousin's not a citizen. He's got a green card that lets him work temporarily in this country. He's got a steady job with a real salary, and he's got a wife and three kids here who speak English fluently. He hasn't seen Serafino in ten years or so. Let's say I stressed to him the importance of calling us if Serafino shows up. I don't think he's going to risk being deported to save a murder suspect he barely knows. I'll leave my card and check up on him every other day or so when I get back. I'll be in on Monday."

"Good work, Pike. We know where Serafino's been and where he's most likely going. All we need is to be patient."

29

"I SWEAR TO Jesus, next year I'm going to plant more green beans. Maybe I'll *just* plant beans."

Kevin Oklund stood with his hands on his hips staring into a field of green stalks. Behind him the noise of the Ventura Freeway drowned out the sound of the dry summer air blowing through his 120 acres of corn.

"At least they can't steal beans as fast as they steal the corn. Gotta look for 'em and pick 'em one at a time."

The thieves he was referring to were the people who periodically stopped at the side of the freeway and entered his fields, picked his corn, and drove away.

"It's a war," he growled to Serafino, who stood at his side. "A goddamned range war. Me against *them*." He pointed to the cars zipping by at sixty-five miles per hour. "You know, I've been here forty-nine years, and there was a time you could see nothing but orange trees and fields for miles with just a scattered house or two. Now look.

Houses everywhere with a scattered field or two."

Serafino had made a calculated decision when he left the Healys. He walked north to Highway 78, then west to the ocean, believing the coastal route to Fillmore would be a direct one, which reduced the risk of veering off in the wrong direction.

After three days he'd exhausted the money the Healys had given him. Tired and hungry, he would have to find temporary work somewhere in the small pockets of farmland alongside the busiest of the freeways. Just north of Los Angeles Serafino stopped at a convenience store for a cold drink and ran into a group of laborers from northern Mexico. Kevin Oklund, they said, needed a man to help stand guard over his field. They'd pointed him in the direction of the Oklund farm, and there he was offered a job.

It was not the kind of job one stayed at for long. There was not much Serafino would have to do. Walk around along the paths that bordered the freeway. Wear a bright red shirt that Mr. Oklund supplied. Make himself seen by the people in the cars. That alone was usually enough to keep them away. If he wished, he could remain in the fields at night and carry a small beeper. If there was trouble, someone would come to help him. For this work he would get fifty dollars a day, an amazing amount of money.

"And it's too bad. Farmers just have a different way of looking at the world."

Serafino stood mute as Oklund ranted on, only nodding his head when he clearly understood what the man was saying.

One thing was right for sure. Just as the farmer told him, Serafino could not smell the corn or hear it rustle in the wind during the day. But at night it was different. If the air turned cool and there was a breeze, Serafino could hear the sound of the plants and he could smell their sweetness. Here too he did not feel compelled to dig himself into the ground to sleep as he had in the canyon. He slept in the open with the stars above him, and in the middle of the night when the noise and exhaust from the freeway were gone, he listened and smelled.

He told Oklund he would stay for two weeks. Then he would walk northward for two more days and be safe with his relatives in Fillmore.

30

THE HOUSING PLAN lay exposed on Franklin Talbot's library desk. After dinner Irene had wandered into the room to sit, as was her custom. The seventeen-by-eleven-inch rendering in blue ink on white paper was impossible to ignore. She was familiar with such plans. She'd been raised with them and had developed opinions of her own on what the middle-income family looked for in affordable housing. These homes looked nice. Really nice. Tile roofs and front patios on the two-story model, wood shingle roofs on the other two. She stood admiring the plans for Las Montañas (The Mountains) and its three Spanish-style tract home models. Vista Del Rio (View of the River), El Lago (The Lake), and Tierra Santa (Sacred Ground).

"Do you like those?" her father asked, seeing her at the desk and entering.

"They're beautiful. The best ever. I especially like the one in the middle here."

"It's a two-story model I helped lay out myself. You'll have to take a look at the interior of it. I don't have it here, but it's got those French windows you like so much and lots of wood."

"I like that."

"I want a real California rustic look to them. With quality wood, too. Oak kitchen cabinets, hardwood floors, and a step-down living room. Earth-tone interiors. You know, the greens and blues and beiges. I'm even thinking that in the two-story model there could be a raised dining area that looks out over the living room. We're still working on the concepts."

"Have you decided where this development's going in?"

"Not yet. But there are several sites I've had my eye on for a long time. We're in the negotiation stages right now—won't wrap it up until December or January. But if we do, and the city permits don't go too slow, families will be in those homes in two years. I'd say two years or less, but we don't have Uncle Rex cutting through the red tape for us anymore. I have some new folks discussing my interests downtown, but none of them are quite as good as Rex was."

Irene sat down in her father's desk chair.

"You just never cease to amaze me, Daddy. You just don't stop. Ever. Building, I mean—always building. When I was little, I used to wonder why you loved it so much. It was such messy work."

"Why do I do it? Because the land's there. It needs to be used. In case you haven't noticed, the days of raising cattle are gone. And the farmers can't make it anymore. It wouldn't matter if I was here building houses or not. Raw land's a thing of the past in California. And you know why?"

"The land's too expensive. Everyone knows that."

"Ah, shit no!" He grinned and shook his head.

"It's why it's expensive that's the reason. Water. Water, honey. There's no *water* for farming. It costs too much to get the water down here to the southern part of the state. And the water that's here costs farmers thousands of dollars to cover an acre! People like me, we've seen it coming for decades. The good farm land in Southern California dried up a long time ago. The row crops—the tomatoes and strawberries—they can't be raised anymore and make someone rich like they might have years ago. Oh, the power crops are the avocados and the flowers up in North County. But they're marked crops too. It's just a matter of time. When I'm long dead, you'll be telling my grandchildren what a prophet I was, how I prophesied the water doom."

"And you just buy up the land."

"That's exactly what I do. I offer enough money to make it feasible for farmers to make a decision about changing their income levels—upward. If the water situation's bad enough, they sell. No, Sugar, and I won't ever stop. Not till I fall over and you all carry me away. I wasn't made for a lot of things, but the one thing I know I was made for is that." He pointed to the building plans. "Most people aren't any different than the farmers. They want land—their own land. That's what I give them. Their own land."

Irene looked at her watch.

"Well, I need to get back to *my* own home. I've still got a lot of work in front of me tonight."

"Important case?"

"Toxic poisoning."

"You mean different than the ones you've already got?"

"No, it's the same one. The little boy whose eyes were burned, Daddy."

Talbot was rolling up the diagram of the models when his daughter blurted out the question.

"Daddy, what would you make of a large-scale poisoning in the farming community up near McGonigle Canyon?"

"Why, I'd say it's impossible. That's not a toxic dumping area."

"No. I mean herbicide poisoning."

"You actually have evidence of that?"

"Oh, I sure do. Not just a little evidence, either. If my case investigators are right, there's poisoning all over the canyon. The only question is why."

"Well, it's *clear* why. If something like that's happening, it's because the farming community's misusing these toxins. I can tell you horror stories about crop dusters hitting the wrong farms, even hitting people and laborers. If you've uncovered anything like that happening, it needs to be rooted out before more innocent people are permanently damaged."

He was adamant. Thinking of the laborers. There was nothing in his voice she should fear. Yet she was so uneasy. She'd needed to ask him, tell him about her findings. Yet he'd jumped on the farmers with nary a hint of suspicion there might be other causes of the poisoning.

"Peter Delgado was telling me that this Serafino Morales, the man they think killed a laborer in the canyon, might have been involved."

"You mean this *Serafino* might have been poisoning the fields?"

"They don't know. Not for sure. That's one of the strange things. Serafino kills Carrasco, and Carrasco's got a paper that says Serafino *knows something*. If they catch this Serafino, they'll find out."

"What else does Peter say about Serafino Morales?"

"That's it. Just that they've tracked his cousin down in Fillmore, and that's where they think he's heading."

"They're goin' to intercept him there, I hope."

"I think that's the plan. Daddy?"

"Yeah, Sugar. Hey, it's getting late here if you're going to work tonight."

"I asked this before, but I'm still curious—and it bothers me. . . ."

"Ask away."

"Uncle Rex was supposedly giving Carrasco money—"

Talbot cut her off.

"Well, now, that's a coincidence, is all. Tell me, is anyone interested in what Rex was doing out there when he was unfortunate enough to get bit by that snake?"

"No. Not that anyone's told me."

"Then don't worry about Rex. Let the man rest in peace. He did a lot of good deeds in his time, believe it or not, and I'd like to remember him as having been doing good deeds when he died."

The force of his conviction in the matter of Rex Cutter was a relief to Irene. And as for her father's quickness in blaming the farmers, well, he'd offered a new theory, one she hadn't heard before. And it was that Serafino had been poisoning the crops. Perhaps that was the truth of it. After all, the man had killed someone else for no apparent reason. Such a person might harbor ill feelings about his work—ill feelings so strong he'd cause damage to the crops and the foreman who was supposed to be protecting them.

The feeling she had, that there were pieces of a

puzzle missing in her toxin case, were figments of her own lawyer's imagination. When all was said and done, it had to have been the farmers, or Serafino or both who were dumping poison. But for now, there was really no reason to doubt her justification for filing the case.

"I'm going to try to remember Uncle Rex doing a good deed too, Daddy."

Irene Talbot worked late into the night. By morning she'd reviewed the final draft of Raúl Ignacio's complaint against the Tanekawas. By the afternoon it was filed in the San Diego County Superior Court. The prayer for relief requested total damages in the amount of ten million dollars for the child and four million for his mother. The cause of damage was specified to be the purposeful and/or negligent spreading of toxins on all acreage farmed and the negligent and/or purposeful disposal of toxins in the irrigation and water supplies in and around McGonigle Canyon.

31

JUDITH WAS AT her desk, her fingers drumming the ten-page complaint filed by Irene Talbot in Superior Court that morning. Normally Judith would not receive civil complaints, but Pike had delivered this one to her after hearing on the news the preceding evening that the daughter of Franklin Talbot was filing a multimillion-dollar lawsuit against one of San Diego County's biggest growers of vegetables. It took him only an hour to copy it, read it, and deliver it to Judith along with a copy of an article in the morning newspaper announcing the lawsuit. She'd taken the time to read the complaint itself twice and skim through the news account of the case.

The lawsuit fascinated her. A child physically injured by mystery toxins on the land where his mother lived and his father worked. A giant lawsuit filed by the daughter of Franklin Talbot. Another piece of some much bigger something. Periodically both she and Pike strained to connect Carrasco to Talbot Construction Company but the only thing she could say was that coincidences were at work. Now here was another one.

Then Peter Delgado, accompanied by Pike, came through the door.

"Pike just came to tell me Irene Talbot filed her lawsuit," Delgado said.

"Yeah. And it's a big one. Millions of dollars."

"Against the Tanekawas?"

"That's the name in the complaint. I have a copy here if you're interested in reading it."

Judith picked the complaint up from her desk and handed it to Delgado, who sat down and began to read through it. Halfway into the document he stopped reading. He had a decision to make. He'd told Judith that during his meeting with Irene at the canyon they discussed only the general problem of toxic wastes. He'd been no more specific than that because he'd promised Irene he wouldn't divulge the breadth of her concerns. But she'd done that herself now with the filing of the complaint alleging the land had been poisoned by the Tanekawas. He saw no need to hold back any information any longer.

"Her real concern's out of the bag."

The comment caught Judith by surprise. "What concern's out of the bag?"

Pike also expressed surprise that some bit of information had slipped past him undetected. "You mean there's something we didn't know about?"

Peter was uneasy. "I promised I wouldn't repeat what Irene told me, but it's all right there," he said, setting the complaint on the desk again in front of Judith, "in that complaint against the Tanekawas."

"So don't keep us guessing. You can't mean this was all some great secret? It couldn't have been. I knew about the boy's eyes. Pike knew. She told

Pike and you about it when you met with her that first time in her office."

"Well, we didn't know the entire truth of the matter. When she called here to talk with Pike, and you sent me up to talk with her, we met out at McGonigle Canyon. What she told me was that her investigators found widespread poisoning in parts of the stream and in irrigation areas. Even the ground had been contaminated."

"So what's so important about keeping that a secret?"

"She wasn't sure where the poisoning was coming from."

"It was troubling her?"

"A lot."

"She knew the land was the Tanekawas'," Judith said.

"She knew, but she said the poisoning was too scattered and pervasive. She didn't think any farmer would do something like that to their own fields. If they wanted to get rid of the land, they could just sell it off for development."

"Was she concerned about filing the lawsuit?"

"I think she was. There's got to be a big ethical problem filing a suit against someone that you believe, or know, isn't at fault."

"Well she must have resolved her ethical dilemma based on that complaint. I read the whole thing. Twice. She's accused the growers of rampant and negligent poisoning of the areas where the field hands work and live."

"The only thing I can think of is that she's comfortable pinning the wrap on them."

"Who else could she pin it on?" Judith asked.

It was a rhetorical question Delgado did not attempt to answer.

But her own question led her into an area she'd never thought about until now, until the discussion of widespread contamination. Her eyes narrowed, and for several moments she seemed to look past the two men into some space beyond them.

"Peter?" she finally asked.

"Uh-huh?"

"Do you know anything about how this stuff, this toxin, gets into the dirt and the water?"

Delgado tried to remember if Irene Talbot mentioned how widespread the poisoning was. She really hadn't.

"She only mentioned it was spread out over hundreds of acres. Why?"

"Well, the stuff doesn't just pop up in the soil. You've got to put it there. You don't drop it from airplanes, do you?"

"No, I think it's got to be spread by hand or by machine somehow. Someone's got to carry it to the locations where it was found."

He could tell Judith's mind was racing, and it took him only a few moments to catch up with her.

"Peter?"

"Yeah."

"Who would be the most likely people to spread the stuff—whether they knew they were doing it or not?"

The simplicity of what she was saying surprised him but not Pike.

"The field laborers," Pike said flatly.

"But, Pike, there's no proof that any of them have been poisoned, just the Ignacio boy," Delgado protested.

Judith wasn't interested in challenging her own ideas just yet. She pointed to the complaint lying on her desk.

"At fourteen million a pop it doesn't take many."

She was saying and thinking of ideas faster than she could put them together. She'd already moved on to the next question.

"Assuming something like that *was* going on—with the field hands spreading this stuff—why would field laborers do something like that?"

"Maybe they didn't know they were doing it," Delgado said.

"Maybe they did," she shot back.

"What do you mean?" Delgado was lost now. And Pike was listening only, a giant antenna piecing together what the two were saying. Then Judith paused, having led herself to a precise, startling conclusion.

"Maybe they were getting *paid* to do it," she offered.

Complete silence gripped the men as they stared at Judith. She looked directly at Pike before she spoke again, repeating herself except for several important words.

"Maybe *he* was getting paid to do it."

Pike spoke first.

"Are you saying—"

"I'm not *saying* anything, Pike. I'm just thinking out loud here."

"Well, let me think out loud with you," he responded.

Now it was Peter Delgado's turn to observe, to watch the two of them piecing thoughts, fragments of thoughts, together as Pike continued.

"Judith, are you thinking that Carrasco might have been involved in spreading this toxin?"

"It's not beyond the realm of possibility, is it? I mean if . . . if . . . *if* field hands were involved in spreading that poison, why not Carrasco? This would maybe explain what the man's doing with so much money. Maybe he was getting paid to do it."

"Paid by whom?" Delgado asked innocently.

Pike and Judith could have answered that question in unison, so completely in tune with each other were they at where this discussion was leading them. But it was Pike who spoke first.

"There's only one person we know for sure was giving money to Carrasco."

Until now Delgado hadn't been privy to the Carrasco-Cutter connection. He had been on his own track, out on the periphery of the murder investigation. And so his next question wasn't a surprise to Judith or Pike.

"Who was that?"

Judith answered. "Rex Cutter. A lobbyist for Talbot Construction."

"Wait a minute. Are you both saying a lobbyist for Talbot Construction was paying a field hand to poison the water and the ground?"

Judith couldn't resist. Leaving Delgado's question unanswered, she looked at Pike and said, "Serafino *sabe*. Serafino knows."

She returned to Delgado.

"This is all theory, Peter. There's not a shred of evidence Talbot Construction is paying *anyone* to do *anything* illegal out in those fields. Not a shred of evidence."

"Why in God's name would anyone do a thing like that? Most of all Talbot Construction?"

"Does Irene Talbot know money was found in an envelope on Rex Cutter and that the envelope had Carrasco's name on it?"

"She knows," Pike answered. "I told her that when Peter and I went out there to her office."

"I want you to tell her that we've learned Carrasco was on the take from Cutter and we're not sure just why yet."

"But that's not true. We don't know if he was on the take from Cutter. I'd be lying to her. I can't do that."

"Yes you can," Pike said.

"He's right, Peter. She's not a suspect in anything."

"Yet," Pike added sarcastically, and to himself.

Judith continued. "Even with suspects the law allows law enforcement officers to, let's say, withhold the truth."

"Lie," Pike added as Judith shot a look at him that temporarily silenced him.

"Here's the thing that occurs to me," Judith continued. "We have a murder victim who potentially was on the take from Talbot Construction. And we have a murder suspect out there somewhere wandering around the freeway systems who might know why. What if this Serafino knows something about what's going on in the fields? What if that had something to do with the murder? Even if we never get into the poisoning of the fields itself, don't you think we ought to investigate what motivations for murder might exist on Serafino's part?"

Delgado understood, but his concerns had now shifted elsewhere.

"Why would Irene Talbot be bringing this huge lawsuit if her father's own company was involved in this?"

"Frankly, that's what I'd be curious to find out. Short of finding Serafino himself, the next best thing we may have is Irene Talbot."

"Okay. I'll call her. What do I say?"

"Tell her you saw the newspaper article about the widespread poisoning. Tell her you talked with me and I mentioned there was some kind of evidence that Rex Cutter was paying Carrasco money to do something out in the fields. That'll be enough. We can see just what happens, if anything. She may be totally in the dark, and we may be so out in left field on this that nothing happens. On the other hand, she might be the catalyst we need to shake Franklin Talbot loose."

32

THE TOMATO PLANTS were brown and wilted. They hadn't lasted the summer, and Peter Delgado, dressed in a snug T-shirt and Levi's, spent the morning digging out the old plants and replacing them with the new ones his father had set near the vegetable garden. It would take a few weeks for another crop of the fruit to set, but it was the planting he was enjoying, having somewhere he could think clearly. So engrossed had he become, that he'd spent several evening hours trying to plot out an eye-pleasing garden, finally deciding that flowering borders were for next year.

The sight of Peter digging outside gave his father great joy, and occasionally he would walk outside to tell the younger man of his approval. At other times he would stand at a distance and watch him. This afternoon as his father approached, Peter heard the announcement of a telephone call for him.

It was Irene Talbot. He'd called her the previous day, and when she was unavailable, he'd left his home phone number, asking her to call him there.

"What are you up to?" she'd asked, and expressed mild surprise when he told her he'd been planting tomatoes all morning.

"And you?" he asked.

"Working. I have a lot to do this weekend."

"On the toxin case?"

"That and about a hundred others," she exaggerated. It was a nice segue into the topic he wanted to raise with her.

"I was talking with my supervisor, Judith Thornton. You know how they were thinking Rogelio Carrasco was taking money from someone named Rex Cutter? Well, they have some evidence—no one's told me just what—that Carrasco was being paid to do some work out in the fields for him."

Irene Talbot's surprise was genuine. "They *what*?"

Delgado repeated what he and his colleagues believed was a lie.

"What could Uncle Rex possibly be paying that field hand to do?"

"I don't know. They don't want to make it all public. It's part of the investigation."

"Peter, what do you *think* he could have been paying him to do?"

"If I knew, I'd tell you, Irene. They're keeping me in the dark too for now."

"If you find out anything, will you let me know? I can't tell you how distressed this makes me, Peter. Uncle Rex didn't have any business out there that I know of. He worked for Daddy and, my God, Daddy . . ." Her voice trailed off, leaving her thought dangling.

Delgado knew he'd placed her in a terribly awkward position. She'd already expressed her concern about who might be poisoning the field, and now they'd handed her a clue to her own mystery. It was not a clue, however, that could possibly make her comfortable. She was a smart woman in the middle of the same mystery they were. And, after all, the whole reason for calling her was to make her feel uncomfortable enough to do something. Just what she might do they were not sure.

"Keep me posted, Peter, will you? You know how everything going on out there in the canyon is important to me right now." There was a hint of desperation in her voice, which made him feel worse about his lack of candor.

"I know. And I promise to call you if anything else happens. But you call me too, will you?"

She promised. Delgado, struggling with his conscience, called Judith Thornton to tell her the trap, such as it was, had been set.

33

THE OFFICES OF Talbot Construction Company were housed in a burgundy-colored wood ranch house with white-framed windows. The one-story structure was the same one Franklin Talbot moved into four decades earlier. It was still sitting smack in the middle of twenty green acres of rolling lawn and trees, offering sharp contrast to a man whose life was devoted to covering empty space with buildings. Beyond the green grass and trees was yet another ring of land, this one brown and covered with orange construction equipment: tractors, cranes, and bulldozers of various sizes.

Irene Talbot had been visiting the offices since she was a child, and Yvonne Eddy, the receptionist who had been at her post for twenty-five years, was both a friend and confidante. She thought nothing unusual about Irene's coming to the office just as she was about to close up for the evening.

"Don't worry, Yvonne. I'll lock up behind me. I need to track down a few sketches for my father."

"Can I help find something before I go?"

"No. But can I ask you a couple of questions about Uncle Rex?"

"Oh, yes. Dear Lord, that poor man. Dying like that out in the middle of nowhere with no one to help him. He must have suffered horribly."

"We were all devastated by it too. I've been wondering if his office here has been packed up."

"Well, I straightened things up, packed some of his personal belongings, but everything else as far as I know is still in there. You know I wasn't allowed to do his filing. He did it himself."

It was true. Rex Cutter's job was so confidential, he preferred to keep his own employment logs and share nothing with the support staff. Even his telephone bills came directly to him unopened.

"His little office is still intact as far as I know. The door's been locked since they found his body. Your father went through it once right after the funeral, but even he hasn't been in there in a while."

Irene waited until the receptionist's car was well out of sight down the road before she tried the door to Rex Cutter's office. It was locked, just as the woman had told her. Undaunted, Irene searched the receptionist's desk drawers for any kind of pick device that might dislodge the lock mechanism. Finding nothing there that might serve her purposes, she looked in her purse and pulled a nail file from an interior pocket.

Several minutes later the lock was broken and the door opened. She would have to tell her father something to excuse her breaking the lock, and she decided to leave a note for the receptionist saying she'd left an important document in the office while visiting Uncle Rex and she needed it back. In all probability Yvonne would have the lock fixed on her own without ever telling her father. It took just a moment to write the note, and she placed it strategically on the seat of the receptionist's chair.

Irene Talbot turned on the lights in Rex Cutter's office. She seldom came into the place, even to visit with him, and she was impressed with its spartan furnishings. There were no green plants to liven the four-hundred-square-foot room or soften its pale blue walls. Only one painting, of a stampeding herd of mustangs, hung on the wall directly facing the dark walnut desk where Cutter worked. Aside from the plush gray carpeting and a four-foot-tall wood file cabinet, that was it for furniture.

Irene walked to the file cabinet and began looking for key words on the files. Carrasco? No. Rogelio Carrasco? Nothing. She tried "paraquat" and even "pay." The name Serafino Morales appeared nowhere. She ran her fingers down the protruding file tabs, quickly eyeing the subject matter of each. Nothing caught her interest. Then, suddenly a name she was familiar with, Las Montañas.

Irene thought back for a moment to her father's library, to her compliments on the three new floor plans of the Las Montañas development. The one the land had not yet been purchased for.

She pulled the file from the drawer and sat at Rex Cutter's desk. She opened the file to find an assortment of notes and letters. A smaller duplicate of the model styles she'd seen on her father's desk was folded in the file. Halfway through the contents of the file, a piece of lined paper made her stop and utter a slightly audible gasp. She recognized the handwriting. It was Rex Cutter's. It was written to nobody specifically and appeared to be a reminder to himself: "Carrasco to help—Las Montañas."

Nausea swept over Irene Talbot as she held the piece of paper limply over the open file. Rex Cutter *was* involved with the murdered field hand. And Carrasco was helping somehow with her father's newest housing project.

There was nothing in the file she needed to take with her. She closed it and carefully replaced it in the file cabinet. Then she left, knowing there was only one person who might tell her exactly how Carrasco was helping with Las Montañas. There was one stop, however, that she wanted to make before she could talk to her father.

Irene Talbot knew the rules that apply at every step of a lawsuit, whether it's criminal or civil in nature, one being that the parties to a lawsuit do not talk to the opposition lawyers or their investigators. What she asked of Kevin Tanekawa was unorthodox and violated every rule of conduct she'd been taught or had learned in the heat of trial combat. She wanted to talk to the patriarch of the family that owned the farmland where the Ignacio boy had been injured. She had called him directly, and he had responded directly, refusing her candid suggestion he might want to discuss the matter first with his defense attorney. He would meet with her in his home at 10 A.M.

Kevin Tanekawa, a short man whose once straight black hair was now almost gray, answered the doorbell himself. He was dressed in casual clothing, a green knit polo shirt and plaid walking shorts. He was cordial, smiling and extending his hand to her first, shaking her hand and immediately offering her something cold to drink.

Tanekawa ushered her onto a small enclosed patio, to a white wicker chair next to a waterfall and fish pond. Encircling the patio were tropical plants.

"They're beautiful," Irene remarked of the large gold-and-white fish peering out of the water at Tanekawa. "What are they?"

"Koi. Very valuable. Very old." He laughed. "Two of them are ninety years old, older than me, but not by much, I think."

"Have you owned them long?"

"Long enough to think of them as my children. I keep them in this patio enclosure because it's safer for them.

"Now, Miss Talbot. Why have you decided you must speak with me against all rules of this lawsuit game we must play?"

"I felt I needed to talk with you, Mr. Tanekawa. I'm alleging in the complaint that—"

"I know what you are alleging, Miss Talbot. You are alleging I am poisoning the people who work for me. You are also alleging I am poisoning my streams and my land."

"What do you think about the lawsuit? I mean, I know that's a pretty broad question."

"Not really. No. I can tell you what I think. It think it is a disgrace. I think, respectfully, Miss Talbot, that you do not do your profession good. Would I poison my own fields? *Why* would I poison my own fields? The earth is something I love. It is something that if I harmed it, I would be harming myself. You see, I don't have any reason to destroy what I've spent my whole life creating. I've been here farming on this land for longer than you've been alive. If I wanted to destroy the land, there are a hundred other ways I could do it, ways that would earn me a considerable amount of money. Without the poison my land is worth hundreds, thousands of dollars an acre. *With* the poison it is worth a lot less. Tell me, do I look like such a fool?"

"No, no you don't, Mr. Tanekawa. Not if you wanted to stay in farming."

The man laughed again. "Miss Talbot, look at me. I'm seventy-five years old. What else could I do?" He looked down at the water beside them, then back at her. "Maybe start a koi farm?"

"Mr. Tanekawa, how could this happen to the water, to the land without you knowing about it? Who else would do it?"

"If I could tell you that, your case would be over, Miss Talbot. If you can prove what you are charging me with, it is, indeed, a grave problem I have on my hands. It will put me out of business. I haven't been the best of businessmen. And I have had some bad times with the government and the unions. But don't confuse that with disdain for my land. That is not the case. Everything I do, I do to make my land work. To make it profitable. I have not succeeded. My children want nothing to do with this. They think I am a crazy man for continuing. Perhaps they are right. We will soon find out, won't we?"

"I guess we will, Mr. Tanekawa."

"You know, Miss Talbot, your lawsuit will break me long before a jury comes in against me. This lawsuit will cost me my name and my workers. If what you say is true, the government will shut me down."

"I'm sorry. I don't know how else to do this. Somewhere down the line we will talk about settling the case. You know the Superior Court has a mandatory settlement program."

"Oh, I think it will be over long before then for me."

"What do you mean?" Irene asked, suddenly catching a different drift to the conversation.

"I have been offered a great deal of money to sell the land."

She was afraid to ask, but it was now necessary to confront the inevitable.

"By whom?"

"You do not know?"

"No, I don't. Please tell me."

"Your father is Franklin Talbot?"

She nodded.

"This is a surprise, truly a surprise you do not know your father has offered to buy all of my land. He has wanted this land for some time. He's made many offers. And each time there's an offer, it gets lower and lower. Now"—again he smiled and raised his hands—"well, it's rock bottom. The lawsuit has driven the value into the ground. No pun intended. It's a very difficult situation. If I sell, perhaps I can stave off further damage to my reputation. Maybe use the money to pay this boy for his damages. If I fight you in court and I lose, I will have nothing left."

"The lawsuit has lowered the price of your land?"

"Miss Talbot, you cannot be so naive as to think otherwise."

She stood and he did also.

"Mr. Tanekawa, I'm sorry I imposed on you. You've helped me, really."

"How can I have helped you? That is an odd conclusion, Miss Talbot."

He walked her to the front door, and the two

said good-bye. In a tone of resignation, Tanekawa's last words were "See you in court."

Irene Talbot was in turmoil on the drive back to her condominium. She had confirmed what she feared for months. Tanekawa hadn't poisoned his water or his land. Someone else had. And she knew only one person who might tell her why.

34

"HE'S THERE!"

Pike burst through the door to Judith's office, causing her to jump.

"My God, Pike, *who's* where?

"*He's* there. Serafino Morales is at his cousin's up in Fillmore."

"You're sure of that?"

"I just got a call from his cousin himself. He knocked on the door this morning."

"Let's be sure he doesn't take off anywhere."

"Oh, he won't. He's been walking for two days, and he doesn't suspect anyone's onto him. His cousin hasn't said a word and hasn't asked about the canyon or mentioned the murder."

"How do we stand as far as picking him up?"

"The arrest warrant's been issued. I've already notified the Fillmore police, and they'll be there as backup. I don't want them picking him up till I get there. I'm going to get the warrant now and any paperwork in the file." Pike was ebullient. "Hell, I'm going to take the whole damn file with me!"

He rubbed his hands together. "You comin' with me?"

"Nope. Not this time. I don't find the thrill of the chase as exciting as you do, Pike. I trust you can handle him. But while you mention it, why don't you take Peter with you. He's worked on the case, and it'll be good to have him see the arrest process. Let him take a look at the file and the warrant on the way up with you." She glanced at the desk clock. "It's three o'clock. It's going to take you about four hours to get there if you leave after the Los Angeles commuter traffic. That puts you there tonight at what, maybe nine o'clock?"

"That's close. I'll call and get the locals up there coordinated. We'll nab the scumbag as soon as the sun comes up."

35

---◆---

SERAFINO WAS DREAMING. He was in the doorway of his small adobe house looking outside. The cornfields were green, and he could see them for miles. There were voices in the distance as he stood looking at the white clouds, and the voices got louder until he could tell they were coming from the sky.

Serafino was jolted awake by rough hands everywhere on his body. His arms were pulled to his back and cold metal was clamped around his wrists. In the haze between sleep and wakefulness, his first thought was that someone had jumped him. Robbers out to steal all the corn. How could he have been so stupid! Then he remembered. He was no longer in the fields guarding Mr. Oklund's crop. He was with his cousin in a place called Fillmore in a county called Ventura. Only when he comprehended this and his eyes were fully opened did he see the police surrounding him.

A heavy man was suddenly standing in front of him reading something from a card. He shook his head, and the man stopped reading and turned to the young Hispanic man, a handsome young man in a white shirt. The young man spoke in Spanish, and Serafino understood much of it. He was under arrest for the murder of Rogelio Carrasco. He had some rights, and the younger man was going to read those rights off the small card.

Serafino was dizzy, and the inside of his legs were wet with his own urine.

The younger man, the one who said his name was Peter Delgado, told the older man with meaner eyes that it did not look as if Serafino could run anywhere. Delgado sent his cousin for a clean pair of pants for Serafino to put on before they drove back to San Diego.

36

PETER DELGADO SPENT the four-hour drive to Fillmore reading the contents of Serafino's file. The information there was scant and sterile. On the other hand, the arrest was a crushing combination of noise and humanity that sent his mind racing and his heart pounding. And for what? Twelve men with guns drawn surrounded and subdued one old man. Why, he had asked, was it so violent? Why were so many people needed for such a simple task? Pike had answered him coldly and with the efficiency one would expect from an experienced law enforcement officer.

"You can't drop your guard for a minute, not a second. All it takes is one moment of misplaced compassion and you're a dead man, or your buddy is a dead man."

Peter looked into the mirror at the reflection of Serafino seated on the bench seat back, his arms still twisted behind him. They did not speak to him. *They* could talk about the crime. They could take down and use against him anything Serafino voluntarily said about the crime or his participation in the crime. But they did not initiate any conversation with him because Serafino did not speak English, and until an interpreter could be found for him, one who understood his language and spoke it clearly, it might be coercive to talk to him. It could lead to misunderstandings. Better to remain mute.

Still, Peter Delgado stared at Serafino. So this was what a first-degree murder suspect might look like, with his shoulders hunched forward and a sad, distant look on his face. He supposed murder could come in a variety of packages. But in so old a man? It was hard for Peter to separate what he knew and had been told from what he saw.

"How about some coffee?" Pike asked. "I could use a cup."

By driving straight down Interstate 5 they'd reached Orange County in a little less than two hours. "There's a couple of drive-through restaurants coming up. I don't suggest food. Our guy back there might be hungry, and if we eat, we might create an oppressive environment."

Delgado couldn't tell if Pike was being sarcastic.

Several minutes later Pike turned the car into a drive-through and asked what Delgado might like to drink.

"Just water, cold water's all. With a straw."

When the drinks were delivered, Delgado shoved the straw into the hole on the plastic top, turned back to Serafino, and held the cup of water up. "¿Agua? Water?" he asked, inviting the handcuffed man to drink from the straw. The old man looked up and into Delgado's eyes, then shook his head and looked down again, absorbed only in the grief that he might never see his village or his family again. Only once did he mumble something in his language.

"He stole my children's food. He stole their food."

"What'd he say?" Pike asked.

But neither man understood.

Later, after Serafino leaned back and fell asleep, Delgado asked in a muted voice, "Why do you suppose he did it?"

Pike's voice was a whisper. "I don't know if he did it at all. Remember, officially he's still only a suspect." Pike leaned heavily toward Delgado, and in a barely audible voice, taking great care not to have any of his words reach the sleeping man, said, "Frankly, I can't wait to see if he tells us what it is he *knows* about Carrasco."

37

THE MESSAGE PETER Delgado left on Irene Talbot's telephone answering machine was clear and simple. Serafino Morales had been arrested and was in the San Diego County Jail charged with murder. Perhaps now they would find out what Serafino knew about why Cutter was paying Rogelio Carrasco. The news shook Irene Talbot. She'd already reached several conclusions, and the thought of Serafino Morales's now confirming her beliefs frightened and angered her.

Kevin Tanekawa was not poisoning his own fields, but she was in the process of putting the man out of business by alleging he was. That was the principal conclusion Irene Talbot had come to after hours of agonizing over the pieces of a puzzle that seemed to have fallen so neatly into place. By the time she arrived at her father's house, she'd worked herself up into a storm of emotion.

"You're doing it, aren't you?"

Franklin Talbot looked up from his scrambled eggs and bacon to see his daughter, angry and red-faced, charge through the front door.

"Doing what, Sugar?" He was as calm as if she'd casually walked in and announced what she'd bought from the grocery store.

"Doing what?" she mimicked. "You're using me, the same way you use everyone."

"Come here and sit down, will you, and tell me what in the hell you're talking about. You're going to scare the help."

She threw herself on the chair across from him.

"I know what Uncle Rex was up to out there in the canyon."

"Well, then, perhaps you can let me know too," he drawled, totally nonplussed by her emotional level.

"He was paying Rogelio Carrasco to dump poison out there."

"He was what?"

"Was Rex doing it at your direction?"

"Of course he wasn't! Why would I want to do a thing like that?"

"You tell me. No, wait. I'll tell you. If the land's poisoned and the farmers can't use it, it's worthless. Then some big-time developer comes along and rescues the farmer by offering to buy up the land, only it's a lot cheaper than the offer made two years ago. And it's even better if there's a lawsuit against the farmer for dumping the toxins in the first place. That'll really nail the coffin shut. Neat and tidy. I'm the nail in the coffin, aren't I?"

"I'd say you've gone and lost your senses. I don't need any more land. And if I wanted more land, why would I go through anything as bizarre as what you're describing?"

"Then why was Uncle Rex enlisting Carrasco's help to build the Las Montañas development? Carrasco lived in the canyon up there. That's where you're putting the development, aren't you?"

"How do you know where I'm planning to put Las Montañas?"

"I saw it. I saw Uncle Rex's files. It's in there."

Talbot wasn't interested in how Irene had gained access to the files. He was more concerned with minimizing the damage and containing his daughter's anger.

Talbot was condescending. "Now look, Sugar, it's a *possible* location. The land's not mine."

"Yet," she shot back.

"Okay, it's not mine *yet*. So I did make an offer to buy land around the canyon. And I did make the offer to Tanekawa. That doesn't put me in bed with Carrasco. It doesn't put me out there poisoning the dirt." His voice was rising and he caught himself. "I'm not going to say this again, Irene. I haven't done the things you're conjuring up. As for Uncle Rex, he always did what he wanted; he always courted the fringes, shall we say."

Irene was agitated. He was explaining himself, but she was not receptive.

"I want to believe what you're telling me."

"Then believe it."

He reached across the table and put his large rough hands on hers, covering them completely. His eyes were on hers, looking deeply, unflinchingly into them.

"Sugar, would I ever do anything to hurt you?"

Here was the final blow. Beyond the anger and frustration in her father's manipulation of the Tanekawas, of Cutter and Carrasco, was the searing pain that he had used her as well. Her trust, her respect for him meant nothing to the man.

The tears spilled from her eyes and dripped onto

the table. She lowered her head and shook it, trying hard to keep from sobbing.

Talbot stood and walked behind her, placing his hands on her shoulders and massaging.

"Look, Irene, you're distraught. We lost Uncle Rex. That's a pretty substantial blow. At the same time you've taken on a tremendous responsibility with this toxin case, and you're being very courageous waging war with the big guns out there. And don't let them fool you. Tanekawa's a shrewd son of a bitch. Don't let them corrupt your cause. That's what they're doing, you know. They're making you doubt yourself. Whoever's planting these ideas in your mind is not your friend."

While he was talking, Irene regained control of herself. She wanted to believe him. She wanted to make the turmoil go away. But it wouldn't.

"There's no one planting ideas in my head. It's just me. There's too many unexplained pieces out there, and they're all related in some way. I'm just trying to put them together so they make sense, and the one way they make sense is not one you'd want to hear."

She rose to leave, her whole body feeling heavy.

"Look, honey, after you get this case set for trial, why don't you take a little vacation? Maybe head over to Hawaii and sit in the sun for a while. It'll be a gift from me."

Irene continued toward the door without acknowledging the offer.

"Irene, you know I wouldn't do anything to hurt you. I believe in your cases right along with you."

She turned and smiled weakly at him. He'd beaten back her anger, the same way he beat everything back that threatened him. It was useless to fight with him. At least it was useless to do so on his terms. But she had her terms as well.

"I want to believe that. Maybe they'll find out something from Serafino Morales. Peter Delgado left a message for me on my tape recorder at home. They've arrested him and he's back in San Diego. According to Peter, this Serafino knows who Carrasco was taking money from and maybe why he was taking it."

"They have this man in custody?"

"Yes, they do. He'll probably be arraigned tomorrow morning."

"Maybe, Sugar, that'll put this whole horrible episode to rest, and you can get on with our trial."

"Maybe. Maybe it won't. I want to know what he knows. About what Uncle Rex was paying Rogelio Carrasco to do. I want his deposition and I'm going to ask the court to let me subpoena him in the Ignacio case. I want to know what Serafino Morales knows."

Talbot lowered his head and glared at his daughter.

"Be careful, Irene. These wild accusations are harmful."

"Oh? To whom?"

"To all of us, honey."

"I have to know, Daddy. I *need* to know if I'm destroying a man, destroying his livelihood for no reason except greed. And if Serafino Morales knows, he'll talk. I'll make him talk."

His countenance softened. "I'm begging you, Irene. Let this rest."

The expression on her face was pained. "I can't, Daddy. I can't. You control it all. The lights, the mortgage, my cases—which ones I file, which ones I reject. You can't control this."

"Just promise me you'll think about what you're

doing. I haven't done what you're saying."

He watched as Irene walked to the front door, then followed her out onto the front steps.

She was not yet out of sight when Talbot went into his library and closed the door.

38

IT WAS IMPERATIVE that cases initiated in the criminal justice system commence properly, and Pike was giving Judith an update on the status of the case of the People versus Serafino Morales. From the arrest warrant through transfer back to San Diego, from booking to housing, everything looked to be on target and within the time frames set by the California Penal Code.

"He hasn't talked to anyone yet, as far as I know," Pike reported.

"Has he had a chance to meet with an attorney?" she asked.

"Not yet. He didn't ask for one as far as anyone can tell. Even though he speaks some English and Spanish, we need to find an interpreter who speaks his Mixtec language fluently."

The absence of an interpreter might be a problem. Serafino could not be required to participate at any step of his criminal case unless he understood what was happening to him and could communicate with his attorney. This was impossible without someone to interpret for him.

Most of the time there was no problem securing court interpreters, and in San Diego there was an abundance of those who spoke good Spanish. Finding interpreters who could speak the more exotic dialects and the related Mixtec Indian language, however, was a problem. Absence of an interpreter could cause a delay in the proceedings, and that was always risky given the strict time frames required for criminal cases. Most often a defendant in such situations would waive the required time periods to allow time to get an interpreter, but there was no guarantee Serafino or his attorney would be cooperative.

"How long do you think it'll take to get one?" she asked.

"The interpreter's coordinator has two women on the list, and they've made calls to them both. They're hoping that by the arraignment tomorrow one of them will have responded."

"Have you gone through the preliminaries?"

"Yeah, in fact I've brought you the booking material. There's a couple of good booking photos in there, Judith."

Pike handed the manila file folder to her, and she laid it on the desk in front of her.

"Have you notified the victim's family?" Judith asked, opening the folder and removing a booking photo of Serafino.

"I have. They've been so belligerent at times that I've made a point to tell them what's happening every step of the way just to keep them under wraps. I called and talked to Carrasco's cousin Ricardo, and I think he and a few of the other relatives are planning to come in for the arraignment tomorrow."

"What time's the arraignment set for?"

"It's the afternoon arraignment, one-thirty in Department Nine. That'll hold if we get an interpreter. I'm assuming the public defender's going to pick up the case. The guy's worse than destitute. If that happens, I'm not sure who'll be assigned, probably someone who has some knowledge of the language. We'll need to wait on that one. But since we're talking trial matters here, Judith, have you given any thought to who's going to handle the prosecution?"

"I'm not interested in handling it, Pike. I've got a major violator case coming in on a man picked up in Fresno over the weekend."

"Are you taking Carrasco into the turkey shoot?"

It was an option. Each week the trial attorneys from the Major Violator Unit met for half a day to discuss pending cases. In particular, they looked for the "turkeys," the cases that couldn't be won or would be difficult to try. A case might have an evidence flaw or witness problem. Experience dictated in such cases that they offer a plea bargain and get what they could in the form of punishment. Still other cases they might recommend handing off to the newer deputies for experience, realizing the chances of winning were slim.

"I thought about the turkey shoot. This one's a potential candidate. But I was thinking maybe Peter ought to handle it. What do you think?" She needed to ask Pike his views, given his finicky attitudes and the fact any trial attorney would have to work closely with the chief investigator.

"Well, a couple of weeks ago I might have given you some trouble about it. Now? Well, I think he's a good match for it. What's he got, two trials under his belt?"

"Uh-huh, two. And they were both turkeys. In

some ways, mostly the public relations area, this is a big case, though. It might be risky. It's one of those cases that has some potential to cause community concern, but the case itself is run-of-the-mill."

"I don't really mind the kid, like I've said. He's coming along fine. He's been involved in the investigation and arrest. He can put the case on."

"The other thing, Pike, is that it's going to be a tough case to put on. We've got a victim who was an outright SOB. Half the jury's going to end up wanting to give Morales a medal if this turns out to be a self-defense case. As for Morales himself, just look at him. Does this look like a mad-dog killer?"

Judith flashed the booking photo at Pike.

"No, and you should see him in person," Pike added, shaking his head. "Lots of sympathy's going to happen out there in a trial. The jury's going to hear how he works in the fields for a few dollars a day and gets pushed around by bullies like Carrasco. I call this one a less than even shot at winning. Maybe having it tried by a Hispanic's going to give us a little more credibility with the jury. My only concern is that our potential wonder boy *want* to win this case."

"Whoa, what do you mean?" Judith asked.

"I watched Peter on the drive down with the defendant. There's this *feeling* he has—I can't explain it. There's a connection between the two of them. I watched the way he helped him into the car and held a drink up for him. It was a look in his eyes when the old man bowed his head. You and I know, Judith, if you don't believe in your case, you won't win it. You just won't."

"I'll keep my eye on him, Pike. He can't help

being the same nationality as the defendant. It's something he's going to have to deal with on his own."

Serafino lay on his cot thinking about what might happen to him the next day when he would be arraigned. Arraignment was not about sorting truth from untruth. It was not about focusing on humanity or the art of advocacy. It was about process, pure function and efficiency: securing the necessities of a fair trial, appointing counsel, setting hearing dates, and fixing bail. The average defendant may come in as one of twenty or thirty cases to be heard. They exit with counsel, hearing dates, and if they are lucky, with bail. With freedom to leave the courtroom, the jail, and return home.

That was how arraignment was explained to Serafino by Víctor Benavides, the public defender who'd been assigned to defend him. He spoke in short sentences to keep the interpreter on track, but still she would occasionally stop the attorney and explain there were several ways to say what he wanted said, and then the attorney would have a choice of what to say.

Serafino tried to remember what his attorney told him.

Don't expect a miracle in court. We'll ask for bail, but you won't get it, and if you do, you can't afford to post it. Forget freedom. But keep your spirits up. Wait for trial. That will be the time to tell what happened and why. Think about home.

Serafino tried to think about home, but it was hard to do so. Although he slept on a cot and not the ground, and he went to a large cafeteria where he received a tray of food, he was in a cage with thick bars and no windows, and the men surrounding him were angry and hostile to everyone. There was nothing—nothing—Serafino had ever been in that resembled this; there was no smell so bad nor sights so wrenching. What must the attorney be thinking? It was not, he thought, any place for the soul to relax, and he despaired for the men who he heard weeping at night in corners of this place, for they might be innocent like him.

In his heart Serafino truly believed his killing Rogelio Carrasco was not wrong. Yet behind his heart, behind the knowledge that Carrasco tried to kill his children, the voices of his father and his grandmother told him these nights in this place, whether he saw the daylight again or not, were his earthly punishment for all the wrongs he had committed in his lifetime. And so he would accept it and pray for redemption.

If God granted him redemption, he would be free again.

The bailiff in Department 9 stood at attention with his hands behind his back when he announced Judge Margot Humphries was about to take the bench. "Please come to order!" he shouted to the men and women milling about at the courtroom door.

The command brought the courtroom to complete silence as a short, red-haired woman in her mid-forties entered through the door behind the bailiff, climbed three steps, and sat on her oversize brown leather chair, her head and shoulders just clearing the bench.

Department 9 was the arraignment department, one of the busiest courtrooms in the building. In this courtroom all criminal cases would first pass to allow the defendant to enter his plea to the charges and obtain counsel. All preliminary hearings would be set to determine if there was enough evidence to send the defendant to trial. It was a constant stream of people, and so it was not a judicial assignment for the faint of heart or the weak in spirit. Nor was it a place for those judges who disdained administrative work.

To the right and three feet lower than the bench sat the courtroom clerk, a two-foot-high pile of case files before her. One by one she would call the name of the defendant appearing on the file, and the man or woman would either step forward from the audience if they were not in custody, or if they were in custody, stand up in the glass-enclosed holding area nearest the door exiting to the holding tank in the basement.

Because Serafino Morales was in custody, he sat with the others, their hands handcuffed in front of them, in the glass enclosure, and he watched as the other defendants' names were called. One by one they were allowed out of the enclosure to join the public defender, who was seated at a counsel table. As was the custom, one public defender handled all the arraignments and searched quickly through his own pile of manila folders and files for the paperwork on the defendant whose name was called. And the same was true for the prosecutor. One deputy district attorney, seated at another table, handled all the cases for the prosecutor. For some defendants, like Serafino, other attorneys who had already been assigned stepped forward when the case was called.

When Serafino heard his name, he rose and the bailiff motioned him to come out of the enclosure and stand before the judge, where he was joined by Víctor Benavides. Serafino had spoken to his attorney again before the arraignment this afternoon, and now could see the attorney's eyes were sad pools of brown. *He must not sleep well*, thought Serafino, noticing the dark circles under them. He noticed even more about the man now that they were in court. His clothes were not like many of the other attorneys' in the courtroom. They were baggy and drab. He did not look snappy like the attorney in the fine three-piece suit who'd stepped forward to answer for a defendant who came from the audience instead of the holding tank. But there was an enthusiasm in his attorney that gave Serafino hope. They'd talked for only thirty minutes today, but even in that short a time, he seemed to understand what had happened to make Serafino take another man's life, and Serafino wanted him to explain it now to the judge. But the attorney again said he must wait. This was not the time. The time would come later. Serafino would have to be patient.

Serafino stood, bent forward between his attorney and the ever present interpreter, who repeated all the English into the Oaxacan's language.

Serafino did not notice Peter Delgado, who was seated next to the deputy district attorney. Delgado did not rise when Serafino Morales's name was called. He had asked to watch the arraignment.

"Mr. Benavides, I understand you will be representing Mr. Morales?"

"Yes, Your Honor. I'm here by special assignment for the Public Defender's Office because I understand some Mixtec, which is the language Mr. Morales speaks. He also speaks some English and Spanish. We do have an interpreter present as well who speaks the language of the Mixtecs."

"Is your client prepared to enter a plea today?"

"Yes he is. He enters a plea of not guilty, Your Honor."

"Do you wish to enter a plea of not guilty?" the judge repeated, looking coldly at Serafino.

The interpreter repeated what she'd said and Serafino nodded.

"Please tell the defendant he must speak out loud," the judge told the interpreter, who in turn told Serafino to say he wished to plead not guilty. Serafino said "not guilty," and the interpreter then repeated it in English.

"Okay, the plea is entered."

And so the proceedings continued with the interpreter repeating the date and time of hearings set. Serafino, who had lowered his head after he'd entered his plea, did not raise it again until the judge began talking about bail and whether he would be set free.

"It's my understanding the People are asking for high bail in this case," the judge said, reading from the file before her.

"That's correct, Your Honor. Mr. Morales is a flight risk. He fled after the homicide of Mr. Carrasco and was brought back from Fillmore. He has no home here, no ties to the community. His family resides in the southern part of Mexico. If he's released, there's a very high risk he will leave the jurisdiction."

"Does the defense wish to be heard?"

Víctor Benvides offered an argument to release Serafino. Bail must be set, he urged. Mr. Morales is old and has lived in McGonigle Canyon during the growing and picking seasons. In any event, bail should not be set too high because it exists only to ensure that the defendant will come to trial.

"Bail will be set at five hundred thousand dollars. Thank you, Counsel," the judge said, smiling at Víctor Benavides.

The attorney's prediction was correct. The court was not going to let him out.

The interpreter told Serafino the hearing was over, and he looked at his attorney.

"Tell him I'll see him this evening," Víctor Benavides told the interpreter as Serafino was led back to the holding area.

Serafino watched his attorney pack his briefcase and leave the courtroom with the interpreter behind him. One by one the remaining defendants came forward and returned after their brief hearing before the judge.

From what Serafino could tell, none of them had bail as high as his. A half million dollars! It was so strange, he thought. What a sum of money he was worth when he was locked up.

Delgado, who'd remained seated during the entire arraignment calendar, watched Serafino leave the courtroom. He'd seen the photos of Rogelio Carrasco and heard all about Carrasco's mean-spirited nature. How, he wondered, could this man, so hunched over and meek, successfully take on the camp bully? Was his strength so superior? This was what the jury would ask. How would he answer it?

Delgado thanked the calendar deputy for letting him sit in, and he rose and walked toward the spectator area where Pike had been observing the proceedings too.

"That's high bail," he said to the detective.

"Not in a murder case it's not. It's also meant to keep the public safe. And as far as I'm concerned, that includes the defendant." As he made the last comment, he glanced over his shoulder at the three burly Hispanic men seated at the back of the courtroom. They waved, unsmiling, at Pike. "Those rather polite-looking men back there are Carrasco's cousins," Pike whispered. "If Serafino sees the light of day, he'll be dead within twenty-four hours."

Peter Delgado was finished for the afternoon. He picked up his file on Serafino Morales and left the courtroom, stopping at the small alcove midway down the hall for a cup of machine-brewed coffee. He didn't want to return to his office just yet. Pike's last comment weighed heavily on him. And he wanted to think about it, here, now, before sitting at his desk again. Serafino was so at the mercy of everything around him. Everything. From the weather that made crops possible for picking to these vengeful men who would kill him in the blink of an eye.

"No jury's going to convict him, you know."

The man's voice came from behind Delgado, and he turned, leaving the paper cup filling behind the plastic door of the vending machine. It was Serafino Morales's attorney who extended his hand to Delgado.

"I'm Víctor Benavides. Please call me Vic; everyone does."

"Glad to meet you. Peter Delgado."

"You're new with the District Attorney's Office?"

"Yes, I've been with them just a few weeks, really. I'll be trying the Morales case."

"Well, it's good to see you in court. I think your coffee's ready there."

Delgado pushed the door open and took the hot

paper cup from the machine. He lifted the cup to his lips and flinched.

"Too hot!"

He walked to one of the empty benches lining the hallway and, setting the cup down on it, turned to Benavides, who had followed him the short distance.

"How long have you been with the Public Defender's Office?"

"Twelve years in December. Before that I was with your office, the D.A.'s office here in San Diego. I'm afraid I identified far too readily with the downtrodden. I lasted with the D.A. about two years. Before that I tried my hand at civil law, but I didn't want to spend my life counting up the number of hours I could bill to clients. So now I've got long hours and lots of other people's grief. Every once in a while I get some nice guy who's just been beat up by life; they punch back and they just get beat up some more. I'm not playing one-upmanship, but it's going to be a tough one for your office. You know that, don't you?"

"No, actually I didn't."

"He tells me this Rogelio Carrasco beat him and stole money from him."

Delgado picked up the cup of coffee and judging it cool enough, took a sip.

"Last time I looked, the law said you don't get to kill someone because they took money from you."

"Not for you and me, but it's different out there in the canyon."

"Different how?"

The more experienced attorney shrugged.

"Have you ever seen a child starve to death? It's okay. You don't have to answer the question.

Serafino Morales comes to this country for one reason only: to make money to feed his kids. He doesn't want to live here. He wants to make money and send it home. If he doesn't send it, his children don't eat. If they don't eat, they die. If you steal his money, you starve his family. Carrasco stole his money and wouldn't give it back. Serafino lost his temper."

"He tried to make him give it back?"

"That's about it."

"But there are other legal ways to report theft."

Benevides laughed. "Have you ever been to McGonigle Canyon?"

"Yes, I have."

"Does it look like a place nicely plugged into the police stations? Don't answer that one either. The question answers itself."

Benevides looked at his wristwatch.

"Oops . . . gotta go." His question was thoughtful: "Have you ever been to Mexico?"

"Of course I have."

"Have you ever *seen* Mexico?

The question stopped Delgado. His answer was stilted and slow. "I've been there to school. And I've had a chance to meet the people."

"Well, I wondered. If you've seen the people, then you know why Serafino killed Carrasco."

Delgado watched Serafino's attorney disappear down the hallway and into another trial department. For a moment Peter envied him.

39

IT WAS PIKE who brought the news to Judith.

"Serafino Morales is out."

"Out where?" It never occurred to her that "out" meant out of custody.

"Someone posted bail for him. Can you believe that?"

"Who would post bail for him?"

"Are you ready for this?"

"No, I'm not ready for any of this. If he's out, he's gone for good." She was only repeating what Pike already knew. An itinerant field hand would have no reason to stay in San Diego and face murder charges when all he had to do was travel fifteen minutes south and disappear across the border.

"The papers from the bail bondsman say it was Franklin Talbot."

Judith's shoulders sloped forward as if someone had hit her on the back with a heavy weight.

"Franklin Talbot posted Serafino Morales's bail? Why?"

"I'll be damned if I can tell you. Champion of the poor?"

Judith waved his reason away. "No, no. That doesn't make sense to me."

"When he was released, he was told he had to stay in the area. He gave his address as the grower's up in McGonigle Canyon. My guess is he went back to the canyon to wait for the trial."

Suddenly Pike's eyes began to blink. Recognizing the reaction as an indication Pike was under stress, Judith asked, "What's the matter? You've thought of something. What is it?"

"Carrasco's cousins. They'll kill him if he goes back to the canyon."

"You've got to get to him, Pike. Find him. You've got to explain he may need to stay out of there."

"I'm going now, Judith. Right now!"

"I want to come out there with you. I think I need to talk to Carrasco's cousins."

Judith got up from her desk chair and moved toward the door, but Pike was ahead of her, on his way to find Peter Delgado, the one person they could call on quickly who could translate the terrible danger Serafino was in if he remained in the canyon. As Judith followed him down the hallway, he looked at his watch and turned back to her.

"We can get to the Oaxacan encampment in forty-five minutes. I hope to Jesus we get there before Carrasco's family finds out he's there."

Serafino Morales did not know the man who put up the money to release him. He was only happy to be free of the foul-smelling jail.

He reached the encampment in three hours—still midmorning—taking a combination of buses along a route explained to him by the Spanish-speaking jail attendant who helped process his release. His first stop once he reached the encampment was to the place in the ground where he'd slept. It was still there, intact. Only the wood planks covering the top needed organization. He placed the jail papers in the hole. The papers told him when he was to come back for trial. He would have to remember to call his attorney the next day and explain his good fortune in being freed. He supposed his attorney would be surprised someone would want to pay the money needed to free him. He could not believe it himself.

It did not take long to discover the tomato fields to the south of the encampment were being worked this afternoon. Several men who were too ill that day to work told Serafino the job was a large one and men from all the encampments were picking.

The sun was directly overhead. Noon. If he hurried, he might find an hour, maybe two, of work waiting for him.

Pike was behind the wheel and Judith at his right in the front passenger seat. Delgado, who hadn't stopped talking from the moment he got into the car, was in the back.

"I can't understand Talbot bailing him out. I can't. There's something else happening here; there has to be."

"I've been thinking," Pike said, his eyes blinking. "We sent Irene Talbot back to her father hoping she'd do or say something that would make him play his hand in this whole thing, maybe do something to connect Talbot Construction to Carrasco's murder. He knows the only person who has any information about that connection is Serafino Morales."

"Are you thinking he's played his hand?" Judith asked.

"I think he just might have," Pike said.

It was Delgado who spoke next. "What's he to gain from getting Serafino released?"

Pike's response was fast, terse. "A dead man."

No one seemed to mind the deep ruts in the encampment road. They were almost a welcome sign to the trio that they'd reached the location where Serafino might be found.

They were, however, too late. The same men who had told Serafino of the available work in the fields also told them that Serafino had left and might not be back for hours.

"That won't do," Judith responded when Delgado interpreted the bad news. "We have to find him right now. Ask where the fields are located."

Delgado talked with the men for several minutes while they gave directions and pointed to the west, where the tomato crop grew. They got back in the car, and it took off again, bumping its way toward Serafino.

Serafino had come to the fields too late. There was no more work to assign for the afternoon, but there would be plenty more work the following morning. Serafino was told to return then.

The news did not dishearten the old man. The last few days had been grueling. The sky was blue and the breeze cool. A few moments to rest here in the fields by the stream would be all he would need today. He wanted only to see the sky and think of home. He would answer to the police for what he did to Carrasco and he would explain. But if he could just stay out of jail until the trial, that was all he could ask for.

*　　*　　*

The man with the rifle walked to the small ridge, to where he could see more clearly. He would be patient. He knew it was there in the canyon, and sooner or later it would show itself. His rifle was old. Perhaps, he thought, it would not fire properly or perhaps the bullet would not shoot as far as it needed to. But he would keep a watchful eye.

Judith, in high heels she swore never to again wear to the canyon, raced ahead of the two men; the warm, sweet odor of tomato plants enveloped her as she felt her heels sink into the soft dirt along the access path to the fields. The field hands, stooped low to the ground, raised their heads as she and the two men raced by. She heard, somewhere off to the side, a long low wolf whistle; obviously someone was surprised and impressed with the sudden appearance of this woman in office clothing racing through the tomato fields.

It took several minutes for Delgado to locate the supervisor, who explained that Serafino Morales had come to him in search of work but he had told him to come back in the morning. He didn't know where he'd gone, but seemed to recall he walked out toward the trees that served to buffer the crops from the wind. He'd been there minutes before. Perhaps if they hurried, they might catch up with him.

Serafino was completely at rest, his back to the tree. Tomorrow he would go to the catering truck early and buy something to bring for lunch. For a moment his mind wandered. The strong odor of the fields surrounded him. It was just like home. Just like his small village . . .

When the sharp crack split the air, Judith, Pike,

and Delgado stopped in their tracks. Pike knew the sound all too well.

"God, Pike, run! It came from over there." Judith pointed in the direction of the trees. It was Delgado, however, who sped from her side, outdistancing them quickly.

When Judith and Pike reached Delgado, he was kneeling at Serafino's side.

"He never had a chance," he said, looking up at his two friends. "It hit him in the chest."

Serafino sat, his back still against the tree, his eyes open but glassy, a red circle of blood on the front of his T-shirt.

Pike knelt down on the opposite side of the stricken man and placed his fingers over Serafino's carotid artery. He could hear Judith's heavy breathing above. "He's dead, Judith." Pike stood and looked out through the trees to the hills beyond. Nothing moved. There was no sound except that of the field boss in the distance, yelling at his laborers, "¡Apúrense! ¡Apúrense! Faster! Faster!"

"I'll call homicide," Judith volunteered, still struggling to catch her breath.

"Do you think it'll do any good?" Pike asked. He broke the long silence that followed. "I'll call the coroner. Why don't you come back with me, Judith." She looked down at her feet and saw she'd lost a shoe somewhere during the run through the field. She reached down and took the remaining shoe from her foot, then, barefoot, followed Pike back to the car.

Neither of them noticed Delgado's face was wet with tears.

PART FOUR

INHABITANT OF THE CLOUDS

40

TERESA, A WREATH of orange and yellow paper
flowers on her head, lay on the cane table in front of the
altar of the house, a small waxen doll in a blue cotton
dress, surrounded by flowers and lighted candles. In
front of her Serafino stood crying at the sight of his child.
His wife and three of the women from the village are
sitting on the floor mats behind him, trying to maintain
a happy countenance, smiling and wailing at the same
time. If the people were not joyful the little angel would
not go directly to God. They sat as Serafino's father
stood nearby, his cheeks wet with tears.

Occasionally the women spoke of the thirteen-month-
old baby's sudden death, only three days after the onset
of el vómito; one opining it must have been the bad eye
of the night—mal ojo de noche—that struck the child
when she was taken outside in the dark.

As they continued to wail, Serafino's attention was
drawn to the children who were playing near the door
outside. One of them had a cold, he could tell. Her nose
was running, and her face looked flushed. As she started
for the door to enter, Serafino stopped her.

"Do not come in," he warned her, *"or you will be-come even more sick."*

The old woman sitting nearest the door agreed, telling the child she herself was once sick with the fever and was not cured until she stopped going to funerals and wakes. She stood and called the child, handing her a cup of chocolate and two rolls before sending her away.

Antonio García, Serafino's neighbor, arrived distraught and sobbing, so much so that Serafino for a moment forgot his own grief and went to the man's side to comfort him.

While the village prayer maker chanted and sprinkled the baby with blessed water, Serafino lifted the child into the white wood coffin and nailed the lid shut. Raising it first to his shoulder, then to the top of his head, he led the procession to the cemetery. Behind him, his wife and children followed with the musicians and the villagers, who brought the altar flowers in a basket. Serafino's own father—now stooped and bent with arthritis—struggled to keep up along the rutted road.

It is ever so, *Serafino thought to himself as the weight of the casket began to grow.* It is the dead punishing the living with misfortune, misfortune that ends only with death.

41

JUDITH SPENT TWENTY minutes reviewing Carrasco's file; then she closed it and in black ink wrote across its front "Close File—suspect deceased." She placed it in the outgoing file basket to be screened by her secretary and then sent off to storage. Attached to it was a second file, that of murder victim Serafino Morales.

Normally a suspected murder case remained open. In California there is no statute of limitations for murder. Next month, next year, or twenty years from now the clue could come, the big break occur that would set up a murderer's arrest and prosecution. The decision whether to leave a case open rested on set office policies. Serafino's homicide file would be sent to Pike. The prospects for solving it were bleak. The bullet that killed Serafino, much like the one removed from Pike after he was shot at the canyon, could not be tied to anyone. Nor did the caliber of the bullet match any gun belonging to Franklin Talbot or anyone who worked for him. As for Carrasco's cousins, they all had strong alibis. After Serafino's death, nobody in the canyon would talk to Pike or Delgado about their possible involvement in a murder. As for Franklin Talbot, he could be no more than hailed for releasing a poor ignorant farmhand. There could be no thought of pursuing him in the matter. For all intents and purposes the case was over.

Across Serafino's file Judith wrote, "Refer to open homicide storage, lead detective Pike Martin."

The twenty-four hours since Serafino's death brought mixed feelings. It was not the kind of situation that developed at times with a bad actor being murdered by another bad actor. In such cases, everyone breathed a little faster but always with an unspoken thought lingering that an innocent in society had not been murdered. But the death of Serafino Morales seemed to have cast a pall over her and, in particular, Delgado, for the death of the man ended legal issues and raised others, more mundane, perhaps, but certainly of human interest.

Serafino's body was yet unclaimed. Although she did not have to take any further action, Judith telephoned the Mexican consulates in San Diego and in Los Angeles in an attempt to determine where his remains should be sent. The Mexican officials in San Diego promised to try to contact Serafino's relatives in Oaxaca, but there were no assurances they would be reached in time to properly dispose of the body, and besides, it was highly unlikely the family had the financial ability to travel to the United States even if the paperwork could be processed to allow that to happen. They could contact the county and bury him in a pauper's grave. Such arrangements could be made. They assured her the matter would be taken care of, particularly since there were relatives in Ventura County.

Judith took a break for coffee, and when she returned, there was a note from Peter Delgado on her chair seat. It was a short message, saying only "please call me." Several minutes later he was standing at her desk.

"I was thinking, Judith, that I'd be happy to take responsibility for getting Serafino Morales back to his family in Oaxaca. I mean, the county wouldn't have to be involved if I could act as a friend of the family. I'd be willing to pick up the costs of transporting him home and the funeral expenses here as well; I know there will be some expense involved in that. Maybe there will be red tape, and I could help cut through it. I've talked to my father, and he's willing to help. Would I be acting out of school, so to speak, if I did that?"

Judith stood and circled the desk to where Delgado was standing.

"No, not at all, Peter. I think the family would be very grateful."

"I want to do this. I don't think he was a bad man, Judith. Maybe I shouldn't feel that way—I mean, I would have had to prosecute him for murder, but that's how I feel now. And I want to see where he came from. He wanted to go back there, and I'd like to see he gets there."

"Make whatever arrangements you want to, Peter. If I can help, let me know. And keep me posted on the days you'll need off."

"I already started the process."

"Has his family been notified?"

"The consulate says a telegram was sent to a relative in Oaxaca, and his cousin in Fillmore has given his permission as closest next of kin to allow me to take the body back."

"Have you spoken to Irene Talbot since Serafino's death?"

"I called her, yes. And I told her what I was going to do. I think she was greatly moved by it. She's an honorable woman, Judith. And she's got a big decision to make. Although she didn't say it in so many words, it sounds as if she's going to persuade the Ignacio family to drop the lawsuit or settle for damages that'll cover the boy's expenses. I think she feels the damage has been done to Tanekawa, though. There's not a whole lot she can do about it at this point, either. She thinks he'll sell out to her father."

"Her father. Right. There's no doubt in my mind he was behind paying Carrasco to poison the land. We'll never pin anything on him, though. There's just no evidence."

"It's Irene I feel sorry for," Delgado added. "She's reconciled with her father, but she'll never trust him again."

"She was used, Peter."

He smiled and glanced sideways at her. "You want to know what I think? I think everyone got used. Some more than others."

Judith reached over to the corner of her desk and retrieved a square white envelope, the kind routinely sent from the larger law firms announcing new partnerships and associates.

"Take a look at this," she said, handing the envelope to Peter.

Peter slipped the stiff card from within and read the raised black lettering. The law firm of Mason, Henderson, and Stalling was announcing the association of Miss Irene Talbot into its firm and her specialization in immigration law. A broad smile spread across his face as he pushed the card back inside the envelope.

"It's a good start," he said, handing the envelope back to Judith. "At least she'll be free from Talbot's financial control."

"My guess is she's not totally clear yet. I'll bet he's going to throw a big party to celebrate her new job and invite all the power brokers in the city."

"I guess that leaves me out," Peter said with a mock sigh.

"Oh, I don't know," Judith said. "If he knows what's good for him, he ought to put you on his invitation lists starting now."

"She'll call me again sooner or later," he continued. "I don't think I'm going to be a welcome addition to her family dinner table, ever. But who knows. Her father's never admitted any wrongdoing in the canyon, and she has to accept it."

Judith glanced at the files of Carrasco and Serafino Morales. "I guess we accept it too."

"He's a powerful man."

"Very powerful. I haven't been on the battlefield with anyone quite like him. And I'd just as soon not have to be."

"I think I'd like to meet him eyeball to eyeball again sometime, somewhere."

"Well, I hope you get to do that, Peter. I'd like to see it. When are you leaving for Mexico?"

"Tomorrow if the body is released and customs allows it. You know, bodies are considered 'intangibles.' "

"Well, good luck, and call when you get back."

42

THE GEARS OF the old white Ford pickup truck shifted noisily as Benito Salas wound his way through the mountains. Occasionally the passenger, Peter Delgado, turned to see whether the particleboard box holding the steel blue coffin of Serafino Morales still lay securely tied in the bed of the vehicle. He'd purchased the coffin himself, a commodity available to only the most wealthy in the rural countryside. The driver, a goateed employee of the Mexican funeral home that accepted Serafino's body from the United States, was philosophical.

"His family will grieve and it will be much pain to see, but it was his time to die. It was God's wish. With time, they will adjust. They all adjust."

"What do you mean, they all adjust?"

"This is not the only man to come back from the United States like this, in a box. Twice, even three times a week I drive the bodies back. Not all of them are men; no, some of them are women. Even children—babies. They all come back here."

Delgado spoke little on the ride. He found the

land arid and the people tired and withered, like so many dried leaves on the corn stalks lining the road. Yet his task was one he was anxious to see completed. He was an emissary of sorts, bringing back to his homeland a man who would have chosen never to leave if only it had rained more often in his small area of the world. And there was something else much deeper inside Delgado now. Perhaps a better understanding of himself, perhaps an acceptance that had not been there six months earlier. He was not so afraid to see himself here in this land.

At last Delgado saw ahead of them, down the road, a group of brightly colored adobes. Yellow and blue and pink. An attempt to bring some life to this brown place, he thought.

The truck ground to a stop next to a brown adobe. A steady stream of people from all parts of the village came to greet them. Upon seeing the box in the bed of the truck, the women began to wail. From the house three boys and a young child came, crying, their arms encircling one another as they walked. In the middle, a short, frail woman wrapped in a black shawl wept. It took only moments for Delgado to see they were Serafino's wife and children.

They were expecting Delgado. Word had spread that a rich American, a Mexican, had befriended their father in death. They grabbed his hand and kissed his fingers as the men of the village patted his back gently. When he reached into the bed of the truck to begin the task of removing the box holding Serafino, they stopped him, and five of the village men helped Benito Salas pull the casket box off the bed and carry it into the house. Delgado followed, watching the men set the box on the floor and then gently pry the particleboard away from the coffin. There were murmurs of surprised approval as the shiny blue metal coffin appeared. They turned to loud wails once again as the coffin lid was raised and the people inched forward.

Serafino's body, naked except for a white cloth covering from his midriff to his knees, had been placed in a clear plastic bag. It would be for the family to dress him in his final clothing for burial. Delgado looked with the mourners on Serafino's remains.

In his lifetime he had seen only one dead body, that of his grandmother. He was five years old, barely able to understand she was not sleeping. She was wearing a pink silk dress lying in a white coffin covered with flowers. In death her face looked as he remembered her in life. In the funeral home death was masked, softened with fine cloth and the smell of roses. Peter could see Serafino's face through the plastic. The dead man's mouth was slightly open, the bottom edges of protruding front teeth forming a thin white line between his lips. And its left eye, open barely a slit, gave the impression the cadaver was winking at the mourners. The emaciated body in the coffin before him was an honest presentation of death, untouched except briefly and inartfully by the embalmer's hands.

Benito Salas, standing behind Peter, whispered in his ear, "This is how they all come back, poor things. Looking like that for the families."

The sound of plastic crackling under the trembling hands of Serafino's family mixed gently with the murmurs of grief and the wailing and the thick musty incense intended to cover the smell of death.

"He looks so old, so old!" one mourner called out.

"He was too young to die. Look what they have done to him!" cried another.

Peter swayed forward, then back. The strong hand of Salas landed firmly on his shoulders, steadying him.

Holding his hand to his chest, Peter turned to Serafino's wife. Nodding good-bye, he took a step back, away from the coffin, as hands now more determined pulled away the cloth covering Serafino's lower body.

"Come with me," Salas said, leading him away.

As the family prepared to dress Serafino for burial, Delgado was led to the home of a villager down the dirt road, to a cot in a room of his own. The neighbor, it was explained, had been to the United States many times and had earned enough money for a larger home with a bathroom. There he would have some privacy.

Delgado did not sleep, but the separation from Serafino's body was welcome. Within the hour Salas returned and asked if he wished to head back. He explained the family would be honored if he stayed for the funeral, but they would understand his wish to return to the United States. Delgado was equivocal. He would like to stay but was unsure how and when he would be able to return. Salas offered an alternative. He could spend the night with friends not far from the village and return the following evening to pick Delgado up.

Delgado spent the night with Serafino's neighbor, awakening only once to walk outside and stand in the darkness, staring up at the stars, smelling the earth Serafino had so longed to return to. The United States and his desk in the District Attorney's Office were in another world. Here there was only life and death and, in between, survival.

He thought of Víctor Benavides, Serafino's lawyer. He could tell him now that he had seen the people of Mexico. He thought of Irene Talbot and the civil lawsuits that created issues that destroyed people's lives without just cause. He thought of her father. He thought of the icons who paid homage and were paid homage for good deeds camouflaging greed. And his thoughts were of McGonigle Canyon and Serafino. And hundreds of Serafinos from this village who would willingly allow themselves to be used for enough dollars to fend off starvation. They would plant and pick and be returned themselves to the soil. And finally, finally, he thought of himself. Could he return to his small office and become a prosecutor, learn to try cases and then learn to file the civil lawsuits? When his eyes became weary, he returned to his cot and slept uninterrupted through the night.

The following morning, Delgado rose early and was offered a breakfast of bread and chocolate. He walked with the neighbor in whose home he'd stayed, up the path to Serafino's house. There he found Serafino's eldest son standing above his father's body, resting in the coffin, his head to the west. Long ago, Delgado's grandfather had cautioned that the children's beds should not point westward, as that resting position was reserved for only the dead.

The room where Serafino lay was dark and musty with the heavy smell of incense. Surrounding the coffin were flowers and candles, some lit. Serafino was dressed in a thin black suit. His hands, crossed over his chest, were held together with a rosary under which rested a picture of a saint. A plate behind his head held a few coins and several packages of cigarettes, offerings from those who had come to pay their respects to the family of the dead man. To Serafino's belt was tied a small cloth bag containing a gourd of holy water, a cup, and small tortillas to carry on his journey to the pueblo underground, Delgado had been informed by Serafino's eldest son.

When the musicians arrived, Serafino's friends and two of his eldest sons lifted the casket and placed it on a horse-drawn cart. The family and villagers, crying and wailing, followed the improvised hearse to the cemetery accompanied by a slow dirge. Serafino's casket was lowered into the ground, and wet cement, flowers, and then dirt were placed on top of it. Now the novena would begin, nine nights of prayers and *las alabanzas*, chants, to aid Serafino's journey to the pueblo beneath the ground.

By evening Delgado had paid his last respects to the family and was on his way back to San Diego.

43

JUDITH WAS THE first to greet Peter Delgado on his return to work. She walked to his office and found him looking through the files and memos that had accumulated while he'd been away.

"Glad to have you back. I trust you're happy to be back too."

"It's like I never left," he observed.

"That's about right. The paperwork never stops. It's always full employment around here. Hey, why don't you join me for coffee? Not here. Down the street. I was about to walk over to the coffee store on the corner and get a real cup of coffee, maybe even a latte."

"Thanks, I'd like that. I think I could use a walk."

Judith and Peter took the elevator to the ground floor and exited through the door to Broadway. The street was teeming with lawyers hurrying on their way to eight-thirty calendar calls, and cars were backed up in the right-turn lane onto Broadway, looking for parking spaces long since occupied for the morning.

"Let's sit," Judith said when they'd ordered their coffee. "I'd like to talk about your case load for the next month or so."

When they were comfortably seated, Judith began outlining her plans.

"I'd like to see you in felony trials by the end of the year, Peter. I think you'll be ready. Maybe you'd like to try a hand at another murder trial then."

Delgado took a sip from his coffee cup and set it down again. He folded his hands together on the table as he spoke.

"I'm not sure how to tell you this, Judith, but—" He looked down at his hands, avoiding her eyes. It was a hesitation she understood.

"But you're not going to be here at the end of the year, are you?"

"Like I said, I don't know how to say it."

"Are you going back east?"

"No. I'm staying here in San Diego."

"That doesn't leave many options. It can't be civil law. You won't ever practice civil law."

He laughed and shook his head.

"I know," she continued. "You're going to become a public defender. I knew it. McGonigle Canyon has turned you into a defense attorney."

"No. Actually, I've been talking to my father about politics."

Judith clutched her throat.

"Oh no, not that!" She took her hand from her collar and took another sip of coffee. "I could never do that," she said. "As a good friend of mine once said, 'I don't think I could like that many people for that long a period of time.' " She waited a moment. "You're serious, aren't you?"

"I said that's what I was doing. I'm going to finish out the year with the office. During the next couple of months I'm going to move to Peñasquitos, get myself a little condominium there. At the beginning of the year I'm going to work with one or two of the community groups and get to know the area and the problems there. Then I'm going to run for the seat opening on the city council in two years."

"That's the district McGonigle Canyon's in, isn't it?"

"Yeah, it is."

"Well, I'm impressed. I'll be sorry to lose you. But I never really thought our office would keep you for long, not from the moment you told me you'd be happy to take on the Talbots of the world. There were always other battles out there. You just needed to find out what they were. Hey, if it helped being in the office with us, that's good for everyone. Pike'll be disappointed. He figures he just got you trained. How about your father? Is he happy with your decision?"

"He's thrilled. He's looking forward to having a Hispanic governor in the family."

"It could just happen," Judith added. "It could just happen."

44

MOST OF THE trial attorneys were gone by six o'clock. But Peter Delgado was hard at work in his office, preparing for a trial the following day. He had several months yet before he would be leaving the office, and Judith was assigning him only those trials that would take less than a week to put on. She'd offered to help him find an interim job, but it wasn't necessary. He'd been offered and had accepted the job of aid to the councilman whose place he wanted to take two years hence.

There'd been some ribbing about Peter, of course. Comments to the effect that he must be leaving because he couldn't take the pressure. And there was the occasional subtle aside that he'd only been hired in the first place because he was Hispanic. She tried not to respond to them. The substance of the comments was true. And it would have taken too long to explain that Peter Delgado's decision to alter the course of his life was caused by the death of a farm laborer who had killed a man.

Judith looked at the personal phone directory lying on her desk. It was nine o'clock in Canton, Ohio. Too late to call her aunt Margaret. A late call would scare her. She'd think someone was dying. Maybe tomorrow morning she'd give her a call to let her know her sister was still doing okay. Right now, she needed to think about getting home. Elizabeth was coming back tonight. Steven promised he'd have her back from vacation by seven o'clock. Judith couldn't wait for her return. The house was far too quiet without her. The solitude brought feelings the house was too big now for them, too much for her to handle. When Elizabeth came home, the yard would be filled with her friends and the hallways littered with Barbie dolls and plastic horses. In the course of a day or two Judith could push back the doubts.

The soccer field was still wet from the night's coastal fog. Annette, one of the senior trial deputies in Judith's office, persuaded her Elizabeth should join Annette's daughter's soccer team. The first morning of Saturday practice the two women sat alone on wood bleachers, talking as the girls and older boys teams worked with the three coaches.

Discussion ranged from Peter Delgado's imminent departure to whether Judith would be interested in meeting one of Annette's friends who happened to be unmarried. If and when Judith planned to resume a social life was inevitably a subject of interest to her friends. When she declined the invitation, Annette turned to her professional plans.

"There's talk Larry Farrell's going to make a run for the federal bench. If that happens, the seat's open, you know," Annette commented, watching Judith's reaction carefully.

Judith knew what Annette was alluding to. She'd read Farrell's name in articles about the new judgeship. The same articles mentioned her as a candidate for district attorney to replace him. She never understood where such rumors started or how they ended up in newspaper articles written by people she'd never talked to.

"I'd have to think about it."

"But you wouldn't rule it out, would you?" Annette pressed.

"No, I wouldn't rule it out. But I'd have to think about it. Political campaigns are grueling." She shook her head. "With my mother so sick and Elizabeth still so young, I'm not sure this is the best time to hit the campaign trail. Besides, I'd really like a state judgeship sometime. A political position would derail that option indefinitely. The only thing that—"

Judith's thought was interrupted by a man sprinting toward them. It was one of the coaches. He ran past the women to the drinking fountain behind the stands. They heard the water splash to the ground. When it stopped, the coach sat down next to Judith. He pushed back thick strands of black hair from his forehead and ran his wet hand over his throat. Without looking up, he simultaneously retied his shoelace and at the top of his voice yelled, "Keep playing!" presumably, Judith suspected, to his team of older boys on the field. Then he stood up and ran off again.

"Wow," Annette said, her eyes widening.

"Wow, what?"

"Gareth noticed you."

"Gareth who?"

"Gareth MacCauly. The soccer coach from England. That dark-haired guy who just came over and sat down right next to you. It's his second year coaching the traveling team. He noticed you."

"Whatever makes you say he noticed me? He didn't even say good morning. Or hello for that matter. In fact, I thought he was rather rude."

"All I can say is, he doesn't just come and sit down next to people like that."

Judith started to laugh. "He got some sweat on me. What's that mean?"

"Don't laugh. He's got eyes like a hawk. He can see everything happening anywhere on the field—all at once. Watch him."

"I'm sorry, Annette, really I am. It's just very funny. Look at him out there. Does he look interested in me?"

Annette squinted in MacCauly's direction. "I think he is, yes," she said defiantly.

"Oh my God, Annette, really!"

Still, Judith was curious. From what she could tell, his complete attention was riveted on the boys he was coaching, albeit he did seem to occasionally look in one direction and yell at players who were behind him. In the hour they were at the field, not once did the coach appear to look in her direction or, for that matter, away from his players. He ran, yelled, pointed, and yelled some more. Then he collected the equipment as the boys ran laps around the field.

At last Elizabeth ran toward the stands and announced her practice was over. The two headed for the car, parked on the street. When they reached the automobile, Judith unlocked the doors, and as Elizabeth got in, Judith looked over her shoulder toward the soccer field. MacCauly, his players now practicing again in front of him, had stopped. For the first time that morning he was standing perfectly still, looking in the direction of the stands where she had been sitting minutes before. His head turned and he looked out over the field, as if he was looking for someone.

From behind her, Annette yelled, "See you next Saturday!"

"Wouldn't miss it," Judith called back.

Epilogue

THE OLD WOMAN leaned the broom against the side of the wood hovel that had been her home for seven years. She had swept the dirt floor all morning and now it was clean; every blade of dead grass, every hair had been brushed away. Soon the men from the city would carry away the boxes containing her possessions.

As she waited for the city trucks to arrive, the old woman walked down the encampment road one last time. "Where are you going?" she asked the man ripping his cardboard home apart, the precious wood supports lying in a heap next to the path. The man shrugged and pointed down the road. "I'm taking my wood to the next canyon, just over the hill there." He was philosophical. "Life will not change all that much for us. We will be near the fields still."

The old woman and the man could not have known that by nightfall the city bulldozers would have demolished every hovel, every canton left standing in McGonigle Canyon. Gone would be the vacant rusting cars and the clotheslines sagging with work pants. Gone would be the makeshift churches and restaurants and the circle of houses where young men flirted with the young girls celebrating their fifteenth birthdays.

Within the month the places where the canyon fell sharply would be leveled and filled in. The stream would be cleaned of debris, and the eucalyptus tree grove where the catering truck blared its horn to announce the morning coffee would be cut down. And the people of the canyon would have scattered to the wind, like so many seeds looking for another place to take root.

With the canyon stripped of its wretched humanity, an ornate blue-and-gold sign would be placed prominently at the end of the old encampment road. The sign, attached to a metal pole driven deep into the dirt, proudly announced Talbot Construction Company was converting the entire area into an exclusive new housing development called McGonigle Canyon.

Acknowledgments

As usual my endeavors have been made easier by a number of friends and associates.

My gratitude must first be extended to Peter Kaye, writer, political analyst, and television producer, whose extensive knowledge and keen sense of humor have been shared with me for twenty-five years.

For whatever truths emerge in the writing of this book, whatever insight into the human condition, my thanks to my good friends John Carney, a not too subtle critic, and Kevin Wirsing, always an inspiration.

A special debt of gratitude to Adam Kaye and Howard Fisher, my guides into the encampments. They were also my drivers on those wild rides through the canyons. Without them the description of the labor encampments would not have been the same.

As always there is my assistant Lorna Luthy, whose belief and devotion to my endeavors sustain me in all of those difficult moments.

And there are those who have from the outset lent invaluable personal support, prominent among them Tom Blair and Dr. Abigail Dickson.

Finally and most of all there is my gratitude to my husband, Don, and our boys, Mike and Peter, for their love and support in the hardest of all endeavors.